With Wisdom and Courage

Ric DelleCave

Cover art by: Animus Graphics
Photos by: Firefly Fantasies Photography

Turos Books
Trafford, PA 15085

Dedication

This book is dedicated to my brother Flavius (Pete) Rhodes who has been my hero since I was a child. Integrity and honor has been the hallmark of his life and was an inspiration in the writing of this book.

Acknowledgments

As always I must express the deepest gratitude to my wife Mary who spent many days and hours edited and correcting this book. Her advice was indispensable and made the process less tedious.

I would also like to thank the following people for their willingness to proofread and offer advice:
Jonathan DelleCave, April Reinke, Tracy Dankmyer, Jill Mossburg and Susan Dewitt.

Prologue

The last two years had been a whirlwind of political activity. No one anticipated how easily the nation could accept such egregious maneuvers to limit individual liberty. New legislation had been enacted on the heels of devastating disasters.

In December 2014, two large mine cave-ins in central West Virginia trapped one hundred thirty miners. Federal regulators quickly moved in to assess the damage and loss of life. President Freeman announced the creation of the Mine Oversight Committee (MOC) and issued an executive order giving power to the MOC to seize control of all coal production. A firestorm of criticism was leveled at his administration from conservatives, all to no avail.

On April 1, 2015 an international flight was highjacked out of Boston. Three Islamic extremists executed sixteen passengers. No one could explain how they had smuggled handguns aboard. The news media vilified handgun manufacturers as mercenary millionaires. As one reporter opined, "The gun industry has turned a deaf ear to the cry of the populous. Numerous watchdog groups like Stop the Slaughter are calling for tougher regulations!"

One cable news outlet gave prime time coverage to gun control advocates calling for the legislature to pass new laws limiting the sale and ownership of handguns.

Politicians spoke of the public good and the need to reinterpret the second amendment stating, "The founders were unable to foresee the horrors of a future that unrestricted ownership of weapons would ultimately create."

"The second amendment, as currently interpreted, is a relic of a more brutal, uncivilized time," said one silver haired Senator from New York State. "It is time for a more rational approach to the blight of handguns and assault weapons that will not infringe on the rights of legitimate collectors and hunters."

The debate raged for several weeks, resulting in the passage of a bill that banned the sale of handguns and required confiscation of all registered weapons. Those granted the right to keep their handguns were involved in legitimate law enforcement or in the military. President Freeman signed it into law with great adulation from news outlets and commentators. Only a minority warned of the danger of reinterpreting the Founders' intent.

When the deadline for voluntarily surrendering weapons expired, heavily armed squads from the newly formed Office of Handgun Reclamation, known as the OHR, began forced confiscation. Isolated pockets of resistance simultaneously formed in Montana, Arkansas and Texas in response.

Within the first three weeks of the rebellion, one thousand four hundred civilians were killed. Three hundred OHR officers also lost their lives.

The uprising in Montana and Arkansas was put down in the first two weeks, however, the fighting in Texas was vicious and the OHR appealed to Congress for military assistance.

Two weeks after the request, Congress passed a law called the Texas Pacification Act that suspended the Posse Comitatus Act of 1878. Some conservative groups warned of grave consequences if this precedent was set. These warnings were largely ignored by a populous frightened by the armed conflict within their borders. Governors, Mayors and average citizens vigorously implored Congress to pass the Texas Pacification Act and restore order.

Simultaneously the Texas legislature voted unanimously to secede from the Union. Immediately the Texas national guard was mobilized to assist the beleaguered militias.

The battle between the Texans and the American military raged for six months. During this period an uprising began in Pennsylvania, Tennessee and several midwestern states. The U.S. military was spread thin and incapable of quelling the unrest. Citizen militias in these states sent reinforcements to assist the Texans.

The Gun Rebellion, as it had been labeled in the media, ended northeast of Laredo in a previously unknown oil town called Seven Sisters.

President Freeman and several high ranking military officials signed a peace agreement with the newly formed Republic of Texas. All military action ceased on July 7, 2016. The last of the United States military withdrew from Texas on October 23, according to the provisions of the treaty.

Chapter 1

Corbin sat staring at the headline. He was not sure why he felt such dread. Something foreboding clung to the edges of his mind, a sense of pending doom that he could not quite grasp.

He had read it several times hoping he had misinterpreted its meaning. Yet its plain implication was unavoidable.

"Why Corbin, you look like you've seen a ghost!" Abigail Miller had been married to Corbin for 10 years. She was a dutiful wife who spent her time caring for the house. With her cotton dress clinging to her ample curves she systematically stooped down to place his coffee on the end table.

Corbin glanced up from the newspaper to Abigail. The concern on her face was genuine. She sat on the davenport next to him, careful to smooth out her dress. Her brunette hair was pulled back into a French braid. There was just a hint of gray at her temples though she was barely forty. She was loathe to dye her hair considering it vanity and not worthy of a woman professing godliness. Without makeup or jewelry, she portrayed an unpretentious dignity.

Corbin had been a Pastor for eight years. He had received his Masters degree from John Fletcher Seminary two years earlier. He was slightly overweight, which he blamed on too many invitations to dinner. His dark wavy hair was meticulously combed straight back, revealing a prominent widows peak. Studious and conscientious, he prided himself on his mental acumen. He looked at his wife and smiled. Her presence was always a comfort. He sat for a while looking into her eyes. Her eyes were so expressive and the deep emerald green was captivating.

"What is it Honey, something has upset you?" Her voice was soft and reassuring. She placed her hand softly on his thigh.

"I'm not sure," he replied, his hazel eyes fixed in thought. "The headline in the paper struck me. With the chaos lately, I'm not sure what to think." He handed the paper to Abigail.

Scanning the article, she periodically looked at Corbin, then back at the paper. When she finished she folded the paper and placed it on the davenport beside her husband. "Corbin, what does it mean? Why would they need to do that?" There was a slight hint of unease in her voice.

"I don't know, I need to call Doctor Crenshaw. Maybe he understands what's going on."

****

Doctor Albert Crenshaw sat slightly slumped at his desk, his thin frame barely filling his suit. The wisps of hair on his balding head were whisked about by the ceiling fan.

As was his habit when deep in thought, he nervously stroked his chin with his right hand.

"Sister Beckwith," he called, his voice barely audible.

"Yes, Doctor Crenshaw?" She replied. MaryAnn Beckwith had been with the Evangelistic Christian Union since she was a young girl. At seventy-five, she had worked with more than fifteen different Presiding Elders. Doctor Crenshaw would be her last. She intended to retire at the end of the next conference year. She had seventeen grandchildren and wanted to spend time with them before the Lord called her home.

Rising from her desk, she slowly made her way into his office. Arthritis had taken its toll on this once vibrant woman. Her shoulders, weighed down by the years with her slight frame, gave her the appearance of fragility. Her steps were slower, but her mind was sharp.

"Yes, Doctor Crenshaw?" She repeated.

"Oh, yes, yes," he said briefly looking over his glasses at her. "Sister, I need you to schedule an emergency meeting for the District Assembly. Friday the twentieth, to be exact."

"But, sir, that is only ten days away. We have pastors that have to travel great distances."

"I am aware, Sister Beckwith. This is important. There have been some changes in the law and we must be prepared. Let them know that we'll be discussing new compliance issues. Also, set the time for nine-thirty. The earlier the better."

"Yes, Doctor." She glanced briefly at the paper on his desk. The letter head read:

Department of Communication and Speech
Division of Verbal Equity and Faith

MaryAnn Beckwith walked slowly to her desk. The country had changed so much since she was young. People seemed so frightened. The changes in the church were just as stark. There was less preaching on personal holiness and responsibility. The majority of sermons she had heard recently were on self-esteem, social justice and community awareness. A chill came over her. Approaching her desk she mechanically put on her sweater. She began the task of calling each pastor in the district, then would send a follow up letter. Dialing the first number she shivered again.

****

The official government notice he received still lay on his desk. Doctor Crenshaw picked it up and scanned it's contents again.

"Those fools," he muttered as he rose from his desk to close the office door. Picking up the phone he hastily dialed Roger Thurman's number.

"Hello," a husky voice answered.

"Roger, this is Doctor Crenshaw."

"Yes, Albert, I was anticipating a call from you."

Doctor Crenshaw recoiled. He took offense to anyone calling him Albert. He had spent many years earning the title of Doctor and resented anyone who ignored it. Having corrected this arrogant bureaucrat several times, he had finally given up and accepted his disrespect.

"Roger, you had assured me that this, this intrusion wouldn't be announced for several months. I was going to meet with my leadership and soften the blow. I have many conservative thinkers in the church and they are not going to take this well."

"They have no choice," he said indifferently.

"You can't just foist this on them willy-nilly!" His voice rose. He tried to calm himself. As a doctor and leader of the largest denomination in the country, he had to maintain his poise. It would be beneath his position to give way to such crude expression.

"Some of these men are still married to individualism and will resent what appears to be the imposition of political control."

"I don't think I need to remind you, Albert, that any belligerent behavior that supplants the good of the community will need to be controlled. These are dangerous times. We need a steady hand from leaders like you."

"Yes, of course," he sighed. Doctor Crenshaw was pleased that he recognized his importance.

"Anyone that you believe will not be a community player, let me know. We have developed remedial classes to help them come along. We will talk again at the appointed time."

"Yes, of course..." The phone went dead before he finished the sentence. Returning the handset to its cradle, he leaned back in his chair and took a deep breath.

"Sister Beckwith," he cried loudly. It took a few minutes for his office door to open. Standing in the doorway, MaryAnn looked haggard. He wondered how much longer she would live. "Sister, get me some coffee. I have much work to do. Friday will come quickly."

"Yes, sir," she replied.

Chapter 2

Corbin had been surprised by the suddenness of the District Assembly meeting. Doctor Crenshaw had been evasive when he called him. This new government division of *Verbal Equity and Faith* was disconcerting. The idea that the government would intrude into his practice of faith frightened him.

In the past six months, Corbin had read many accounts of pastors being fined or imprisoned for hate speech. Mostly for declaring that homosexuality was a sin, or refusing to bless their activity in marriage. Some for preaching against adultery, drunkenness and immorality, and even for making negative comments about Islam. This type of preaching had been declared judgmental and divisive.

The recently established National News Alliance had a two hour special on this issue. Corbin had watched in silence. He no longer had the will to protest, not even to himself.

"These men are relics of the past. Tolerance for this type of hate has ended. These men who think they're better than everyone else should be silenced. After all, how arrogant do you have to be to think you own the truth?" All but one on the panel nodded in agreement.

Out of the twelve participants only one held an opposing view. "What about freedom of speech and religion?" she asked. Barely finishing the sentence, she was interrupted and silenced by the eleven.

"They have the freedom to say whatever they want as long as it doesn't call into question the character of others. They have free speech within the confines of the law," said a middle aged gentleman with dark wavy hair. His smile never waned as he slowly leaned back in his chair.

"We cannot have incitement to violence against a specific group of people. People are who they are, and their right to live their lives is of greater importance than the ability of haters to say whatever they want," said a beautiful twenty-something blonde, scolding her opponent.

Each member of the panel had similar comments, each reinforcing the view of the one before.

Corbin had noticed that this lone opponent was overweight, her dress was slightly rumpled and her hair, though not messy, looked like it had been pulled up into a hasty bun on her head. When she spoke, her voice was raspy and she used words like "ain't" and "shoulda." In contrast, the other members of the panel were well groomed and articulate.

The rest of the special highlighted the intolerant actions of religionists, especially Christians. In the end, the rumpled woman was asking forgiveness and gently weeping, while the others comforted her and celebrated her enlightenment.

After the special report, the conclusion was that something had to be done to ensure that the American people would be shielded from this form of verbal inequity.

Corbin and Abigail were appalled. They sat in silence, Abigail obviously praying.

"Abbie, what will we do?" Corbin's voice was barely audible. "What will become of us?"

"Corbin," her voice soft, but full of strength, "we must preach the truth." Corbin looked up from his lap. His hands were still fidgeting.

"But Abbie, I have my ministry to think of. There are people who need me. Besides, can't the truth be taught without offending anyone?" His eyes were pleading.

Abigail did not answer. Instead she took his hand, looked into his eyes and said, "I know you will do what is right."

****

Pacing in his study, Corbin stopped briefly to pick up his Bible. Holding it in his right hand he stared at the cover. *Holy Bible,* the words were familiar yet foreign. Did he really know what that meant? Did he really believe this Book to be the revelation of *the* God?

He had studied the scripture for most of his adult life. His parents had been devout Christians. He remembered hearing his mother praying late into the night for him. He had rebelled as a teen. At age thirteen he had taken to drinking alcohol and had even been arrested once. He chuckled to himself, remembering how frightened he'd been. So frightened that he had difficulty telling the officer his name and remembering where he lived.

The fear, however, hadn't been enough to arrest his attention. It had been the sobbing prayers of his mother.

"Corbin," she had said to him, "never lose sight of where you've been, who God is, and where you're headed."

Coming home at three in the morning, he staggered to the front door and heard the familiar sound of his mother in prayer. He stopped at the door and leaned close. He could hear her pray.

"Father, tonight, wherever he is, please watch over my boy," her voice cracked with emotion. He heard her sobs, the wordless pleading of a broken heart.

Standing at the door, Corbin began to weep. Losing the strength in his legs he slumped to the porch and prayed. From that moment he lived for his and his mother's God. She and his dad perished in an accident on I-79 shortly after he graduated from seminary.

Looking down at the Book again, he wished his mother was there. He knew she could help him. He also understood that his relationship to God would be determined by his choices.

Reverently setting down the book, Corbin bowed his head and breathed a silent prayer.

****

The drive into Pittsburgh was slow and tedious. The security sweeps at each of the tunnels backed up traffic for hours. The first few months it was infuriating. Two years later it was a natural part of commuting.

Corbin had left three hours early for the District Assembly meeting. Sitting in traffic, he listened to classical music. Adjusting his fedora, he glanced in the rearview mirror. The traffic stretched behind him for miles. He could see the soldiers at the Fort Pitt tunnel check point. He was close and retrieved his national ID from his wallet.

He had forgotten his ID card once and never wanted to do that again. He was promptly forced to pull off the Parkway. After being frisked he was quickly taken to a detention room were he was questioned for what seemed like hours. His interrogator took his fingerprints and after verifying his identity, they let him go. Three days later he received a letter from the Department of Terrorism informing him that he had three weeks to pay a one thousand dollar fine. Many of the pastors on his district and across the nation had made donations to help him pay the fine. Without their help, Corbin would have faced up to five years in a federal prison. Corbin had never been so frightened. The fear of going to prison almost crippled him.

After that incident he always made sure he had the card with him. Holding it tightly between his thumb and forefinger, he handed it to the guard.

The sergeant carefully examined the card and looked intently at Corbin's face.

"Please remove your hat," he said politely.

Corbin quickly took it off. He was feeling jittery. He hated these checkpoints.

"Please step out of the car."

"Why?" he asked reflexively.

"Out of the car, Reverend." The sergeant's voice was even. Yet, the look in his eyes and the slight movement of his hand to his sidearm told Corbin he better obey.

Legs trembling, Corbin slowly exited his vehicle. The air was filled with the smell of automobile exhaust. Looking around, he saw the taut faces of other drivers waiting to be passed through. Though it was mid summer, Corbin shivered.

"Move to the front of the vehicle, please."

Corbin obeyed. Moving to the front of the car, he silently prayed.

Two privates, quickly moved to the vehicle. Opening all four doors, they methodically searched his car. Opening the glove compartment, they removed all the contents and scanned each paper. After ten minutes, they closed the trunk and nodded to the Sergeant.

"Okay Reverend, you can go now."

Corbin quickly sat in the driver's seat and fastened the seat belt. Starting the engine and putting the transmission in drive, he slowly pulled away. The tunnel ahead of him was free of traffic. He could never get used to the random searches. Corbin didn't relax until he could no longer see the soldiers in his mirror.

Chapter 3

The conference room at the hotel was large. Tables were arranged throughout the rectangular room. Each table had a setting for six people. In the center of each was a fresh spray of flowers in white vases. Still standing in the doorway, he surveyed the room, hoping to see Doctor Whitaker.

Corbin had met Doctor Whitaker at John Fletcher Seminary in Wisconsin. Doctor Whitaker taught a class on eschatology and had immediately captured Corbin's attention. His views on the end times were different from what was considered orthodox, and extremely different from what was taught by radio preachers. Doctor Whitaker taught that rather than things having to get worse, God was powerful enough to bring change for the better. This venerable man's optimism was contagious, and gave him a small, but devoted following.

Glancing toward the double doors on his left, he saw Doctor Whitaker enter. At six feet-three inches, Jedediah Whitaker towered over most of the pastors in the denomination. His stately demeanor was enhanced by his snow white hair that was cut short and combed to the right side. His posture was strong and proud. His piercing gaze revealed an intellect unparalleled by his peers. Though he carried himself with authority, Doctor Whitaker was a gentle, thoughtful man, who loved life and his vocation.

"Doctor Whitaker," Corbin called out, not trying to hide the excitement in his voice. His relationship with this aged pastor had moved beyond the formality of seminary. This man was like a father to him.

"Corbin, my boy, how are you?" Jedediah's smile was warm and genuine. Corbin extended his hand. Jedediah grasped it and pulled the young man to him and gave him a fatherly hug. Releasing him, Jedediah patted Corbin on the shoulder as they turned to enter the hall.

"Jedediah," the formality had long disappeared between them, "what do you make of all this?"

"Not now, Corbin," his whisper was almost inaudible.

"But, Jedediah," his words were cut off as the older man raised a slightly trembling hand.

"Not now, Corbin," he said as he stopped to look his disciple in the eye, "Not now. Wisdom and courage, Son, wisdom and courage." Jedediah abruptly turned and moved toward the podium to shake hands with Doctor Crenshaw.

Corbin was stunned. What did he mean by *wisdom and courage?* The context made no sense. Perplexed, he began searching tables for his name tag. He hoped he would know the people he sat with.

Corbin's table was in the back on the left side of the podium. An organist began to softly play hymns. The many voices were a cacophony of sound, a rumble of old friends getting reacquainted. Others were debating fine points of doctrine, a practice Corbin enjoyed, but not today.

Corbin sat in his assigned seat, periodically glancing at Doctor Whitaker as he moved from person to person shaking hands. "Wisdom and courage," Corbin whispered to himself. "What did he mean by that?"

"What did who mean by what?"

Startled, Corbin looked into the smiling face of Jeffrey Arbino. "Huh?"

"You said, what did he mean by that?"

"I was thinking out loud," he replied, surprised that he had verbalized his thoughts. Smiling and rising, Corbin gave Jeffrey a strong handshake. Jeff's smile had not changed in all the years Corbin had known him. Genuine with a hint of mischief, his smile was disarming.

Patting Corbin on the back, Jeff sat in the empty seat next to him. "What were you mumbling about?" He asked, his smile never wavering.

"Nothing," he replied slowly as he turned to watch his mentor continue his greetings.

Jeffrey pastored one of the largest churches in the denomination. His organizational skills and gift of oratory had helped him take a struggling church of twenty-five and turn it into a congregation of over ten thousand in just ten years. Corbin was slightly jealous of his college buddy's success.

Leaning closer, Jeffrey firmly grabbed Corbin's right forearm. The pressure of his grip quickly got Corbin's attention. "We are living in dangerous times." His voice was low, his eyes intent and boring into Corbin's. Corbin looked away from the intensity of the stare.

"Yes, we are," was his reply.

"I have heard rumors that we will no longer be able to preach as God leads us."

Corbin slowly turned toward his friend. Jeffrey's face betrayed a strength of character he had never noticed before. The years they had spent in the seminary together were filled with hard work that was offset by Jeffrey's penchant for mischief. He had never been serious or thoughtful during those days. However, something told Corbin that had changed.

"Yes, that is what I have feared. The creation of the Division of Verbal Equity and Faith is ominous. Isn't that what this meeting is about?"

"We shall soon find out," Jeffrey said as his eyes moved toward the platform. "It looks like Doctor Crenshaw is getting ready to speak."

Corbin's eyes moved instinctively to the podium. Jeffrey patted his shoulder while rising, "Wisdom and courage, Corbin," he whispered, and left him sitting perplexed.

Wisdom and Courage, kept running through his mind. The words were unsettling, yet there was a sense of comfort in them. Was it coincidence that Jeffrey and Jedediah had parted using the same words?

Doctor Crenshaw had just finished the preliminaries. Corbin's mind was preoccupied during the invocation and he had absentmindedly participated in the singing. He periodically looked where Jedediah and Jeffrey were seated. Everything appeared as it should. *It must be a coincidence*, he thought comforting himself, *just a coincidence.*

Corbin's musing was interrupted when Doctor Crenshaw began his presentation. The statistical data on church growth and finances were as boring as Corbin anticipated. Several times he had to stifle a yawn.

"Now, to some important, and I hope, exciting news. As you are aware, the Department of Communication and Speech has developed new tools to enhance our sermon preparation...."

Corbin was shaken out of the fog of his thoughts. Leaning forward, he listened intently.

"The ushers are handing out packets that will outline the procedures all pastors must follow before presenting a sermon to their congregation."

A groan passed through the assembly.

"Now, now, this is for our betterment and it is the law. Each of you will have to submit, in writing, a manuscript of what you want to preach to your district facilitator. He or she will then ensure that you are following the guidelines on hate speech, discrimination and...."

An elderly preacher that Corbin didn't recognize, jumped to his feet. "How dare they and you, Doctor Crenshaw!" His face was slightly red. Corbin wasn't sure if it was from anger or effort. "I have been preaching for 50 years. I will say what my God gives me, not some bureaucrat! I am an American, sir, I have my rights..."

"You will follow the law," a man Corbin did not recognize stated evenly. Corbin had noticed him on the platform, but had not given him a second thought until now.

"Who are you, Sir?" The elderly pastor asked, obviously angered.

"This is Roger Thurman," Doctor Crenshaw replied curtly. *"He* is the Regional Head of the Department of Communication and Speech and will be overseeing our progress."

A collective murmur escaped from the audience.

"My allegiance is to God!" cried the elderly man. "I take my marching orders from the Book, not any man!" His voice was strong and confident. Dozens of amens could be heard on the floor.

"Gentlemen, ladies, order," demanded Doctor Crenshaw. "Let us behave ourselves," he said as he tried to calm the crowd. Many had opened their packets and nearly all were incredulous at what they read.

The voices of protest were many and varied. Most proclaiming their refusal to get government approval for what they would present to their flocks.

Corbin started to rise. Jedediah, staring at him, raised a hand and subtly motioned for him to sit. Corbin stared at the pandemonium around him. He had never seen such anger and fear. After nearly thirty minutes of outcry, Doctor Crenshaw, unable to control the meeting, left without a word.

Corbin noticed several men standing along the perimeter of the tables taking notes. These men, he was certain, were there to record the proceedings for the government. When the crowd began to dissipate, he saw each of these men leaving with Roger Thurman.

Chapter 4

Returning to the small conference room assigned to him as a courtesy from the hotel, Roger Thurman sat at the head table exhausted. This was his fifth meeting in two weeks and they all seemed to end the same.

He was weary from dealing with these religious neanderthals. All of them thought they had the only truth. He was grateful that the legislature had the insight to understand that these were dangerous people and had to be controlled. Their penchant for hate was more than he could bear, and he always felt a need for a shower after dealing with them.

"How many names did you get?" He asked mechanically. Manny, the head of his intelligence task force was efficient and ruthless. He and Manny had discussed these people many times. Both understood the need to eliminate this archaic superstition. Manny's mother had been fanatical in her beliefs, and he resented how she had controlled his life.

Three years ago, Roger had read Manny's file and anticipated meeting him. After getting permission to visit Manny at the maximum security prison that housed him, Roger looked forward to recruiting him. What elevated his interest in Manny was the systematic brutality he had used to dispatch his mother. The police report stated that after having cut out her tongue, he slowly dismembered her, while alive, all the while taunting her to call on her God to save her.

After a short hour interview, Roger was certain he had found the man to keep these mentally unstable people in line.

"At least thirty." Manny's voice was deep and gravelly.

"Good, good, I want a full profile on each. I need to know who to make an example of. Nothing ensures compliance better than..."

Interrupted by the slamming of the conference room door, Roger raised his eyes menacingly.

"I told you this wasn't the time!" Doctor Crenshaw's voice was shrill. "I told you to wait, told you this would not go well!"

Roger placed his hand on Manny's arm and imperceptibly shook his head. Manny relaxed his tense muscles and took a step back.

"I find it's best to get everything out in the open, Albert."

"I've told you, it's Doctor Crenshaw! I have a Ph.D!"

"Calm down, Albert," his voice was even, but menacing. "I told you we will be handling things through the Division of Verbal Equity and Faith. You will do as you're told. We can put anyone in charge of your denomination."

Doctor Crenshaw gasped. He had worked hard to get where he was. How dare this nobody, this uneducated nit presume to usurp his position and authority. "I'll have you know," he began but was stunned silent by Thurman's reaction.

Roger despised this little man. For all his education, Albert understood nothing. He didn't realize he was a pawn in a broader game. The sight of this little weasel, coupled with his cheekiness, made it impossible to hold onto his composure. Slamming his fists on the table in front of him, he stood and leaned toward his adversary. "You will do what you are told," he hissed. "Nothing more, nothing less." Turning he nodded to Manny.

Manny was six feet tall, muscular and athletic. His religion was his body. He worked out two hours a day and only ate the most nutritious foods. Second to this, Manny took his job seriously. He worked many hours gathering information on the enemies of the government. He was both an intelligence gatherer, and enforcer.

Manny moved quickly. The shock on Doctor Crenshaw's face was testament to Manny's strength and speed. Manny's powerful right hand was contracting on Albert's windpipe. Every breath he took wheezed through his obstructed airway. Manny easily moved him four feet to the wall and helplessly pinned him there.

Roger slowly rose from his seat and moved toward the struggling preacher. Aimlessly, Roger withdrew a roll of mints from his pocket. Taking his time he unwrapped one and placed it in his mouth. Leaning close to the weakening man, he whispered, "Defy me again and I'm not sure what he will do next."

Albert was frantically clawing at the powerful man's hands. A lack of oxygen was blackening the edges of his sight. Albert's eyes were wide with fear. He knew he was going to die.

"Let him go," Roger said walking back to the table. Manny released his grip. Albert gulped in air. Sliding to the floor, he began to weep.

Roger and Manny returned to compiling their list. Manny had highlighted the ones that he believed would be the biggest problem.

"As usual, you did a very thorough job," Roger said, praising his enforcer.

Manny grunted in appreciation.

Roger had not noticed when Albert had slipped out. Dismissing Manny, he completed his report of the day's events. One thing he highlighted was his misgivings about easily pulling these bible thumpers into line. These fools believed the tripe they peddled. He had had no problems with the more socially conscious churches. After all, many of those denominations had been useful in initiating the changes needed to make America better.

This group would be tougher. Fishing into his pocket, he retrieved his mobile phone. He quickly dialed and tapped his pencil on the table, waiting for an answer.

"Hello, Lambert here."

"Mr. Lambert, this is Roger."

"Ah, yes Roger, tell me you have some good news."

Chapter 5

Troubled, Corbin slowly made his way through the crowd. He studied the men who were scribbling notes on clipboards. Groups of clergy were huddled and talking in half whispers. All were animated and everyone looked uneasy.

The elderly minister who had first voiced objection to the new plan, was reminding younger pastors that their allegiance was first to God, then Caesar. Corbin noticed one man staring in the old preacher's direction. He was large, and his face was void of expression. His jet black hair was slicked back, revealing a high forehead. His eyes were dark, and despite his passive face, were foreboding. The man had glanced in Corbin's direction which made him quickly turn away. Though he briefly looked in the man's eyes, a sense of uneasiness momentarily touched him.

Glancing at his watch, he noticed it was three o'clock. The traffic going out of Pittsburgh would be horrendous the next three hours. Needing time to think, he fished out his cell phone and called Abigail.

"Hello," came the cheery voice.

"Honey, it's me. I'm going to stay in the city for a couple of hours. I don't want to fight the tunnel traffic right now."

"OK, Corbin," Abigail replied, understanding his avoidance of the traffic. "How did your meeting go?"

"We need to talk, but not now. Not on the phone."

There was silence for a few seconds. That meant she understood that things did not go well.

"Alright, Dear," she answered, "We'll talk tonight. Take courage, Corbin."

Struck by the word, his conversation with Jedediah and Jeffrey rushed to the forefront of his thought. "Goodbye," he said absently and ended the call.

Wisdom and Courage, the words haunted him. It must have been coincidence that they both used the same admonition. Yet, they both emphasized it, as if to give it more meaning. Corbin stopped on Fifth Street and took a deep breath. Too many thoughts were competing for his attention. A feeling of confusion and helplessness threatened to overtake him. Taking another cleansing breath, he noticed his heart was racing. His life, ministry, and nation were collapsing about him.

Breathing a prayer for guidance and strength, Corbin slowly walked to a little restaurant. He had been here before and enjoyed the seclusion it afforded. The counter was crowded with men in suits, grabbing a coffee or soft drink, and hurrying out the door. The smell of burgers frying was pleasant and made him a little hungry. Standing behind a well dressed woman with too much perfume, Corbin stifled a sneeze.

The woman behind the counter was efficient with a plastic pleasantry that sounded too rehearsed. Ordering coffee and a small order of fries, Corbin found a small table for two and wearily sat down. Though always busy, the small dining area was never full. Corbin guessed that most of the clientele worked in town and hurriedly stopped in for lunch or a drink to take back to the office. He could always find a quiet place to sit and think.

Corbin sat silently listening to the commotion around him. A young girl with too much make-up sat chirping to a young man sitting across from her. She swung her hands wildly, apparently emphasizing her point. The young man idly dipped a fry in ketchup while nodding slowly.

An old man sat alone, his pure white hair combed straight back and his unshaven face was littered with stubble. He was talking with no one listening. Periodically he would become animated, which drew stares from the other diners. Corbin's heart went out to the man. He was obviously mentally ill.

Corbin started to rise from his seat, intending to sit with the man and offer him some companionship. Leaning forward to pick up his fries and coffee, he heard the familiar sound of his cell phone. Slightly perturbed, he sighed. Replacing his refreshments, he fished in his pocket for his phone. Struggling to extract it before the call ended, he became more agitated. Once free, he flipped the phone open and quickly said, "Hello!"

"Corbin?" the voice was familiar. It sounded tired and weak.

"Yes, is this Sister Beckwith?"

"It is. Corbin, I have some very sad news. I'm calling all the district leaders so they can pass it on to the other pastors. Doctor Crenshaw was found dead about fifteen minutes ago."

The shock was palpable. Corbin's mind was racing. He had just been with Doctor Crenshaw. He seemed as robust as ever.

"How? Why?" Was all he was able to say.

Corbin could hear the old woman stifle a sob. Her voice was tremulous, and the sadness in it was sobering.

"The authorities say he committed suicide."

The words struck him like a mallet. Suicide! This man had served the Lord most of his adult life. *He would never kill himself, would he?* The shock was disorienting. *Why, why would he do that?* He was unable to make sense of it.

"What happened?" The question was mechanical.

"They said he jumped from the roof of the hotel. Corbin, I heard the police talking. His head was completely turned around!" Her timorous voice broke and she wept openly. Corbin's heart was moved. He offered a prayer for her and was barely able to maintain his composure.

Sitting silently, he was unable to quiet his mind. Before he had ended the call, he had assured Sister Beckwith that he would contact the other men in his district.

Unable to finish his snack, Corbin pulled a dollar out of his wallet and placed it on the table. Pulling out a business card holder, he extracted a card and laid it with the tip. He made these cards to offer hope to those who served him his meals. He hesitated before rising and read the words,

For God so loved the world, that he gave his only begotten Son, that whosoever believeth in him should not perish, but have everlasting life. John 3:16

He had read these words many times, and staring at them now, he wondered if he ever really understood them. Today had devastated his faith. The prospect of losing his freedom to share the Gospel was frightening, but the death of his friend was devastating.

How could you, he thought, *how could you throw away your salvation? Why, what did you gain from such a death?* Doctor Crenshaw had always seemed to be a pillar. Now he was gone.

Corbin walked slowly toward the parking lot that held his vehicle. He didn't remember opening the restaurant door. The blare of the horn startled him. He stopped abruptly, unsure of what was going on. Slowly realizing that he had stepped into the path of a cab, he gestured an apology and backed onto the curb.

Taking a deep breath, Corbin tried to calm himself. He stood on the corner and looked at the world around him. This once vibrant city had been reduced to poverty, crime and hopelessness. The reality of life overwhelmed him because he knew it was all unnecessary.

When the road was clear, he hurried across the street. Once at the garage, it took a few minutes to buy the token needed to exit. He bypassed the elevator and walked the three flights of stairs. It didn't take long to locate his vehicle. Opening the door, he found a paper neatly folded, and lying on the driver's seat.

Curious how it had gotten there, he bent down and picked it up. It was folded once. The crease was crisp, as if special attention had been paid to folding it.

Corbin stood silently staring at the paper. Where had it come from, he wondered? He scanned the parking lot to see if anyone was watching him. Satisfied that he was alone, he looked at the paper again.

Unfamiliar words were written in bold letters. Corbin had studied Latin at seminary. He quietly translated it. Stunned, he repeated it several times in his mind. Finally he whispered, "With wisdom and courage."

Chapter 6

Albert moved unsteadily away from the conference room. The powerful grip of Manny's hand left the sensation of a knot in his throat. Unconsciously he rubbed his neck.

"I have never been treated in this manner," he mumbled. "That brute almost killed me!" he emphasized to himself.

"Doctor Crenshaw, is everything all right?" The question caught him off guard. Stopping he turned toward the voice and recognized one of the young pastors he had interviewed at the last conference. "You look ill, sir. Can I get you anything?"

Albert looked into the young man's face. It was etched with genuine concern. Forcing a smile, he quietly replied, "No thank you Son, I am quite well. The preparations for this meeting have just worn an old man out. All I need is to get back to my room and lie down for a while."

Without waiting for a reply, Albert continued down the hall, pressed the elevator button and impatiently waited for the door to open. Feeling weak, he leaned against the wall.

"I'll contact the Deputy Director," he was mumbling again. "I have never been so humiliated. Don't they know who I am?" The single chime broke into his thoughts. The elevator had arrived. Stepping inside, he pushed the button for the tenth floor. He was alone and the elevator quietly began its ascent. As the elevator climbed, he became more angry.

"Heads will roll. There will be an accounting. After all, I am the head of the Evangelical Christian Union! That thug will pay for what he has done." Albert felt a tinge of guilt for his thoughts of revenge. A mental picture spontaneously filled his thoughts of Jesus on the cross. *Father forgive them.* Albert inwardly cringed at the words. *Father forgive them.* Unsolicited it had a sense of urgency. Albert shook his head trying to silence the intrusion. It had been a long time since he had prayed, really prayed. *I'm too busy,* he thought. *My work Lord, I can't ignore my work.*

The elevator door opened on the tenth floor. Stepping out, he turned left. Counting the numbers on the doors he finally came to 1020. His hands were shaking and he fumbled with the key. Pressing his head against the cool door, he took several deep breaths trying to calm himself. After several seconds he was able to open the door.

The suite was large, consisting of a lounge inside the main entrance. The lounge was furnished with a couch, end tables and a large screen television. A small section of the lounge had a kitchen. The apartment sized stove had four small electric burners. Above the stove was a microwave. To the left of the stove was a small stainless sink. On the opposite wall stood a small refrigerator.

Entering the lounge and looking to the right, Albert moved toward the bedroom. Trying to remove his jacket, he realized that his left shoulder was stiff and extremely sore. Gingerly he lifted his left arm trying to remove the coat. After much effort the coat came off and he threw it onto the queen size bed. He then went into the bathroom.

Father forgive them. Albert could not understand why his thoughts were invaded with the words of Jesus. *I am the leader of the largest denominations in the United States. I deserve an apology and I shall get one.* He had long ago stopped believing that everything in the scripture was true. Only wild eyed fanatics, like Whitaker, believed such nonsense. There were others in the denomination that subscribed to Whitaker's foolishness. They would be forced out along with that nineteenth century throwback.

The thought of cleansing the denomination made Albert feel a little better. Moving to the sink, he turned on the faucet and splashed cold water on his face. Aimlessly, he walked out into the lounge still wiping his face and moved toward the balcony.

He did not notice the hulking man standing in the entryway. Sliding open the balcony door, Albert took a deep breath. The slight breeze was cool and refreshing. Although it was against denominational rules, he intended to have a glass of wine before lying down. It was for medicinal reasons, after all. *Besides, Jesus drank wine, didn't he?*

Turning, Albert froze. Weakness, brought on by fear, made it impossible for him to move. The color drained from his face. Unable to catch his breath, he whispered, "H-h-how did you get in here? What do you want? Haven't you done enough already?"

The large man moved into the lounge. There was an odd sadistic sneer on his face. His hands clenched and unclenched reflexively as he came steadily forward.

Albert tried to scream, but he had no air in his lungs. He had never felt such fear. He understood the strength of the feral beast moving in his direction. He willed his feet to move, but they would not obey. Opening his mouth to scream, the sound was cut short by a powerful jab to his solar plexus. What little air was left in his lungs was force out by the blow. Albert crumpled to his knees. Desperately he tried to crawl away. The lack of oxygen and pain in his chest made it difficult to move.

A heavy boot caught him in the buttocks and sent him sprawling. He tried to crawl again, but this time Manny roughly placed his left knee in the old man's back. The pressure on his frail body made his ragged breath come in gasps.

Manny leaned down and quietly said, "Wanna meet Jesus, old man?" His voice was cold and emotionless.

"Please!" Albert gasped. "Please!" Tears emerged in his eyes. He knew he was going to die. *Father forgive them.* Unbidden, it filled his thoughts. He answered audibly to the thought, "No."

Albert felt Manny's hands. His left palm was placed behind Albert's right ear. Simultaneously he grabbed the old man's jaw on the left side of his face. His powerful arms moved in opposite directions. The last thing Albert heard was the popping of cartilage, then everything went black.

****

The lifeless form of Albert Crenshaw flew through the air. A twenty something woman in a business suit screamed when his body struck the left front fender of an old Buick. She backed up hastily, staring in disbelief. A crowd gathered, gawking at the lifeless form.

Chapter 7

Jedediah was deeply troubled by the news of Albert Crenshaw's death. Albert was many things, but not suicidal. He remembered a time when he and Albert spent hours debating theology and church polity. In those days, Albert had been inflexible. Right was right, wrong was wrong. Over the years as Albert matured, he began to soften on his dogma. That transformation brought him into leadership and eventually he became the Superintendent of the denomination.

Regrettably, he had also seen Albert's convictions wane. Though once a staunch advocate of holy living and dedication to Christ, he melded into a politician protecting his position.

"No, no," he whispered with emphasis, "he would have never taken his own life." Jedediah believed this, not because of Albert's spirituality, but his stubbornness and love of power. With the newly formed Division of Verbal Equity and Faith, Albert's authority would have grown exponentially.

The parking garage was a block away. Though still summer, the slight breeze gave Jedediah a chill. Pulling his jacket tighter, he hurried his pace.

When he reached the lobby of the garage, the elevator was out of order. Several years ago these occurrences were annoying. Jedediah was used to them now. The price of energy had risen so high that practically no one used air conditioning anymore except the very rich and the politically connected. The government had mandated that all thermostats be set at sixty-five during the winter. Anyone using excessive energy faced heavy fines, and gross offenders faced imprisonment. Jedediah had been surprised at how easily people accepted these assaults on personal liberty.

Reaching the third flight of steps, his legs burned and he was struggling for breath. The heart attack he had suffered five years past made him careful not to over exert himself.

"I must hurry," he said aloud. Then continued his ascent.

The battered sedan was a welcome sight. His hand shook as he fished for his keys. Inside, he lay his head back, conscious of the quickness of his pulse. Taking several deep breaths he tried to calm himself.

I must call the brothers. Jedediah had never owned a cell phone. He always believed they robbed you of peace and time to reflect. Other pastors were on their phones constantly. Though he understood the utility of being available to your flock, the benefits were outweighed by the intrusion into your internal life. Now he wished he had a cell phone. The two hour drive home would only delay the plan he was concocting.

****

Roger Thurman sat behind the makeshift desk finishing up a report. He made a sour face after taking a drink of cold coffee.

"Hey, you!" He demanded looking in the direction of one of his staff. He knew his tone was gruff, but he did not care. These men were hired to serve his needs. He could not even remember the young man's name. "Get me some hot coffee, two creams, no sugar."

Obediently moving forward, the slender staffer dutifully picked up Roger's empty cup and headed for the door to fulfill his boss's wishes.

Roger smiled to himself. As regional head of Department of Communication and Speech, he was one of the truly powerful men in the country. He had worked hard to get this position. He had used Manny's talents to eliminate opponents in the past. Manny made each death seem like suicide. Roger never asked for details, nor did he have to explain to Manny what he wanted. Earning this position, though some would say he stole it, had given him power over the media, education and these insignificant religious fanatics.

Threatening a man's livelihood made it easy to get editors and news agencies to fall in line. Teachers were already in the fold, having swallowed the union's dogma and accepting an "us versus them" mentality. These religious fanatics were another matter. Their belief in the Christ myth buffered them from the motives of most men. Though some like Crenshaw were corruptible, many others would suffer great adversity to hold on to their superstition. The only religion Roger believed in was the religion of power.

Roger caught himself grinding his teeth at the insolence of these fools. Crenshaw had angered him. He wasn't used to anyone questioning his edicts. His word was law, wasn't it? Soon after Crenshaw had visited him, he slipped a note into Manny's hand. *Crendshaw* was the only word written.

Manny read the note and looked steadily into Roger's eyes. After a few moments, he nodded and walked out the door. Manny understood the message, having received many before.

Remembering Manny's cold gaze caused Roger to shiver. Though he was certain of the man's allegiance, he feared and envied his ruthlessness.

Glancing at his watch he became anxious. Manny had been gone for over an hour. He needed to know the problem had been taken care of. He was ready to leave this pitiful town.

"Has Manny checked in?" He asked one of his staff.

"No Sir, not a word."

"Let me know as soon as..." He stopped mid sentence as Manny's massive frame filled the door.

"How'd it go?" Roger asked.

"As you expected," came the terse reply.

****

The two hour drive home had left Jedediah drained of energy. Getting out of the car had been an ordeal. Old age had taken its toll on his stamina. It seemed that every joint ached, and standing erect was almost impossible.

The steps leading to his front door were another obstacle. The cement had begun to crumble. Navigating the damage was sometimes difficult. He had intended to get them repaired. The price of materials and finding a competent contractor prohibited the task. The red tape required to get the necessary permits was beyond his budget. The stipend he received for teaching biblical Greek at the local community college barely supplemented his meager pension.

Before he slid the key in the door, he heard familiar whimpering. Samson, his English Mastiff, was one-hundred eighty pounds of baby. Jedediah had been gone long enough to know that Samson would be anxious for his return. Slowly pushing the door open was Jedediah's ritual teasing of his friend. He painfully bent forward and put his nose close to the ecstatic animal's nose. Samson's excitement exploded in a spate of barking and whimpering.

"Hey there boy," he said as if talking to a child. "Miss me?"

In response the behemoth licked his master's face multiple times. Jedediah pushed the door open and stepped inside. Samson's whole backside wagged in time with his powerful tail. Jedediah sidestepped to avoid being struck by it. The older he became, the more that whip felt like being struck with a baseball bat. Collapsing in his favorite chair, he spent the next few minutes petting and hugging his slobbery companion.

Samson had been with him for the past five years. The fawn colored canine had saved Jedediah from several potentially difficult situations. Thirty years ago his neighborhood had been slightly upscale. He knew most of his neighbors, and it was safe to take a walk in the cool of the evening. In the last ten years, the deterioration of the borough was striking. When the economy faltered in 2014, unemployment hit a staggering fifteen percent, from which the country never recovered. Jedediah had watched in horror as his neighborhood became a haven for thugs and addicts. He would have left long ago, but he felt an obligation to the souls of these people.

Samson's size and bark was intimidating to most people. A gentle giant by nature, Samson enjoyed attention and kindness. On two occasions, Samson had defended his master against addicts who would have done Jedediah harm.

One night in particular, a man slit the screen in the living room window and entered the house. Armed with a knife, he had made his way up the stairs to where Jedediah was sleeping.

The creaking of the stairs woke Jedediah from a light sleep. Samson stood near the door his teeth bared, his low growl ominous and a portent of danger. His hackles were erect, his front feet planted firmly, and his head slightly bowed.

Frightened, Jedediah began to pray. He continued to pray as he rose from bed and pressed himself against the wall. The squeaking hinges confirmed Jedediah's fear. When the door was opened wide enough for the intruder to enter Samson's growl became menacing. The man, obviously inebriated, stood in place swaying from side to side. Samson cautiously moved forward, barking, his teeth snapping in warning.

The man stepped forward. Samson moved with surprising speed. His size belying his agility. One-hundred eighty pounds of anger lunged at the hapless man. Without time to react, the intruder was on his back. Samson had torn the flesh off his right forearm, then swiftly clamped his powerful jaws on the man's neck.

At first, Jedediah had been horrified. The man was bleeding profusely from the wound on his arm. His first thought was that Samson had bitten through his jugular and killed the man. Forgetting his fear he moved forward. The man was breathing heavily.

"Please, Mister," he said pathetically. "Please get him off me." Tears spilled from his eyes and he wept uncontrollably.

Jedediah called the police who hauled the man away. Samson had saved his life.

So he always took the time to give his black faced friend all the attention he needed.

Once the reunion was finished, Jedediah walked stiffly to the kitchen to make himself some tea. After filling the kettle, he placed it on the stove and turned on the burner. It would be a while before the water would boil so he grabbed the handset from the phone and dialed.

"Hello," a voice almost whispered on the other end.

"Do you follow the Lord?" Asked Jedediah.

"With the wisdom of Solomon," was the reply.

The code varied from week to week. They could not afford to be careless. They were living in dangerous days.

"You heard about Albert?"

"Yes, we must act quickly."

"I have a plan," Jedediah stated. "When can the Brothers meet?"

"Go to your favorite restaurant for breakfast. You will be contacted there."

Then the phone went dead. The whistle on the kettle screamed. Jedediah methodically made his tea.

Weariness was overcoming him. Back in his easy chair, he picked up his copy of Luther's *Concerning Christian Liberty.* Sipping his tea he read until sleep overcame him.

Chapter 8

The past week had been busy. Roger was hoping for some time off. He loved his job, but there were times that he needed to unwind. His thoughts went to Peggy.

He had met her at a meeting in Knoxville. She was sitting at the bar drinking some exotic drink he had never heard of. Her auburn hair caressed her oval face. Her brilliantly green eyes danced when she talked, and her body language was flirtatious. After a quick introduction, he learned that she worked on the third floor of the Division. She was assistant to one of the Head Facilitators.

He had spent a passionate night with her and called her occasionally when he needed a diversion. He didn't love her. He wasn't quite sure he had the capacity for that emotion. Yet, he was intrigued with the power she had over him and her undivided attention. When he was with her she made him believe no one else existed. Maybe he would call her tonight.

The phone startled him from his thoughts.

"Thurman here."

"Roger," the voice was distinct. Deputy Director William Lambert's high nasally voice was hard to forget.

"Yes, Deputy Director, how are you today?" Roger asked routinely. He despised the man. Lambert's appearance matched his feminine voice. A slight man with a hook nose and extremely pale skin. Though frail and effeminate, he was a dangerous man. He was connected to powerful people who listened when he called.

"I want to know what is happening with that religious sect. I understand that nuisance, Crenshaw, ended his pathetic life." That made Roger smile.

"I'm working on that now, Sir. I have the Assistant Superintendent meeting with me in a few minutes. He is in the waiting room now. We need to hammer out a viable candidate to succeed Crenshaw."

"Do your job and appoint one!" His voice was shrill and Roger sensed his aggravation.

"Well, Sir, their bylaws mandate a special election. Wellborn cannot take over leadership, even though he is Assistant Superintendent."

"Are you telling me you can't appoint a successor?"

"Right now, the law is on their side. They still have some autonomy. Our attorneys are working on a method to subvert that, but until then we can't appear as though we are ignoring the law. The last thing we need is to inadvertently create sympathy for these dying sects."

"Make sure this Wellborn understands his place. Is he trustworthy?"

"He'll do what he's told."

"Good, keep me posted."

Lambert had embarrassed Roger on several occasions. Roger had been more naive at the time. He had learned quickly not to trust the Deputy Director. One of these days, when the time was right, his name would be written down and handed to Manny. The thought brought a smile to his face.

Roger looked at his watch and decided he had made Wellborn wait long enough. He enjoyed making lesser men anticipate an audience with him. He rose from his desk and walked to the office door.

"Doctor Wellborn, please come in." He disdained this plump little man. However, pleasantries were necessary for now.

Charles Wellborn had been educated at the denominational school. He had a doctorate in theology and had no problem reminding his colleagues of their lessor education. Charles considered himself among the new spiritually elite. As others who had been educated in a modern seminary, he had long ago given up the notion that the Christian scriptures were the sole authority of truth.

Charles cleared his throat and struggled to rise from the chair. He was grossly overweight and walked with a slight limp that was due to his girth. His body was ravaged with weight bearing maladies and though only in his early thirties, he had the mobility of a much older man. Standing to his full height of six feet, he struck an odd picture of arrogance and weakness.

"Do you know how long I've been waiting?" He made no attempt to hide his anger. "I have travelled here from Youngstown and resent having to sit here for over an hour! Our appointment was for one o'clock."

Roger stared evenly at the portly figure before him. "My apologies," he said sourly. "I had other concerns that took precedent." Roger smugly toyed with the idea of giving this man's name to Manny. He smiled as he turned toward his desk.

Charles sat in one of the two chairs in front of Roger's desk. Beads of sweat broke out on his forehead. The large man extracted a soiled handkerchief and began mopping his brow. Even though government officials had air conditioning, the units never worked efficiently.

The fat man's discomfort amused Roger. He watched him struggle into his seat. His deep breaths indicated the difficulty he was having with the humidity. Roger had a small cooler with water that he kept under his desk. Ignoring Charles, he pulled out the cooler and withdrew a bottle. He methodically screwed off the cap, took a long drink then placed it on his desk. Charles was looking from the cooler to Roger. He even licked his lips. He would make no offer of a drink to Charles.

"Now Charles, let's get down to business. You were hand picked to be second to Crenshaw and I must say, the information you've provided has been beneficial."

"May God rest his soul." Charles said reverently.

"Yes, of course. Now, if I understand your bylaws, you are obligated to call an emergency session to elect a new Superintendent. Is that correct?"

"Yes."

"You have served the people well. Now I need to know who among your more enlightened and educated members would understand that serving the people is the same as serving God?"

"Roger," Charles began.

"Regional Director, Reverend." Roger reprimanded.

"Ahem, Regional Director," Charles began, "since I have proven myself as a servant of the people, I would have thought that I would be the most appropriate candidate."

Roger hesitated and smiled broadly at Charles. "Of course you have served the people. But Charles, surely you know your physical appearance is your biggest hindrance?" The look of astonishment on the fat man's face was the highlight of his day. He watched intently as he again removed the handkerchief from his suit jacket and wiped his forehead. Charles tried to lean forward, but his large midsection made it nearly impossible. He struggled to his feet and removed his suit jacket. Large sweat stains had formed under his armpits.

He continued, "Surely you did not think that you would ever be chosen as the people's representative? There are other men, better educated and presentable, to be chosen for the job."

"Not only did I think it, I shall make sure that I'm nominated." He said this as he shifted in his seat.

Roger sat quietly. Leaning back in his seat, he steepled his fingers at his lips and stared into Charles' eyes. The effect was beautiful. The preacher's arrogance was waning. After a few minutes, Roger left his seat and walked to the filing cabinets against the North wall. In the five steps necessary to reach the cabinets, he had extracted a key from his pocket and unlocked the first cabinet.

Pausing for effect, he slowly turned and went back to his desk. Standing erect, he tossed a folder down in front of Charles, simultaneously saying, "You will do what you are told."

Charles was clearly taken aback. The puzzled look on his face told Roger he had no idea what was coming. Still standing, Roger leaned forward and shoved the file toward his prey. "Open it," he said quietly.

When Charles didn't comply his voice became sinister, almost feral. "Open it," he hissed.

Obviously frightened, Charles reached for the folder. He spilled the contents on Roger's desk. He made a mewling sound as disbelief changed his features. His hand trembled as he spread the photographs out. Weeping, he looked at Roger pleadingly. "Please don't do this."

Roger was gratified by his sniveling. The pleasure he derived from making men like this beg was almost sensual.

"Please!" His voice was quavering. "It was a mistake, I didn't mean it." His ample frame was racked with sobs.

"Should we actually elevate a pedophile to be the leader of your God's church?" Charles' suffering was intoxicating. He knew Charles would do or be whatever he wished. So much for his God. He, Roger, was now his god.

"You will do what you are told, or these pictures go public. After all, don't I have a civic duty to protect children from the likes of you? Don't you think your church would want to know the kind of man they have giving them spiritual direction?"

"It will ruin me," Charles sobbed.

"So tell me Charles, what will you do?"

"I will do what I am told."

Roger smiled.

Chapter 9

Jedediah turned into the parking lot of the Deep Dish Pizzeria. The meeting place was prearranged on rotation. The Brothers were cautious to protect their identity. The government's antagonism to Christianity had become palpable.

The transformation from tolerance of Christianity to outright opposition had evolved slowly. During the 1960s, prayer in school had been assaulted. Then the legalization of abortion and the passage of the hate speech legislation made it a crime for pastor's to preach on certain subjects because the law construed it as an attack on particular groups.

Jedediah remembered, with sadness, the men whose lives were ruined so the government could make examples of them. His dearest friend, Bob Yoder, had died a broken man in prison. He was convicted of verbal terrorism because he refused to allow an immoral law to supersede what he believed to be God's law.

Law enforcement broke down his door in the middle of the night and spirited him away. Since his crime was considered an act of terror no one heard from him for nearly eight months. His wife, Amanda, who had cancer, died before his public trial.

Other restrictions were imposed on the Church. Conservative churches suffered most from the legal tyranny, being forced to comply or have the doors of their churches closed. Many good men, men that Jedediah loved and respected, left prison broken.

The latest assault on the Church was the newly formed Department of Communication and Speech. Forced through the Congress and Senate, it was quickly signed into law by President Freeman and gave unprecedented power to unelected bureaucrats. The abuses were only beginning to be recognized. Forcing preachers to have their messages approved by this monolithic organization ensured that only government approved ideas could be presented.

When the arrests began, Jedediah and several others in various denominations had met to form a secret order. Their charter was to preserve pristine Christian doctrine and keep alive the vision of individual liberty and freedom as defined by the Word of God. Inspired by the Black Robe Brigade of the American Revolution, Jedediah envisioned a refuge of truth.

Seven men and three women who were leaders in their denominations met is secret and decided, after spending much time in prayer, to adopt The Brotherhood of Solomon as the name of the newly formed group.

They also adopted the motto of *With Wisdom and Courage,* believing both key ingredients to overcome the spreading evil. Over the last five years, the Brotherhood had grown to over five-thousand members. Broken into twenty-five regions, each group developed plans to promulgate liberty in Christ. Only the leaders of each region knew the identity of their total membership. The process of membership was tedious, but necessary. Each new member was recruited by the regional leader, and vetted long before they were approached to join. A recruiter must be convinced that the one they approach was beyond reproach.

Tonight Jedediah would attempt to recruit his newest member. He had watched the life of this young man for years. He knew now was the time to approach him. If he refused, Jedediah would walk away and never broach the subject again.

Stepping out of his car, he noticed a familiar vehicle. "So he did come," he said to himself. Smiling, he opened the door and stepped in. The smell of garlic assaulted his senses. Not unpleasant, but strong. He took a deep breath, enjoying the aroma.

****

Corbin sat at a corner table sipping a soft drink through a straw. He noticed Jedediah, smiled and waved. He stood when the old man approached and shook his hand.

"Good evening, Jedediah." His smile was warm and genuine.

"Beautiful evening, Corbin. Another gift from God."

After catching up, the two men ordered a pizza with everything. The small talk continued until the meal arrived. Jedediah said he was pleased to hear that Abigail was well. Corbin was excited about a new convert at the church, and described the process of them coming to Jesus in great detail.

After they had eaten, Jedediah looked at Corbin for a long while.

"Son," finally breaking the silence, "I have been watching your life for the past several years. I am convinced that your dedication to the cause of Christ is unshakable. But I must ask you, would you be willing to die for that truth?"

Perplexed, Corbin was not sure what to say. He recognized the gravity of the question. It was not meant to be rhetorical or theoretical. There was a gravity behind it that caused a chill to engulf him.

"Jedediah, is there something wrong?"

"Corbin, my Son, we live in dangerous days. I have seen truth tortured and trampled. There are forces working to destroy the gospel of Jesus Christ, unscrupulous and evil men who would imprison or murder all those who name the name of Jesus Christ. So I ask you again, would you be willing to die for that truth?"

Corbin stared into the old man's eyes. There was a sorrow there he had never seen before. The suddenness of the question caught him off guard. He had thought about this many times. He looked deep inside hoping to find a resounding yes, only to be disappointed by his inability to embrace that storm. Jedediah's gaze seemed to penetrate to his soul.

"I don't know," was all he could say. To say anything else would have been a falsehood. He didn't know if he could be brave enough to die for this eternal truth. It would have been easy to say yes, but it would have been a lie.

"Thank you, Corbin. You have verified my faith in you."

"I don't understand?"

"It was the most honest answer you could have given. Had you told me no, I would have walked out. If you had said yes, I would have known you were not ready for what I'm about to tell you."

"Jedediah, you're talking in riddles. I don't understand where this is going. What are you expecting?"

"Come Son, let's go for a ride. I need to speak with you in private."

Jedediah paid for the pizza and left an ample tip. This did not surprise Corbin. His mentor had always been a generous man, especially to servers. He once asked Jedediah why he always left such generous tips. His response was that his mother had been a waitress and had worked long hard hours. Her wages were extremely low and she depended on tips to earn her living. He did it to honor her memory and show appreciation for the hard work of those who served him. This, and many other traits, made it easy for Corbin to love and admire the man.

Jedediah drove his protege outside the city limits into the country. A gospel quartet was harmonizing on the CD player.

"There is nothing like the old hymns," Jedediah said reverently and began to softly sing along.

"Jedediah, what is going on?" Corbin asked.

"Patience, Son, patience. I must make sure we are not being followed."

Corbin looked over his shoulder out the back window. There was a set of headlights several car lengths behind them. Jedediah put on his turn signal and took a side road. The car sped past. He used a driveway to turn around and parked at the end of the road leaving the engine running. They sat in silence for several minutes. Satisfied the car would not return, and with no vehicles in sight, he pulled out on the main road and continued his journey.

They arrived at a little church. The sign was faded and the lawn overgrown. No one had worshipped there for a long time. Corbin was saddened by the thought. Jedediah pulled the car in back of the building turned off the lights and waited for *Amazing Grace* to finish before turning off the car.

"Corbin," he began, "do you believe this Gospel we preach is sufficient for the condition of man?"

"Yes," he answered perplexed.

"Not just his spiritual condition, but every aspect of human life?"

Corbin thought for a moment. He and Jedediah had had these conversations before. They would sit for hours and debate theological issues, sometimes late into the night.

"I believe that the Gospel touches every aspect of our lives," was his reply.

"Do you believe that God's Word teaches us to resist tyranny, and teach men to live free?"

"Why are you asking me these things? Why all the secrecy? Jedediah, I'm at a loss. Tell me what this is about." The concern in his voice was obvious.

****

Jedediah sighed. A sadness washed over him. He suddenly felt the weight of his years. The responsibility he carried was oppressive. He looked at Corbin and his heart was overcome with emotion. He had mentored this young man from the time he had entered Seminary. On him, he believed, rested the answer to the darkness that was coming. Corbin didn't realize his own potential, did not understand the confidence that his peers had in him.

"Corbin," the weariness in his voice was evident, "several decades ago freedom began to die in our nation. The Church was asleep. We missed the warning signs. We were so busy trying to build large churches and garner the praise of our colleagues that the true power of the Gospel was lost in that quest.

"Many convinced themselves that Christianity only pertained to the soul. That spiritual salvation was the only goal of the church. So we tolerated tyranny. We were conditioned for it. Churches practiced spiritual tyranny by using peer pressure to nudge people into choices made for them by the church. The arrogance of this was never challenged. Either conform or be ostracized."

"But Jedediah, doesn't the church have an obligation to guide people in the right path?"

"The church's obligation is to present the truth. To reveal Jesus, to call them to holiness. We made it our business to prohibit innocuous choices. Ecclesial authority began to dictate what could be read, seen or heard. Warnings are one thing, dogmatic demands are another." Jedediah spoke forcefully, perhaps more forcefully than he intended.

"I think I understand. Our sole responsibility is to present Christ. It is up to the Spirit to instruct a person on how to live. But how does the church's failure to do this lead to the tyranny you speak of?"

"We trained our flock to not question, to not think for themselves. They were conditioned to blind obedience. A believer must question. To accept a lifestyle based on the word of men, even if it is laced with scripture, robs a man of his ability to be free. It is a bondage worse than the bondage of sin."

"Why do you say that?" Corbin was perplexed.

"Because binding a man's conscience to another's will makes him a slave. Do you understand that?"

They sat in silence for a few minutes. Corbin was deep in thought. Jedediah prayed silently.

"I do understand that," was his reply.

"My Son, I'm about to reveal something to you that must stay between us, and only us. Will you let me trust you in this?"

"Jedediah, you can tell me anything. You know that."

"Once I have told you, I need to know soon if you will join me or not. If not, I shall never speak of it again. If yes, I promise you that God will use you in ways you've never dreamed. Can I trust your silence?"

****

The urgency of his mentor's words were sobering. He had known Jedediah for many years. He admired and loved this man like a father. He looked at the man before him. His deep blue eyes belied a keen intellect. He noticed for the first time how old he had become. The paleness of his skin, his furrowed brow, and the slight tremor in his hands. At first glance, a stranger would think him feeble and weak, but he was anything but that. Jedediah possessed a strength of character that most would never attain. How could he ever let this man down? Reaching over, he placed his hand on top of the old man's.

"I would never betray you, Jedediah."

"I am a member of a secret society," he began without hesitation. Corbin sat and listened intently as this warrior of the cross explained the purpose of the Brotherhood of Solomon. He never took his eyes off his friend. At times, what he heard stupefied him, yet he was not offended or horrified.

"I am asking you to join us," he concluded.

"What does your brotherhood intend to accomplish?" Corbin asked.

"To preserve freedom. To give men hope and the chance to make their own choices. To be free to serve God according to their conscience, unmolested by government, both ecclesial and federal.

"Corbin, Christianity is more than a spiritual journey. It encompasses life. A person cannot truly be free until the chains forged by his own actions are broken and he possesses the ability to live according to his conscience."

Corbin and Jedediah sat in silence. Corbin knew his mentor was correct. Freedom began with Christ, and was developed in a life governed by God.

The drive back to the restaurant gave Corbin time to think. As they approached the pizzeria, Corbin leaned forward putting his head in his hand. "Jedediah," he said without lifting his eyes, "I need time to consider this. I need to pray."

Chapter 10

The memorial service for Dr. Crenshaw had been touching. The hymns were stirring and those who spoke, did so with passion. The last to speak was Jedediah. He had known Dr. Crenshaw the longest. His words were comforting and painted a picture of hope.

Corbin sat on the left side of the assembly in the second row. He had a full view of the platform, and watched Roger Thurman with curiosity. *The man fidgets more than a child,* Corbin thought. Though Jedediah's message was inspiring, he could not help smiling at the Regional Director's discomfort.

"So today," Jedediah said with gravity, "we have a hope that cannot be shaken. One day we shall ride in the clouds. All our sorrow and suffering forgotten..."

Some of the older preachers let out with hearty "amens." Some nodded their heads in agreement. Jedediah finished his message with prayer. Corbin could not help but glance at Roger. This was an irreligious man. His face was set with scorn as he glared at Jedediah's back. The evident darkness surrounding him made Corbin uncomfortable.

Once the service was completed, the real purpose of the assembly would begin.

Dr. Wellborne struggled to his feet. His girth made it difficult for him to walk to the podium.

"We will call this meeting to order," he intoned with an air of authority. Slightly out of breath, he continued. "As you all know, the bylaws of the Evangelical Christian Union mandate a special election upon the resignation or passing of the denominational superintendent."

Corbin noticed Roger Thurman scanning the group and making notes. Behind him stood a strongly built man. His face was placid. His muscular six foot frame made everyone on the platform seem stunted except for Doctor Wellborne.

Jedediah had taken his seat next to Corbin once Charles took the podium. He gave Corbin a warm smile, and affectionately laid his hand on his shoulder.

Corbin smiled at his friend who fixed his eye on the podium and listened intently.

"At this time the Nominating Committee will read its report."

The committee secretary was tall and lanky. His jet black hair was combed straight back in a vain attempt to cover his balding crown. Clearing his throat, he began reading the report in a stentorian voice that could have been heard without the microphone.

"The nominating committee recommends the following names for the office of Denominational Superintendent..."

Corbin could not help but yawn. These meetings were more ostentatious than suited him. It always seemed to be a competition to prove who was the most important. Corbin was slightly surprised that most of the people nominated were well known for their views of limited biblical authority and vocal opposition to the basic doctrines of the faith.

"... and that concludes the report."

Dr. Wellborne waddled back to the podium.

"And now we will entertain a motion..." he was interrupted as Jedediah rose to his feet.

"The chair recognizes Dr. Jedediah Whitaker," he said, somewhat puzzled.

"Mr. Chairman, I would like to nominate Rev. Corbin Miller for the office of Superintendent."

Roger Thurman jumped to his feet and stormed to the podium. "Ladies and gentlemen, let the nominating committee do their job."

"A point of order, Mr. Chairman," Jedediah said firmly. "This man is not a part of this body and has no right to speak, nor should he be on the platform."

Charles Wellborne nervously stepped to the microphone. Corbin noticed his eyes flicker several times to Roger Thurman. "Jedediah, he is with the government and is here to assist."

"With respect to the man's position, he has no lot, nor part with us. My nomination stands."

Several men jumped to their feet. Some shouted in favor of Jedediah, others called for respecting the wishes of the government agent.

Corbin clasped Jedediah's forearm and pulled him into his seat. "Jedediah, why would you do this?"

"Because God has a plan for you," was his sincere answer.

"I cannot accept your nomination," he said with agitation.

"You must, my Son, you must." Jedediah looked full into Corbin's face. The evident tenderness moved the younger man. "This is the will of God."

*****

Corbin sat silently on the platform steps. Almost everyone had left the meeting. After Jedediah's nomination, near pandemonium had broken out. Those in the denomination who wished to become more compliant with the government's standard of worship had clearly revealed their intentions. Having worked behind the scenes for so long, and believing they had a chance to take control, they openly ridiculed what they called "the religion of the past."

Once the verbal jousting was over, round after round of voting took place. On the last and final ballot, there were two names left. Corbin Miller and his good friend Jeffrey Arbino. Jeffrey had been nominated by an elderly pastor that Corbin barely knew. As the final ballots were passed out, Jeffrey stood to his feet and asked that his name be withdrawn. Then on common consent Corbin was elected as the new Superintendent.

"Congratulations!"

Corbin looked up. It was Jeffrey. Corbin rose and hugged his friend. "Why would you drop out?" He was truly puzzled. "You are the most qualified of us both."

"God has other plans for me, Corbin. This was God's will. Lead with wisdom and courage."

The greeting of the Brothers had become familiar to Corbin. He had not been surprised when he had learned that Jeffrey was among their number.

As with the superintendency, Corbin feared himself not strong enough to serve in the Brotherhood. After leaving the restaurant that night, he had taken the long way home. He had much to think about. After three days of thought and prayer, he made his decision. He would join Jedediah in his quest. The old man's courage and enthusiasm were hard to ignore.

That night he called Jedediah and said only one thing, "Yes."

Two nights later, he sat in Jedediah's living room. Samson sat next to him, occasionally pressing his nose against Corbin's chest and breathing deeply. Corbin had to divide his attention between Jedediah and his dog.

After they had prayer together, Jedediah handed him the Brotherhood's covenant.

"You must speak aloud the covenant and sign it. Once done, you will be a part of the Brotherhood of Solomon. I can then reveal more of our mission."

Corbin reverently took the paper. He was surprised by the brevity of the document. Glancing up, he noticed Jedediah studying him intently.

"I'm ready," he said quietly.

Taking a deep breath he spoke the covenant, "I dedicate my life to serve God with wisdom, courage and honor.

"I affirm that human life is sacred, and will defend it at all costs.

"I will, by the help of God, live faithfully, and share the Gospel of hope to all mankind. I will labor to ignite the spark of freedom in every heart."

"I affirm that I will defend and aid widows, orphans and the fatherless.

"God being my helper, I will live with honesty, integrity and holiness.

"I will protect the identity of the members of this Brotherhood, especially from those who seek to do them harm."

Jeffrey was one of those whom he had sworn to protect. Recent events had only verified the importance of that covenant. Several of the Brothers had been arrested in Knoxville several nights before today's assembly. No one knew what became of them. There were only rumors. The last word Corbin heard was that they may have been executed.

Jedediah approached and interrupted their conversation.

"You planned this!" Corbin said. "Jeffrey, you were in on this too, weren't you?" The look Jeffrey and Jedediah gave each other when the old man approached made Corbin's conclusion obvious.

"We trusted God it would be so," Jedediah said.

"You knew this would divide the assembly."

"Yes, I knew that serpent, Thurman, was handling Wellborne. Charles has been on a tight leash lately. Thurman has seen to that. And, yes, I knew challenging Thurman would cause a division among the preachers. We must be wise as serpents."

"Jeff is far more qualified than I for this," Corbin protested.

"That is precisely why we wanted you," Jeffrey said smiling. "Corbin we need a man like you leading us. You are acutely aware of your weaknesses. Dr. Crenshaw was consumed with power and prestige. Power is intoxicating, even for those who follow the Nazarene."

"The same could happen to me," he protested.

"We will be your advisors," Jedediah smiled. "Courage, Corbin, God has called you for such a time as this."

*****

Roger threw his coat on the bed. He picked up the phone and ordered room service. *What had just happened! That twit, Wellborne, was supposed to keep those rubes in line.*

The knock at the door interrupted his inward tantrum. Moving with haste, he pulled the door open.

"Come in, come in," he said impatiently. Spinning around, he led Manny into the room.

"I have a job for you. This Whitaker. I want to know as much about that old fool as you can find out. He set back any progress we've made with these fools."

Manny stood silently. His hands were thrust into his pockets. He carefully watched Thurman pace back and forth.

Roger stopped and looked at Manny. There was something creepy about the man. His eyes were hollow, no emotion. "Don't you ever speak?" he half shouted in frustration.

"When I need to," was his terse reply.

"Find out about Whitaker. I want his house bugged and his phone tapped. I want to know what time he gets up, and when he goes to bed. When he eats, and how often he uses the john. What are you waiting for? Go!"

Manny waited several seconds, then silently turned and walked out the door.

Chapter 11

Manny walked out of Thurman's room slowly. *One of these days I'll write his name on a piece of paper*, the big man thought. The idea made him smile. Manny never had a need to smile. Happiness was a foreign idea to him.

Thurman was a small man with a small mind. He really wasn't much better than the religious boobs he despised. Still he supplied Manny with entertainment and the job paid well.

Manny had an intense disdain for practitioners of Christianity. His mother had made his childhood a living hell. She would beat him for the smallest infraction. Whenever he displeased her, she would shut him up in a closet for days. As he sat in the darkness he heard her pray and sometimes say amen to the strange cadence of a radio evangelist.

One time he had begged her not to lock him in the closet.

"Please Mama," he had pled. "Please, I'll be good." He still remembered the brutal slap across his cheek.

"You're going to hell, Manny. You are a wicked, wicked boy. You have to learn what punishment is."

As she closed the door to his prison, her voice became more tender, "Remember my baby, mommy loves you. This is what God wants."

On one occasion, he subsisted on one-half piece of bread for a week. Manny smiled again. It had made him strong.

When he reached his teenage years, he began to work out. His intense training taught him discipline and endurance. To work off his frustrations, he would bully kids in his neighborhood. When that lost its appeal, he turned to torturing and killing kittens and dogs. This taught him the value of power.

One evening Manny came home later than usual. His mother was standing inside with a belt in her hand.

"Where have you been?" she had demanded.

"Get out of my way," was his calm reply.

"How dare you!" she screamed, "How dare you!" Her arm came up quickly. The belt buckle struck Manny on the left side of his head. Blood ran freely as she struck him repeatedly.

Welcoming the pain he moved toward her. "Stop!" she screamed, "Stop!" He continued to move closer. "You ungrateful worm, you will do as you are told!"

She continued to strike, screaming, spittle clinging to her lips. He moved closer, feeling every movement of his powerful body. He was keenly aware of everything around him. Backed against the wall she swung the belt again. His strong hand grabbed her arm. She wriggled to get free, but the effort was in vain. Manny was still intoxicated by the ritual he had just performed on someone's pet cat. The smell of its blood was still in his nostrils. He could still hear its pitiful screams.

It only took him a few minutes to remove her tongue. He spent the next two hours torturing her. When he finally dispatched her, it was out of boredom and not mercy.

As he passed through the lobby, he saw Jedediah Whitaker. For a brief moment, Manny thought he had seen him before. As quickly as it came, the thought was gone. This old man would not be much of an obstacle, any more than Crenshaw had been. Killing him would be easy.

Thurman had ordered him to watch the old man and gather information. Manny would comply, but he felt such boring tasks beneath his skills. He did not like it when he could not toy with his prey. Manny knew he was the king of the beasts and he liked to torment his quarry. After he had his fun, he could then devour.

Manny walked over to the paper rack and grabbed a complimentary copy of the evening news, while keeping an eye on his prey.

He kept his distance as the old man exited the hotel. He followed him to the parking garage and used his cell phone to snap several pictures before the old man exited in his car. He scribbled down his license plate number, though he was certain Thurman had the old man's address. He did not want to leave anything to chance. If Thurman did not have it, he would use his security clearance to get Whitaker's address. Then the hunt would begin.

****

In the lobby Jedediah had seen Thurman's man looking in his direction. He was unnerved by his soulless eyes. After saying goodbye to Corbin, he hurried to his car.

As he was backing out he saw the big man again, and an uneasiness settled over him. This was not a coincidence. Thurman had put his dog on his scent. His time was growing short and he must do everything he could to prepare Corbin.

He took several back roads, turning left then right, always checking his rearview mirror to make sure he was not being followed.

Jedediah could not shake a growing sense of foreboding. This man had been Thurman's shadow. There was something dark about him, something evil. *Yes,* he thought, *something evil.*

Satisfied he was not being followed, he made his way home. Samson was there to greet him.

"Hello, boy!" He said with enthusiasm. "How ya been?" Samson replied with some very wet licks, which Jedediah took in stride.

Once the reunion was complete, he began to make plans on how to help Corbin navigate what was probably coming. Somehow he knew his time was short. The mission of the Brotherhood was urgent.

Since Corbin had taken the covenant, he had proven himself a capable leader. His genuinely humble attitude made it easy for the others to accept and trust him. Corbin's greatest strength was his inability to see himself as capable. Not that he was afraid to do hard things. On the contrary, he gave to exhaustion.

Jedediah methodically performed the ritual of making his evening tea. Once settled in his recliner, he took the phone from it's cradle and dialed.

"Hello," the voice was familiar.

"Corbin, this is Jedediah. We need to meet tomorrow at 8 a.m., I need to speak with you. Can you come here?"

"Yes, Jedediah, is everything all right?"

"Everything is fine, Son. I'll see you at eight."

Still unnerved by his encounter at the hotel, he went through the house and checked all the windows. He locked the deadbolt on the front and back door with Samson following at his heels.

Weary, he climbed the steps to prepare for bed, grateful for his companion.

****

Manny took another sip of coffee as he watched the old man's house. The neighborhood would have been considered upper middle class at one time. Whitaker lived in a red brick cape cod. The grass was neatly cut and the flower beds weeded. It stood in stark contrast to the houses surrounding his. Most of the homes were extremely dilapidated.

On either side of Whitaker's house were two story buildings that, in the past, would have provided shelter and warmth to the typical nuclear family. Since the economy had collapsed, and most to the residents of this neighborhood received some form of assistance, no one cared any longer, except the old man, and that intrigued him.

Manny was reading the scant file on Whitaker. He did not want to waste time while waiting. There was nothing illegal in his past, not even a traffic violation. He paid his taxes, his bills were up to date and he had a modest savings. According to the report, Whitaker had been married for forty years. His wife had died of breast cancer. He never remarried.

He attended school in Cincinnati at some Bible College Manny had never heard of. He then earned his Doctorate at John Fletcher Seminary where he would eventually teach. This had surprised Manny. The religionists he had met with were uneducated, ranting fools like his mother.

The front door of the Cape Cod opened and Jedediah stepped outside. He stood for a few minutes looking up and down the street. Taking his time to navigate the steps, he entered his car and pulled out of the driveway.

Manny waited a few minutes then pulled onto the road. He didn't need to stay close. The GPS tracking devise he attached to the old man's car would allow him to follow at a distance. Thurman wanted to know what he was up to. Once that information was gathered, Manny could do what he was created for. That made him smile.

Chapter 12

The trip into Philadelphia was grueling. Getting out of Pittsburgh was difficult enough. The two-hundred sixty mile trip on I-76 was worse. Though still a toll road, the condition of the interstate was abysmal. When Texas seceded, coupled with the continual unrest across the country, the economy crumbled and most roads in the nation had fallen into disrepair. The Pennsylvania turnpike was just another example of the failing infrastructure.

The number of people who could afford to drive on I-76 had dwindled drastically. Many could not afford vehicles, let alone the insurance needed to cover one. Most drivers avoided the turnpike, not having the extra income to pay the toll. This left it in a perpetual state of construction. The other nuisances Corbin met with were the security checkpoints along the route. Each checkpoint meant forty-five minutes to over an hour of waiting. The trip was long enough, but the added inconvenience had rattled his already jagged nerves.

He had been Superintendent for little over a month when Roger Thurman's office called and requested, no, demanded he attend a meeting in Philadelphia. The power this man wielded was disconcerting. Each of the men and women he shepherded were at the mercy of Thurman and his staff. Corbin had butted heads with the Regional Director's staff several times.

"You need to revise this message," Thomas Caldwell had told him. "There is a lot of hate speech in this and the law will no longer tolerate this criminal activity."

Corbin involuntarily shook his head as he remembered the encounter. Caldwell was just one of three Facilitators assigned to his denomination. Thomas Caldwell had recently graduated from college and had majored in speech relations. A college major Corbin had never heard of before. In his conversations with the diminutive Facilitator, he had ascertained that this was a new major designed to prepare eager students for a future with the Department of Communication and Speech. As with many looking to build a career, he was unnecessarily eager in enforcing the will of the Department.

"Mr. Caldwell," he had replied as respectfully as he could, "what part of this are you referring to?"

"You cannot judge people's actions, Corbin. These things you mention, adultery and premarital sex, are your opinion, and quite frankly, meant to demean people who disagree with you. You should really be ashamed. This is why our division exists. You narrow minded religionists have run amok and, thankfully, that is changing."

What saddened Corbin was that this young man was a product of extensive propaganda that he helped fund with his taxes. The thought made him cringe.

That the government had taken on the role of truth's arbiter was dangerous. Their conversation had driven him to his knees. Being forced to submit his message was chafing, but having a bureaucrat approve it was tyrannical.

After several days of soul searching coupled with fasting and prayer, Corbin preached his original message. During the time he spent on his knees, Peter's words in Acts clearly presented to him. Peter and his companions had been beaten and imprisoned for preaching what had been forbidden by the authorities. When they were brought before the Jewish leaders and reprimanded for continuing to proclaim the gospel, Peter stated simply, "we ought to obey God rather than man."

When he took the podium after that meeting, he did so not in defiance to men, but in obedience to God. Initially his hands shook because he knew what the consequence could be. Thurman had the power of Federal authority. Corbin could be arrested as so many others had. The initial fear was almost crippling. *"I could change a few things,"* he had thought, *"I could soften the impact, not mention the questionable points."* When the thought was born, a sense of emptiness and guilt filled his heart. No, his allegiance was to his God. No matter what Thurman could do, no matter the punishment, he could not take the easy way out.

This trip, he was certain, was a direct result of that message. When he had finished preaching he had felt a boldness and peace he had never experienced before. Though his stomach was in knots most of the trip, he was certain God would help him through the meeting.

Corbin took Exit 344 and merged onto I-676. He was not familiar with the area and watched anxiously for the exit toward Broad Street.

Thurman's office was in a newly constructed building for the Eastern Regional office of the Division of Verbal Equity and Faith on Race Street, not far from the Pennsylvania Convention Center. A parking garage had been constructed under the building.

Corbin found the building without difficulty. This allowed him to relax. He pulled up to a staffed guard post. The security officer looked to be in his mid-forties and not very friendly. Corbin rolled down his window as he came to a stop.

"I'm here to see Roger Thurman," he said.

"Name?" He asked tersely.

"Corbin Miller. He's expecting me."

"Photo ID please." Corbin fished out his driver's license and passed it through the window. The guard studied the photo ID and scrutinized Corbin for a few moments.

Apparently satisfied, he handed the license back to Corbin and opened the gate. As Corbin pulled in, he saw two armed men by the elevators. The atmosphere was unfriendly and caused Corbin to speculate on what he would face.

He took the elevator to the eighth floor. The ride was smooth and the music soothing, which seemed to be out of place for such an austere environment.

The elevator deposited him at the receptionist's desk. Corbin smiled cordially, "I'm here to see Roger Thurman, Miss."

Without looking up she motioned to a row of chairs and curtly said, "Take a seat." She made no further attempt to communicate with him.

Corbin walked over and took the first empty seat. He sat fidgeting with his fedora while the time slowly passed. After waiting nearly two hours, he walked back to the receptionist's desk and waited to be acknowledged.

Enduring several minutes of being ignored he cleared his throat, "Miss?" The twenty something woman continued typing without looking up.

"Excuse me, Miss!" He said with more emphasis. Finally exasperated, he leaned closer. "Young lady, didn't anyone ever teach you manners? It is polite to acknowledge someone who is speaking to you. I have been waiting nearly two hours. Is Mr. Thurman available?"

This made her look up. She glared at him and retorted, "He will be with you when he is ready!"

****

Roger sat sipping his afternoon tea. He quit drinking coffee around ten in the morning, having read somewhere that tea was better for your health.

It was nearly four o'clock and he figured Corbin had stewed enough. He relished this show of power. He wanted these nobodies to understand how insignificant they were. They were in his control. This one had defied his Facilitators several times and had encouraged the preachers in his denomination to do the same. So making him wait was just a warm up to what he had in store for Corbin Miller.

Rising slowly from his seat he walked to the door. "Gladys," he said addressing the receptionist, "send in Corbin Miller."

"Miller," she said curtly, "he'll see you now."

Corbin stopped briefly at her desk, smiled and said, "Thank you." A gesture she never acknowledged.

"Good afternoon, Regional Director." Corbin said politely.

"Sit down Miller," he said for effect. Roger watched to see his reaction. He was surprised that there was no outward response.

"Miller do you know why you are here?"

"I believe I do, yes."

"Then you are aware that you have defied the law by using hate speech from the pulpit?" Roger sat back and steepled his fingers and placed them under his chin.

"I am guilty of preaching the word of God," Corbin's response was calm and confident.

Ric DelleCave

"Doesn't your scripture order you to obey the government? Yet, you defy our Facilitators who are there to help you be a better citizen."

"Sir, you put words in the mouth of God. We are to obey the law as long as it is moral, ethical and does not require us to break God's law."

"So you are accusing the leaders of your government of being immoral? Unethical?" Roger was visibly angry. "You act as if you are better than the collective wisdom of our lawmakers."

"God's wisdom supersedes that of any man. I respect my leaders because of their office. However, I serve my God. If I am asked to act contrary to the law of God, I must side with Him."

He watched Corbin closely. Though he readjusted himself in his seat several times, he never raised his voice or betrayed any nervousness. He had hoped to cow this preacher as he had Charles Wellborne. After many hours of research, the worst they found was a parking ticket from seven years ago.

"You love your wife? Abigail, I believe, is her name. You wouldn't want to leave her alone to fend for herself would you?" Roger was satisfied with the reaction this elicited. He believed he saw the color drain from the man's face. This was the direction he needed to

100

go. "You could place her in jeopardy, she could be considered an accomplice to your malfeasance."

"My wife has nothing to do..."

"Yes," he interrupted, "yes, she has everything to do with it." Thurman smiled inwardly. He had found a way to keep this dog on a leash.

"In the future, you will follow the direction of your Facilitator. You will learn to change your hate speech and stop demeaning people with your rhetoric. Is that clear?"

Corbin said inaudibly, "I will continue to obey God, rather than man."

"What's that?" Roger's tone was harsh and scolding. "Speak up Corbin! What did you say?"

Roger was taken aback when Corbin lifted his face and stared into his eyes. It was the look of determination, not defiance that caught his attention.

"I will continue to obey God, rather than man." His voice was firm, there was no fear or submission in his eyes.

"You will do as you are told!" Roger was surprised that he was on his feet and shouting.

Corbin didn't blink. Instead he stood, and without uttering a word, walked out of the office.

Chapter 13

Corbin's encounter with Roger Thurman seemed like a distant dream. He had spent most of his trip home in prayer, sometimes crying openly. The thought of Abigail suffering for his choices was painful.

When he arrived home he told Abigail what had been said and the threats made against her. At one point, Corbin began to weep. She took his hand and placed her forehead against his.

"Corbin, it is as God wills. You are not in this alone. I would die a thousand times rather than see you deny God." As she spoke, tears filled her eyes. Gently placing her hand under his chin, she raised his head so she could look in his eyes. "The name of the LORD is a strong tower: the righteous runs into it, and is safe."

Corbin recognized Proverbs 18:10. He could hear the conviction in her voice. He also heard an inner voice gently prodding and asking, *why did you doubt?*

"Abbie, I don't know what I'd do if I caused you any harm. I am not strong enough to bear giving you pain."

"Corbin, I too serve Christ. Do I not have a right to stand with you? I could not bear knowing that my safety caused you to deny your faith.

With Wisdom and Courage

"For centuries, Christians have been persecuted, tortured and martyred. At one time, we had freedom in this country. It was a light on a hill. That light is being extinguished. We were fortunate for over two-hundred years. Now God is calling us to trust him. It is our turn."

Corbin did not respond. He knew Abbie was right. Why should American Christians never face a crucible? He also knew that his love for God must never wane. He looked deep into her eyes, she was so beautiful. She was his only real love. Yet, he knew he had to surrender her to the will of God.

****

His time had been absorbed in working with the Brotherhood. Over the past ten months, Corbin and Jedediah had organized small groups of dedicated believers to do acts of mercy in their communities.

A bill had been introduced in Congress that was expected to be signed into law that would make any charitable organization that did not register with the government illegal. The penalties outlined in the law would be severe. Anyone involved in an illegal group could face fifteen years in prison. There were also fines that could be levied that would put most churches out of business. It would also be a crime to proselytize, which effectively made it impossible for anyone in the group to share their faith. Many of the Christian charities had already complied due to the pressure exerted on them by the government. The law would just make it easier for the government to further clamp down.

Corbin's goal was to develop groups that would act independently of denominations, yet still share the gospel with those they helped. The Brotherhood established hidden locations that could be used to hide supplies that would be distributed as needed. The network was growing larger everyday.

It was becoming increasingly more difficult to attend a worship service that did not include government propaganda. Most denominations had complied with the new regulations, even to the point of encouraging their congregants to use the new Bible that had the sanction of the Division of Verbal Equity and Faith.

Each of the five main denominations, which included the Evangelical Christian Union, had contributed scholars to work on the new Bible. Once the work was completed, his Facilitator had given Corbin a copy and asked him to promote it to the pastors he led. All references to God as *He* or *Father* had been eradicated. The word *sin* had been replaced with *mistakes*. All references to lifestyle choices deemed to be negative or judgmental were removed. What they produced made Corbin cringe. When asked why he hadn't officially endorsed the new Bible, Corbin retorted, "This is no longer God's word, but a primer of social engineering! This is detestable." That outburst had resulted in an official letter warning him that his attitude verged on sedition.

The strangle hold the government had on the church had convinced him that the true church must begin to go underground.

Corbin's heart broke for the suffering of the people around him. Many could no longer find work, and the stipend they received from the federal government was barely enough to survive on. Crime had risen to an alarming level. Women had turned to prostitution and other demeaning jobs, to try to feed their children. Some simply abandoned their families, never to be seen again. The number of orphans had increased exponentially, many became homeless turning to drugs and crime.

Death among the elderly and very young during the extreme heat of summer and the cold of winter became common. The Brother's meant to change that. One challenge they faced, was providing adequate food and clothing for the growing number of poor.

Corbin and Jedediah had made a trip to Traverse City, Michigan to meet with some of the leaders of the Brotherhood. They had been actively smuggling in supplies from Canada. Most of their cargo had been nonperishable foods and second hand clothing. With winter coming in just a few months, jackets, sweaters and anything that would keep a body warm were in great demand.

The government had distribution sites in the major metropolitan areas for winter clothing. The inefficiency of these centers was appalling. Many were turned away based on income and religious affiliation. The bias against Jews and Christians had grown to a fever pitch.

Jedediah had used his influence to develop a system of moving the merchandise that would not rouse suspicion. Small amounts were moved daily to prearranged locations. Usually packed in the trunks of cars or vans. The drivers were members of the Brotherhood who had learned how to avoid the checkpoints on the main highways.

"It never seems to be enough," Corbin said to Jedediah, as they prepared to distribute the weeks parcels. "The needs grow beyond our ability to meet them."

"Corbin, there will always be poor. Even more so now that the politicians and power brokers oppress the people."

"I know," he said with sadness in his voice. "Jedediah, this seems an impossible task. Look at these people." He swept his hand toward the people waiting for a morsel of food and some clothing. "They have no hope. Look at their eyes. They are empty pools."

"Then give them hope," was his quiet response. "You cannot meet all their needs. But, you can offer them the hope of the nations. Corbin we do what we do for a greater purpose. Let these people find purpose in Christ and you will change their lives. Purpose will inspire hope."

"I know Jedediah, but how do we do that? These people struggle to live. They watch their parents and children die. Many cannot get the medicine they need. Do you see that gaunt woman there?" The woman he pointed to was in her early thirties, but malnutrition had aged her. Her hair was straw like and her skin hung on her bones. "She has three children. She goes days without food to make sure they eat. Her story could be multiplied one hundred fold. We are barely making a dent."

"Son," Jedediah's tone was tender, "every morsel of food we distribute is a testament to the love of Christ. We don't merely fight to save their bodies. Our battle is for the soul. What will it profit these dear people if we satisfy their hunger yet they miss the greatest gift ever given?"

"I am here! Now! I see what is happening and know I'm powerless to change it."

"No, Son you're wrong. We live for eternity. What we do now is preparatory for our real lives after we die. You are making a difference. Some of these here today will walk away ungrateful and perpetrate evil. Others will walk away with Christ in their hearts. These will change the world!"

Corbin watched the line of people move slowly forward. He heard the eager thank you's from the grateful, and was saddened by the brusque expectations of the greedy. His heart melted at their plight. Mothers who were thin and frail, clinging to their children, waited patiently for a meager supply of food. The supplies they gave would last for only a day, two at the most. Most of the people in the small borough of Arnold had long ago given up finding work.

Each parcel of food and clothing contained the Gospel of John. Since the reliable translations of scripture were no longer legal to print, the Brother's had been working on creating pamphlets containing books of the bible from those outlawed translations.

Corbin had struggled with this. It was an act of defiance to the government. In the end, he knew that this was God's struggle and he was just an instrument. This was necessary. The Word of God could not be withheld from the masses. It was a dangerous business, but had to be done.

Many of the Brothers had been arrested for crimes against the state, especially for violating the anti-hate laws. The Christian Scriptures, Talmud and Quran had all been outlawed as subversive. Christianity and Judaism were under constant attack. The Jews had faired worse with many of their Synagogues forcibly closed, and many of their religious leaders either imprisoned, murdered or exiled to Israel.

Nearly every week he received news that another preacher had disappeared, apparently arrested. Some surfaced later during their trials and others were never heard from again. Few of those lucky enough to be tried, confessed to sedition and repudiated their faith. At first Corbin condemned them, then over time realized he had no right. They became a constant matter of prayer. Those who refused to confess were either lost in prison, or assigned to permanent house arrest.

The thought made Corbin shudder. He was tired and missed Abbie. Thurman's threat had made him paranoid. He could not take the thought of Abbie paying for his choices. They had friends in Texas and the Brothers had smuggled her south of the border.

When he first approached her about leaving she had refused.

"Honey," she said, "my place is by your side."

"Abbie I am involved in a dangerous undertaking. Every day my actions make me an enemy of the state. If I were ever arrested they would use you as leverage. Don't you see? I can be stronger if you are safe. I don't want to have to choose between you and God." He knew he was weak, and not knowing her fate would make him weaker. His need to protect her might compromise his convictions.

"Corbin I can't leave you," she said weeping.

"Abbie please," he pled, "I know I am weak. I admit that. I cannot stand the thought of you suffering. What I've heard they have done to others, I could not endure if it happened to you. Please, my dear Abbie, please let me take you to refuge."

It finally took Jedediah's intervention to get her to concede. They had a tearful goodbye.

His mind went back to the day he had met her. She had visited the church he attended while at Bible School in Cincinnati. He was talking to Jeffrey Arbino when she exited the sanctuary. Her long brown hair hung to her waist. When their eyes met, she smiled demurely and slightly turned away. He continued talking to Jeff, but could not keep his eyes off this beauty. Uncharacteristically, he walked to her and asked her if she would like to go on a date. He was floored when she said, "Yes."

He was totally enamored by her. Her voice, smile and everything about her animated him. They dated for several months before he asked her to marry him. He knew the moment he had seen her that she would be his. Again, to his surprise, her answer was yes.

They had a modest wedding. Neither one wanted to go to great expense. With Jeff as his best man, he exchanged vows with the only girl he had ever dated. They had been married for nearly ten years and he loved her with all his heart. They had been unable to have children. That had been a source of deep sorrow for both. Now Corbin wondered at the wisdom of God. Worrying about Abbie was one thing. Having children would have made his situation far more unbearable.

He caught himself smiling. The ache in his heart grew. Corbin did not know when he would see her again, but at least she was safe. He felt a slight twinge of guilt, knowing that others in the Brotherhood had not been as fortunate. Some of the members had been arrested with their spouses. Corbin could not imagine the pain they must feel. When his time came and he was certain it would, Abbie would be safe.

****

Abigail trembled as she waited for Corbin to pick her up. She had packed enough for the trip. She looked at her home through a blur of tears. *Why Lord,* she questioned, *how have we come to this?*

Their house was modest, a ranch style home with three bedrooms. Abbie had longed for the day when she would hear the noise of her children playing. She had imagined teaching them about Jesus, going over their ABC's and helping them with homework. For reasons unknown, God had chosen to keep them childless. Being barren, she thought at the time, had been the greatest test she had ever faced.

Then, in 2014, things had collapsed in rapid succession. No one anticipated the collapse of the American republic. Some said it was prophecy fulfilled. Abbie was not sure of that. America was another nation in history that had a choice between honoring God or facing retribution. The political leaders had chosen the latter.

It was almost impossible to believe that in three short years the nation could be fractured. Texas had seceded. There were militia uprisings that began simultaneously. Washington had so decimated the military that they did not have the strength to deal with it all. She and Corbin had spent hours together praying for the nation.

She carried her bag from the bedroom to the living room. Abbie stood in the center and let her eyes sweep it, probably for the last time. The light blue davenport was faded and frayed on the arms. She remembered when she and Corbin had bought it.

"Which one do you like?" Corbin said with a toothy grin. He and Abbie had only been married two months at the time.

"I like the light blue one. I think it would go well with our carpet," she squeezed his arm and laid her head on his shoulder.

"I like this one," he said, pointing to a lime green couch with light yellow flowers.

"Oh! Corbin!" She exclaimed, "That is hideous!" When she looked at him, she could tell by his laughter that he was teasing her. She punched him in the left arm.

The memory brought tears to her eyes. Though heart broken, she knew she had not suffered as many were. Corbin's position with the Evangelical Christian Union provided for their needs, although she and Corbin lived frugally so they could help their needy neighbors.

That outreach had given her opportunity to share the scriptures once a week with a small group of women in the community. She would miss that as well.

She sat on the davenport and ran her fingers over the familiar upholstery. All of her memories were in this house; photos, knickknacks, everything that meant home and safety. She began to weep.

"Abbie, I'm so sorry," she recognized Corbin's voice. She knew it may be one of the few times she would hear it again.

Drying her eyes, she responded, "Don't be Honey, Jesus paid a higher price for my redemption. I am not better than He."

Corbin moved toward her. She relaxed in his embrace. She wanted to hold him forever. Her love for him was beyond her ability to communicate. She wrapped her arms around his waist and locked her fingers together.

"I love you," she whispered. "Oh Corbin, how I love you." Though she tried to be strong, she could not bear what may lie ahead. She wept uncontrollably.

****

After loading Jedediah's car, the three of them had prayer. Abbie felt more strength after that. When they started their journey, no one noticed the vehicle following them.

It took nearly three days to reach the border of the Republic of Texas. They had made stops in several major cities where members of the Brotherhood had safe houses for them to briefly rest. The first day they stopped in Cincinnati. The next morning they were back on the road with a full tank of gas.

When they reached Shreveport, Louisiana, preparations would be made to cross the border. The Freeman administration had built a twenty-foot tall fence along the Texas border. Since Abbie knew no one was clamoring to enter the United States, she understood it was to keep U.S. citizens from going to Texas.

The Brotherhood had a strong organization within the newly formed nation, and had arranged for Abbie to get a permanent visa. The trick was getting into Texas. The border patrol presence was extensive.

They were put up in Shreveport and moved each night to a new location. Jedediah's car had been abandoned at the first safe house, and he and Corbin would retrieve it later. After a week of planning, the move to Texas would begin.

Abbie grew more apprehensive as they neared the point of entry. Leaving Shreveport they took I-20 until they reached Exit 5. Once on Greenwood Road, they followed the route into Greenwood, Louisiana. In Greenwood, they switched cars again.

"Rev. Miller, Sister Miller, I am Brother Forrester. I will be taking you into Texas. Sister, there is a visa in this folder along with a new identity. The Brother's in Texas were able to get you religious and political asylum. Any ID you have on you now please, give them to me."

"You mean I'm no longer going to be me?" She wasn't sure she liked that.

"It is for your protection, and Corbin's. Unfortunately the U.S. government has operatives in the Republic that have been successful in kidnapping and removing people they consider subversives."

She looked at her husband, "Corbin?"

"You must Abbie. It is the only way to keep you safe."

"There is also another caveat," Forrester said. Tom Forrester was five feet ten inches tall and solidly built. If Abbie had seen him at random, he would have been intimidating. He had black stubble on his square jaw, and a full head of wavy black hair. His powerful build made him look more like a construction worker than a preacher.

"What's that?" Abbie tried to sound brave, but was afraid she had already anticipated what it was.

"You cannot communicate with Corbin directly." His tone was apologetic. He averted his eyes when he spoke. "If you want to get a message to him there are a few things you must do. The message must be type written. Nothing can be said that identifies you or Corbin. Our operatives will deliver one message every month. These same rules apply to you as well." This was addressed to Corbin.

"This is just as important. Once we get you to Tyler, you must say your goodbyes. Corbin cannot know your new identity, or know where you are. These are the rules."

"How will my messages get to her?" Abbie could hear the fear in his voice.

Tom pulled Corbin aside so no one could hear. "Once we leave her and we return to Shreveport, I will give you directions. Any communication for Abbie will be sent to a third party in Louisiana. You will address your message to Reverend Gates. The Brother's assigned to your case will know how to route it. You cannot tell this information to anyone, not even Jedediah. Do you understand? If you fail to do this, your wife could be in jeopardy."

Abbie was quiet as they reached the border check point. Many Americans worked in Texas and had work visas that got them across the border. The guards were members of the New American Liberation Corps. Each were carrying an M16. Every car was scrutinized and all occupants questioned. Corbin and Jedediah were given fake ID's for the border crossing.

When they reached the gate, a young soldier with a baby face rudely demanded they exit the vehicle. Abbie had watched with sadness the change of behavior among America's youth. This young man, no more than eighteen, had been given tremendous power of which he was fully aware. Many youth who had joined the New American Liberation Corps, known as NALC, had unprecedented authority. These young people committed atrocities that were never punished. They were the strong arm of the newly formed American Democracy Party. President Freeman announced the formation of the party after elections had been suspended over the Texas revolt. Though other political parties could exist. None of their candidates ever won elections.

When he barked his order, everyone immediately complied. The shrill voiced youth scrutinized everyone's paper and had the car searched. The process took about an hour. Abbie wondered how people remained patient as she saw the long line of vehicles waiting to go to Texas.

It was a short drive to Tyler. Abbie did not notice anything about the town. She had a tight grip on Corbin's hand. She was cognizant of its warmth. Periodically she would raise it to her lips and kiss his hand gently. "I love you," she whispered.

Tom stopped the car in a park when they were a safe distance from the border crossing.

"Smell that? That is the smell of free air." He smiled for the first time since she met him. "You two need to say your goodbyes," he said looking at Corbin. "We have to get back."

Corbin took Abbie's hand and led her to a bench.

"Corbin," she began, "I don't think I can do this." She began to sob. Corbin wrapped her in his arms and cried with her. "Please let me come back with you. I don't want to exist without you," her voice was broken.

"Abbie, I love you more than life itself. If I could change all this, I would."

"Why do you have to go back? What purpose would it serve." She already knew the answer. She scolded herself for her weakness and selfishness.

"Abbie," he pulled her chin up and looked in her eyes. She saw the compassion mingled with pain. It was unfair of her to do this to him. She knew God had called him for this. He had accomplished so much good in the midst of such suffering. "Do you believe that I love you?" He continued. "This is not goodbye. We will be together again, but my job is not complete. There are many who need me. Preachers that have put their lives in jeopardy for me. We have just set in motion a plan to educate the public about who we once were."

"But, Corbin if they arrest you, you will suffer. I feel this. I fear this." She held his gaze. She wanted to persuade him, find the words that would change his mind.

"My love, there have been many men, better than I, who have been tortured, some murdered. My Lord suffered the worst fate of us all. Am I better than He?"

"Oh, Corbin, it is knowing that God has called you to this that I fear. I know He will protect you. But, I don't know if I can place you in His hands."

"You are the strongest woman I know. Abigail, if I were to die for the faith, we will meet again. This is the time of testing. Before the calamity in 2014, faith was theoretical. The worst most faced was trivial compared to this. Don't you see? We asked God for years to let us show his glory and he is using the circumstances around us to glorify Himself."

She kissed him deeply. With every ounce of her being she knew he was right. They held each other for a long time. She wanted to remember his smell, how his body felt close to her's. She was writing every detail of this moment in her memory.

"Corbin," the voice was soft, "we must go."

Abbie opened her eyes. She noticed the sky was blue, nearly cloudless. The park where they sat was clean and children were at play. People were going about their business, most smiling. She had not seen that in years. God had given her a refuge, a place where she could pray for Corbin. She could support him from here. She was determined to work with the Brotherhood.

Abbie watched the van until it became a speck. She blew one last kiss, then left with a Texas Brother to begin her new life.

Chapter 14

Roger Thurman scrolled through the contacts on his smartphone. Only government officials were allowed to have this type of device. Smartphones, along with unlimited and unrestricted access to the internet, had been outlawed for the general populous. Limiting the mass's ability to get instant information and to communicate quickly had made it easy to elicit compliance to the necessary laws.

People who could afford it had cell phones, but the service was unreliable. Most of the population could no longer afford personal computers. Those who did own them worked mainly for the government.

Finding the name he needed, he prepared a text message.

Come to my office immediately.

He pressed send knowing that Manny would receive it almost immediately. He would waste no time coming to his boss.

Roger leaned back in his seat and studied the file Gladys had pulled for him.

You've been a busy man, he thought as he perused the information Manny had gathered on Jedediah Whitaker. He still chafed at the embarrassment of losing the selection of a new superintendent to Whitaker's man. The old man had pull in the denomination.

What was curious were the trips the old man and Miller had taken together. Something he saw made him sit upright in his chair.

"Texas," he whispered, "how had he managed that trip without my knowledge? How did he get across the border?" Manny would answer for this. That oaf had kept this out of his report. Why hadn't this been reported to him? The one thing Roger could not abide was incompetence. Maybe he trusted Manny too much. Perhaps a few days back in prison would wake him up.

He picked up the phone to call the fool when Manny walked into his office.

"Ah, there you are. Didn't I tell you to let me know anything out of the ordinary on Whitaker?"

"Yes," came the simple reply.

"Don't you think this old man and Miller traveling about the country worthy news?" The irritation in his voice was obvious. "And how could he have gotten to Texas without my knowing it?"

Manny didn't answer. He stared at Roger without moving.

Manny's silence infuriated him. He rose swiftly from his desk with the file and slapped it into Manny's chest. The giant did not flinch, nor did he raise his hand to grab it.

"Take it!" Roger fumed, "Take it!"

Manny's massive hand grabbed the file and threw it back on the desk.

"I want to know everything about this man. I see in the file that no cameras or listening devices have been installed at his house. Why?"

"The old man lives alone and we have his phone tapped. He didn't seem to be that large of a security risk." That was the most Manny had ever said to his boss.

"I want to know when this man eats, sleeps and uses the john. Now get to it."

When Manny left, Roger called Jack Barnes.

"Jack, Thurman here, I have a job for you. I'm going to email you a file. I need an extra set of eyes on two men. I am not confident that the people I have working on this are telling me everything."

He ended the call and went to Gladys's desk. She would have the file to Barnes in a matter of minutes.

****

Leaving the office, Manny reached into his right front pants pocket and rubbed a piece of paper he kept there between his thumb and forefinger.

Manny despised men like Thurman as much as he did hypocrites like his mother. This Whitaker that Thurman despised was unlike both. Manny had been observing him and Miller on and off for months. Both worked tirelessly to help people more needy than themselves. His access to private information revealed that both men had used their own finances to fund some of their work.

Manny had left much of their activity out of his reports. He wasn't quite sure why. Manny considered Whitaker harmless. He was not arrogant like Crenshaw, nor a sniveling sycophant like Charles Wellborne. After hours of following the man, he began to respect his commitment. That was new for Manny. One thing was certain, he despised Thurman much more.

He headed back to his townhouse. He was back in Philadelphia for three weeks and would head back to Pittsburgh in seven days. The work he did for Thurman paid well.

All his records had been scrubbed and he technically did not exist. This made it convenient for him to exterminate those on Thurman's list.

Whenever Roger wanted him to dispatch someone, he would type their name on a small piece of paper and hand it to him. No words were ever spoken. This, Manny was sure, was to protect Thurman in case anything went wrong.

He finally reached his home. He unlocked the front door and threw his keys on an end table. Manny's townhouse was comfortably furnished. He had abstract art hanging on the walls. He had no idea what most of them depicted. He bought them because he could afford them. He saw no beauty in them, yet the chaos of color and brush strokes somehow connected with him.

The living room had plush leather chairs and a couch. The north wall had a working fire place. Since it was mid-autumn, he would build a small fire. Once the fire was prepared, he poured himself a glass of wine and sat in an overstuffed chair.

For some reason he was troubled about what he must do. It was curious. He had never believed he had a conscience or soul, but somehow these two men troubled him.

After finishing his wine he fell asleep to fitful dreams.

Chapter 15

Manny was surprised when he received a call from Jack Barnes before leaving for Pittsburgh. He informed Manny that Thurman assigned him to tail Whitaker and Miller and would send him whatever intelligence he gathered. Manny accepted having a new partner, although Thurman's lack of trust would merit closer scrutiny. Reflexively he put his hand in his pocket to feel for the paper and rubbed it between his fingers.

The trip from Philadelphia to Pittsburgh was uneventful. Manny had unlimited use of the department's private jet. The jet was comfortable and could seat six. Manny would be the only passenger tonight. Once the pilot leveled off at thirty-five thousand feet, Manny poured himself a drink and read Barnes' first briefing report.

His unrestricted use of the jet made it easier for him to move about the northeastern states for his boss. Once they had landed, he waited patiently as the pilot taxied to a stop. Stepping off the plane he took a deep breath of the cool autumn air. The attendant retrieved his bag and directed him to a waiting SUV.

Manny climbed into the driver's seat and retrieved his smartphone from his pocket. He sent a quick text message to Thurman to let him know his time of arrival.

It was 8:30 in the evening and traffic into Pittsburgh would be light. The jet had landed at a private strip near the Pittsburgh airport. The Department had mandated the construction as imperative to security. Manny knew the real reason was the convenience of the bureaucrats who loathed rubbing shoulders with common citizens. Not that he found fault with that logic. He just despised their dishonesty.

Whatever the reason, it served his purpose. He was a ghost. He had no past, thanks to Thurman and did not exist. There was no DNA record, fingerprints or any other identification that would verify he even existed. To protect his anonymity, he never used commercial flights where security cameras were sure to capture his image. Though the security at this official government airport was extensive, most of the cameras were focused on the perimeter. No one had access without going through an extensive pre-screening.

His travel arrangements took him from the flight directly to his vehicle, avoiding any surveillance. Manny waited for the attendant to load his bag into the back of the vehicle. He did not bring a change of clothes. What he had to do would be quick and he would be back in Philadelphia by morning.

The private road leading from the airport deposited him onto I-279. As he anticipated, the traffic was light. He found a classical music station and lost himself in the music. He did not consider himself a connoisseur, and really did not care who composed the music. Normally he liked the silence, but the soft melodic tones helped him to concentrate.

He was not sure why Thurman found this Whitaker so threatening. He was an old man. His religious superstitions were irrelevant to current society. That was why Manny had not expended much effort monitoring him which resulted in Jack Barnes being assigned to get information on him.

Barnes' surveillance reports were in his bag. Once he got to his destination he would review them again to make sure he did not overlook anything.

He turned down the music to answer his phone which was ringing with urgency.

"Yes," he said tersely.

"Manny, this is Jack. Are you in town yet?"

"Just landed. I'm headed to my destination. What do you have for me?"

"The old man is with Miller in Erie. Some small meeting about prayer and personal responsibility, nothing of note," his monotone voice grated on Manny.

"The meeting is about to end, and then they plan to return to Pittsburgh."

"Let me know the minute they leave," Manny's voice was cold. He hung up before Barnes could respond.

Barnes' call was necessary, but chafed him. He turned the radio volume higher than before and lost himself again.

The GPS system had been programmed by some unseen agent at the airport. It's female voice notified him that the Churchill exit was approaching. He took the exit and followed the sultry voice to his destination.

He drove past Whitaker's house slowly. No lights were on and the neighbors had their shades closed. The neighborhood had been upscale in the past. Though the decay was not as visible in the darkness, the abandoned cars and corner drug deals dispelled any doubts.

Turning left at the next corner he drove several blocks and parked. He pulled out the reports that Barnes had filed and using a small pen light, perused the information. He was not surprised to see that the old man and Miller spent considerable time together.

Whitaker was gone quite a bit, taking trips to nearby cities and was involved in some small illegal activity distributing food, clothing and other necessities to families in each location. He also noticed he had a dog, although the report didn't specify breed or size.

The dog would not pose much of a problem. Even if it barked, the neighbors would probably ignore it. Manny smiled. He had dispatched enough of these creatures in his youth. He did not fear them. He was the king of the beasts. He had perfected prolonging the agony of these creatures as a child. It was when he ended his mother that he realized the torture and killing of humans was much more fulfilling. His inability to feel empathy for anything that drew breath was what had brought him to Roger Thurman's attention.

When he met Thurman, he had been in solitary confinement for three years. His need to kill had ended in the dispatching of several hardened criminals. Their deaths had been slow and painful. When he was working, he liked to take his time. The death penalty was no longer legal, so solitary confinement was the only option prison officials had to protect other inmates.

On August 6 (he remembered the date because that was the day his life began) he was taken into a small room. The room was a pale green with a tile floor. He was led to the metal table that was bolted to the floor. The shackles on his ankles made it difficult for him to walk. Led by two guards, he shuffled to the room. Once he sat down, his restraints were secured to the table.

When he first saw Thurman, he imagined how easy it would be to crush him. Small, thin and pale, Thurman's demeanor was effeminate. The tiny man sat in the chair opposite him. He sat upright not letting his back touch the chair. His voice was surprisingly deep for his appearance.

"How would you like to get out of here, Manny?" He began the conversation.

"Who are you?" He was suspicious of this waif.

"I'm your savior, Manny, I'm going to give you a new life!"

Manny stared into his eyes. He was surprised the man did not flinch. He held Manny's gaze. The smile on his face was plastic, one that a politician would wear.

Manny leaned forward, his voice cold, "Do not toy with me." This made the man flinch. Manny leaned back in his chair. "You're wasting your time," he said after a few moments.

Thurman opened a folder that was placed by his right hand and slid a small pile of pictures to Manny. Thurman nodded to the guard and he removed Manny's cuffs. Surprised by this show of trust, Manny spread the photos on the table in front of him. Though he remained expressionless, he relished the images before him. He glanced up and saw Thurman's toothy grin. This, he was sure, was an honest smile. His urge to crush this man was almost overwhelming.

"I have the authority to get you out of here," Thurman said, after some silence.

"I like being alone."

"Not out of solitary, out of prison. You would work for me doing what you like." He motioned toward the pictures on the table. "You would get to play with whomever I choose."

Manny stared at the man. He imagined how loudly he could make him scream. How long he could endure before he died from relentless punishment.

Three months after that meeting, Manny was freed from prison. He had been working for Thurman ever since.

He finished reading the file, and retrieved the bag from the back of the SUV and returned to the driver's seat. The bag contained the listening devices and cameras he would install in Whitaker's house. He removed the tactical knife and sheathed it on his belt. He was already wearing his silenced handgun. He did not like using guns, they were too quick. He liked to savor his kills. Before exiting the car, he hung a balaclava on his belt. He would put that on a block before the house.

Though he was a ghost, there was no reason to be careless. He did not want his picture circulated among local law enforcement. Outside the vehicle, he pulled the hood up on his zip up sweat shirt. He hunched his shoulders, put his hands in his pockets, and started toward Whitaker's block at a fast pace.

The streets were dark. The streetlights had either been broken, or had burned out. The economic depression that was crippling the country made such expenditures impossible. Half a block ahead he saw three figures. By their height and build, he knew they were male. As he drew closer, they separated. One of the men stood in his path and the other two stepped behind him.

Manny felt a rush that ignited his senses. The man in front put his hand in the center of Manny's chest.

"You goin' somewhere boy?" His voice was a low growl.

Ordinarily Manny would have ended him right there.

"Don't make this mistake," was his simple reply.

"What are you gonna do? Huh?" The obviously inebriated young man was raising his voice. That worried Manny. He could not afford to draw attention to himself. To be a ghost, you had to be unseen.

In a swift motion he drew the knife from it's sheath. The reverse grip placed the spine of the blade against his forearm. Before the young man could flinch Manny grabbed his left shoulder and moved the knife across his throat. The razor sharp blade cut deep.

Clutching his throat and unable to scream, the man went to his knees. Blood covered Manny's legs. Without hesitating, he spun and plunged the blade into the second man's chest. It punctured his heart. Letting go of the knife's handle, he pulled his handgun and the night's silence was interrupted by the clack of the gun chambering. The boy's head snapped back and he fell on his side.

Manny had not broken a sweat. He smiled to himself. "Still king of the beasts," he whispered. Extracting the knife from the dead youth's chest, he wiped it on the kid's jacket. Then he put away his gun, he grabbed two of the fallen boys by their collars and dragged them behind a stand of untrimmed bushes. After retrieving and hiding the third victim, he continued on his mission.

****

Jedediah was weary from the trip. He and Corbin had been traveling through Pennsylvania, Maryland, Ohio and southern New York. They had only returned to Pittsburgh briefly before leaving for Erie.

He worried about Samson. He knew these protracted trips were stressful on his friend. His neighbors, the Kessler's, had been old family friends. They loved Samson and made sure he was fed and taken out. They kept him with them during the day. They would return him home for the evening. For some reason, his companion would not cease whining in the evening until he was back home. Jedediah anticipated their reunion. Before their meeting in Erie, he had stopped at a pet store and bought his friend some treats.

He and his late wife, Lydia, had spent many hours with the Kessler's. They were devoted to each other, and to Christ. Reminiscing made his heart ache for Lydia. After forty years of marriage, he spent the last three watching her waste away. She had been diagnosed with breast cancer a week before their thirty-seventh wedding anniversary. They had spent the day in prayer. Lydia silently wept. A trip to the oncologist gave them hope.

She was in the early stages of the disease, and stood a good chance of survival with the proper treatment.

The national healthcare system had been in place for nearly 10 years. Considering her age, Lydia was refused treatment. The doctor could only prescribe pain medication and his beloved Lydia suffered greatly and died needlessly. That was the first time that Jedediah really understood the consequences of the slow erosion of personal liberty. Human life had inexorably lost its value. Lydia's death awakened a dormant fear of a soulless bureaucracy. Her death had been the impetus that began the Brotherhood. He had no desire for revenge, only to alleviate the suffering of the unfortunate and preserve the knowledge of freedom. Corbin had been a Godsend. His humble spirit, ability to organize and motivate other believers, had given the Brotherhood a broader influence.

"Jedediah," Corbin interrupted his thought, "have you noticed a vehicle following us?"

Jedediah turned in the passenger seat and looked out the back window. He recognized the vehicle. He had seen it behind them before. "Yes, I've seen that car before. Corbin, take the next exit and see if he follows."

Jedediah watched out the back window as Corbin moved into the right lane. At the last minute he put on his turn signal and took the exit. The car was several lengths back.   As they reached the stop sign, Jedediah notice the car on the exit ramp moving at a slower pace.

"We're being followed," Jedediah's tone was serious.

"I know," was Corbin's reply.

****

It only took Manny a few minutes to reach the old man's house.   Why Thurman had demanded he do this personally puzzled him.   Barnes would have been capable of bugging the house.   His talents were usually reserved for more permanent solutions.

The house was dark.   Only the wealthy could afford to leave lights on at night.   He had pulled the balaclava over his face a block before he reached the house.   Manny readjusted the bag on his shoulder.   He move silently to the back of the house.

The backyard was surrounded by a ten-foot high privacy fence.   This would give him added cover.   He went to the back door and tried the knob.   No use expending extra energy breaking in if the door was open.

The first job he had done for Thurman was a cluster.   He tried to enter the mark's house through a side window.   Frustrated by his failure to breach the window, he had taken a rock and broke the glass. Once inside he discovered that the back door was unlocked and simply testing it would have gotten him in sooner.

The noise of the breaking glass had aroused his subject. Manny had to dispatch him, his wife and three children. Thurman was not happy. Only the man was to die.

Satisfied the door was locked, he inspected it more closely. Like most kitchen doors, it had windows to allow the sunlight to brighten the room. Each little square of glass was set inside a wooden frame. Manny removed the duct tape from his bag and completely covered the pane closest to the lock. Placing the tape back in the bag, he then removed a rescue tool and with two sharp taps, shattered the glass. Some glass tinkled on the floor. Most of the shards still adhered to the tape which he removed, then discarded.

He paused and listened for Whitaker's dog. *No barking, good sign,* he thought as he reached through and disengaged the deadbolt. Manny was not concerned that anyone would pay attention to him breaking into a house. The neighborhood's high crime rate and retribution against witnesses ensured that no one would interfere with his business.

Entering the kitchen he turned on his pen light and placed his bag on the kitchen table. He was surprised to see how clean the kitchen had been kept. There were no dishes in the sink. Nothing that would indicate a bachelor lived there.

He started for the dining room, but stopped short when he heard a low growl. *Dog,* was his first thought. He cautiously stepped into the room. The dining room table had a centerpiece of artificial flowers. There were six chairs neatly placed around the oval table. Manny swept the light through the room to see if he could see the source of the growl.

He stopped and held his breath. Not because he was frightened. He did not want his breathing to interfere with his ability to hear. The low growl was coming from what must be the living room. Walking cautiously, he moved with deliberate steps toward the sound. When he breached the doorway he was struck hard and driven to the ground.

Disoriented, Manny first assumed he had been tackled by an adult. The searing pain in his right forearm told him otherwise. The dog's teeth had sunk deep into his flesh. Manny squirmed to his left only to have the massive animal drive him to the ground as it bit his right shoulder. The dog's weight and size kept him from reaching either his handgun or knife.

Manny drove his left fist into the dog's ribs. The animal yelped, yet did not let go of his shoulder. Manny winced in pain as the dog renewed its hold. He punched the dog in rapid succession. The blows gave him the opportunity to roll away. He rolled quickly to his left and hit the wall. Trying to get to his feet, he was knocked off balance as the dazed animal lunged at him again. Manny punched its massive head and pulled his tactical knife slicing the animal's left shoulder. He was surprised when the dog lunged for his throat. He felt the heat of its breath on his face while simultaneously plunging his knife into the dog's chest.

He felt the warmth of its blood on his hand as he removed the blade and plunged it into its chest again. This time the animal crumpled to the ground. Its breath was jagged. The animal was whimpering and obviously in pain.

Manny leaned against the wall breathing heavily. He had never had such a challenge before.

"Still king of the beasts," he said under his breath.

He assessed the damage to his arm and shoulder. He was bleeding heavily from his forearm. The shoulder had been partially protected by his Kevlar vest. He uneasily stood to his feet, staggered to the wall and turned on the light.

"A Mastiff?" He was surprise by the old man's choice in dogs. Barnes had failed to mention the breed. He would have to discuss that with him when he saw him.

Manny struggled to the kitchen. His hands were shaking from adrenaline. He ran water over his forearm and steeled himself against the pain. He wrapped it with a dish towel and went to the bathroom to see what the old man had for emergencies. He found an old roll of gauze and wrapped it tightly around his forearm.

He went back to the kitchen, fished out his smartphone and sent a text to Barnes.

ETA?

After several minutes, Barnes responded.

Less than an hour.

Though in pain, Manny finished his task. Thurman's bugs were all in place.

Chapter 16

Corbin knew he had been under investigation. As head of the ECU, he was responsible for the conduct of the group's pastors. Three of the preachers in the denomination had recently been questioned. Eric Bandon and John Corless were the most recently incarcerated.

Corbin had called Thomas Caldwell, the Facilitator responsible for the arrests. Caldwell had refused to talk to him.

He and Jedediah were on their way to Caldwell's office. Though he was not close to the two who were arrested, he knew their reputations. Both were young fathers and had done nothing but faithfully serve their God. After several hours in prayer he and Jedediah concluded they had to intercede.

Corbin glanced at his mentor. Jedediah was looking out the passenger window. His concern for Samson was taking its toll. Since the attack on the animal, Corbin had become a permanent guest. He was afraid to leave his old friend alone.

That night when he and Jedediah had arrived at the house, they expected to be greeted by Samson. Both were surprised by the silence they met. Though extremely large and nearly one-hundred eighty pounds,

Samson was quite agile. On a typical reunion, Samson would be at the door, tail wagging and spinning in circles. That made him a bundle of lovable lethality. Corbin would usually dodge and side step, especially to avoid being hit by his massive tail.

"Samson," Jedediah's voice was filled with concern as he opened the front door. "Samson," he called a little louder.

"Maybe he is still with the Kesslers," Corbin offered.

Jedediah ran his hand up the wall and switched on the light. Scanning the room he saw Samson lying on the floor. It was strange that he did not move.

"Samson, come here boy. Come here. Corbin, there is something wrong." Jedediah moved quickly to his companions side. Samson was lying in a pool of blood.

"No, no, no!" The old man's cry was full of sorrow. Samson gave a feeble whine as his master touched him. Jedediah sat down hard. He gently lifted the animal's head and laid it on his lap. He was oblivious to the gore that soaked through his trousers.

"What is it?" Corbin was still at the door.

"Oh Corbin, he's been shot. Who would do this. Why?" The old man began to weep bitterly. He hugged the dog tightly and kissed him tenderly on the cheek.

Corbin hurried through the dining room, then into the kitchen.

"There's been a break in. He was protecting his home," Corbin called to him. He picked up the phone and called the police. Next he called Ben Johnson, who was a veterinarian and part of the Brotherhood. Ben came from Lower Burrell and arrived within the hour. He and Corbin placed Samson on a heavy blanket. All three men gently lifted the animal on the impromptu sling. After much effort, they placed the dog in the back of Ben's van. He took the dog back to his home to try to keep him alive. It took the police three hours to arrive. Neither Corbin or Jedediah anticipated any action.

Since that night, Jedediah mourned for his friend. Once their business with Caldwell's was finished they intended to visit Samson.

Caldwell's office was austere. There were no pictures on the walls, nor did there appear to be any personal items on his desk. He wore a starched white shirt and a nondescript black tie. His black hair was cut short and his face clean shaven.

"How can I help you?" he asked after his assistant ushered them in.

"We're here about the three men you have arrested," Corbin said this less cordially than he planned. The spate of recent arrests and detentions had pushed him to the limit.

"That is none of your concern."

"It is my concern," he interrupted. "I am responsible for these men. These are good men who have done nothing to deserve the treatment they are receiving."

"Take caution, Reverend," his words dripped with sarcasm. "You might not want to admit responsibility. These gentlemen have been arrested for sedition. Are you fully aware of the implications of that?"

"Sedition? How can that be..."

"They have encouraged the mob to resist the law. I've heard the prosecutor may also add the charge of treason. They face life in prison. If convicted of treason, they could be put to death. That is the only crime where the death penalty is legal."

Life in prison... death... Corbin was stunned. The lengths that the government had gone in the past to elicit obedience had been limited to financial ruin and loss of property. Though such sanctions could be devastating, a person could recover from financial setback, this was new and brutal.

"Mr. Caldwell, these men are not traitors, they love their country. How could this happen?"

"These men have preached sermons that question the authority of the government. They have encouraged people to horde food to distribute to whom they choose. They give out copies of Christian scriptures that have been banned. All of this is illegal."

"Surely you understand these men have the right to preach what they believe to be the truth? What about free speech?"

"They are free to say whatever is legal. The laws were created for a purpose. Unguarded speech led to the Republic of Texas and the anarchy in the Midwest. Some of the militia are still active.

"This free speech you mention is nothing but a plea for insurrection. It will no longer be tolerated."

Corbin looked at Jedediah who had remained silent through the entire exchange. His face was drained of color. When he returned Corbin's gaze, his eyes were fearful. The crack down they feared was beginning.

"If you want to take responsibility for these men, that is an admission of culpability. I would be glad to take your statement." Caldwell's smile was smug and dark.

"What of their families? These men have wives and children."

"Unfortunately for them, the Anti-Sedition and Terrorism law makes them accessories. Though they will not be arrested, they are not eligible for state assistance.

"Also," he said this with emphasis while looking Corbin in the eyes, "anyone offering them food, shelter or finances will be in violation of the law and would face twenty-five years in prison."

Corbin rose to his feet. Jedediah did the same.

"Please excuse us, Mr. Caldwell. We must be going."

Corbin turned and walked out the door. He felt nauseous. The unlimited power of the federal government was being leveled against anyone who loved freedom. How could they fight against such evil?

Neither spoke until they were clear of the building. The sun was bright and felt warm on Corbin's face. He stopped abruptly. He wanted to weep. *How could men survive such oppression? Don't you care Father? We are only men.* Tears ran down his cheeks and dripped off his chin. *What do you expect of us? What will these men do, their wives and children?*

He felt Jedediah's hand placed gently on his shoulder. His shoulders shook with sobs. The purposeless throng moved around him. Most just stared. Others hurried past. No one stopped to offer comfort or help.

Standing on the corner of Fifth and Liberty, surrounded by a decaying city, Corbin received the answer. *Inasmuch as ye have done it unto one of the least of these my brethren, ye have done it unto me.* The words permeated his mind. They accused and consoled all at once. The price he paid in walking away from Abigail was small compared to the price these men and their families would pay. His faith could no longer be a matter of convenience. It must be laced with unwavering conviction.

The cost of following Jesus was no longer theory. It was no longer the sum of a sermon speculating on the consequences of faith. Most would not accuse him if he walked away. Prison or death would be a high price to pay. If he walked away now, he knew he would be an anathema.

In a brief moment his conscience and will melded into one. The inward struggle ended. Working with the Brother's, though dangerous, had netted inconvenience. He thought he had made himself safe sending Abigail away. He now realized that she had never been his weakness. It had always been himself. The words of the Apostle Paul filled his mind. *I protest by your rejoicing which I have in Christ Jesus our Lord, I die daily... Awake to righteousness, and sin not; for some have not the knowledge of God: I speak this to your shame.*

The full realization of the Gospel message hit him at once. For years he had played at faith. He had faced setbacks and temptations, all of which he understood were miniscule. *Do I have the faith to believe you even in death?* This prayer was different. He knew he was speaking to God. Many times he had prayed merely out of habit, simply because it was expected. Today he stood empty, helpless, wretched. *I cannot do this, I am weak. Give me strength, strip me of cowardice.*

At that moment, God answered him. It was distinct and powerful, full of hope and foreboding. *Follow me and I will show you what great things you will suffer for my name's sake.*

Corbin's unease vanished. He understood his path.

"Jedediah, we must be going." His voice was unusually calm.

"What is it, Son?" Jedediah sensed something different. An assurance that had been absent just moments ago.

"We must hazard our lives for the cause of Christ."

Chapter 17

Corbin sat at Jedediah's dining room table. He stared out the window. A starling was hopping about on the window sill, periodically bobbing its head to pick up bread crumbs. Morning and evening Jedediah would place small crumbs on the window sill.

"I like watching them dance for their food," he said one morning while he and Corbin ate breakfast.

Watching the creatures bob and hop, Corbin concluded that they did indeed appear to be dancing. The starling picked up a large crumb and flew to a nearby bush. Then flapping its wings, it disappeared within its branches.

"Lord, how have we come to this?" He breathed this prayer as he read the letter detailing the arrest of the two men. The crime they were accused of was predicated on an immoral law.

"Thirty years ago, our nation would not have tolerated such tyranny," came a familiar voice.

Corbin turned toward Jedediah. "Thirty years ago, we ignored the inevitability of this. How could we have been so blind?"

"Corbin, hope sometimes stifles common sense. Everyone assessed the future based on the precedent of the past. Those who did warn of these abuses were seen as extremists. We still had a modicum of freedom and never truly believed this could happen."

"They have taken everything." Corbin lamented. "Good men risk their lives for voicing their opinion or preaching the gospel. Politicians pretend that limiting speech to what they approve of is, in some twisted way, freedom of speech. Religious liberty has been eliminated. A once strong and self sufficient people have been reduced to penury and fear."

"Corbin, learn from the past, don't lament it. Looking back is crippling. We will never be there again. Those days are gone and may never be reborn. The future will be whatever it is. Our calling is to have an impact on the present."

Corbin sat silently for a moment. He felt helpless. What could he or Jedediah do against such darkness? Frustrated, he rubbed his face with his palms.

"These men," he said not looking at Jedediah, "are paying a price they do not deserve. Their families are suffering want. I encouraged them to live according to their conscience, to preach the gospel. I sent my wife to safety, but who will look after their wives and children? I am responsible for this…"

Jedediah held up his hand to silence him. Corbin stopped in mid sentence. Jedediah was like a father to him. He respected the man, not just because he was a minister, but for his consistency and integrity. Jedediah had always been honest with him, even if the message was unbearable.

"Corbin, you cannot take that upon yourself. You spoke the truth and they made a choice that was between them and God. You did what God and your conscience required just as they did. Every person is responsible for his own choices.

"This institutional evil is not of your making. Darkness is all around us, Corbin. Men devoid of compassion and principle will always try to force their will on others. In the end they will fail."

"How?" Corbin was perplexed. "Wicked men seem to ascend to power. They hold all the power!"

"Because the one thing they cannot control is in here," he said touching Corbin's chest. "Men have the power to force the body, but they cannot truly control the heart. The innate desire for freedom can never be regulated or destroyed. That is why they must use force. They can kill the body, but not the soul.

"Great men throughout history have defied the odds and been triumphant. Who would have thought that a lowly carpenter from Nazareth would birth the greatest religious movement the world has ever seen. No one believed that Gandhi could lead the Indian people out from under the burden of the British subjugation. Do not underestimate the power of one unwavering person.

"God has chosen you to lead a movement for spiritual freedom. Once a person finds freedom in their soul, every other form of liberty will follow. It is inevitable, it is the power of the gospel."

"Jedediah," there was sadness in Corbin's voice, "I don't know if I have the strength for what I know I must do."

"No man can take away who you are. They can rob you of property, health and even life. But, and remember this, they can never rob you of who you are in Christ.

"Who you are is the person at your core. A man who compromises his convictions for safety never truly held them. The question is, Corbin, what are you willing to die for? When you find that out, no man will ever rule your spirit or break your will."

"Ah, there you are," Jedediah said playfully as Samson limped into the room. Though completely healed from his wounds, the damage done to his tendons forced his friend to limp. Samson shook his head, his ears slapping the sides of his face. Jedediah laughed and hugged his massive neck.

"Come on boy, let's go outside." Padding behind his master, Samson followed him to the door.

Corbin turned his eyes toward the window. A black bird was chasing the remaining starlings away. This living shadow used its size and strength to terrorize the smaller creatures. Undaunted, the sparrows would fly back to the sill and land long enough to snatch a bread crumb. They came so fast, and in such numbers, the black bird was incapable of guarding what it had stolen. After a protracted contest, the bully bird flew away empty beaked.

Corbin sat straight in the chair. It always amazed him how God could take such a small interaction to instruct him.

"Thank you Father," Corbin prayed, "I understand now. We will take back the freedom we squandered, one crumb at a time, until there is nothing left for the usurpers."

Chapter 18

The meeting went longer than Corbin had expected. He was heartened to see the young faces that were there. For far too long, the church had been aging. Twenty years ago, young adults, especially males, seemed to have lost interest in the gospel. Looking back, Corbin realized, with regret, the shallowness of Christian teaching.

Lamentably, even he had embraced the self-help culture of the church. It seemed the leaders at the time, including him, had thought that using pop psychology would somehow make the gospel more palatable to the masses. So they encouraged people to improve themselves to see their value and potential. Though he was certain these things were not bad, he was convinced these ideas robbed believers of the ruggedness of faith. Many anticipated ease, and when the culture collapsed, the Church was ill prepared to truly be relevant.

In the past year, Corbin had met many young men who were eager to carry the gospel. He and Jedediah had traveled across the eastern states recruiting men and women to spread hope. The past six months had been especially fruitful. He had organized thirteen groups of young adults who were moving from city to city calling people to embrace freedom.

These cells of itinerate preachers organized prayer groups, preached the gospel and educated the masses on the history of freedom. With the assistance of missionaries from South Korea and Africa, the itinerate arm of the Brotherhood distributed scriptures and copies of the works of such men as Jefferson, Hamilton and Paine. Though the debate had raged among academics whether these men were Christians, their belief in, and respect for Christian principles was indisputable. One of the goals of the cells was to proclaim liberty to the whole person.

Sitting on the platform, Corbin's heart was heavy as he looked across the audience. Of the forty volunteers in attendance, he knew that most would be arrested and some would lose their lives. Each one who would suffer these losses were men and women he had recruited. The price incorporated more than the threat of arrest or death. These volunteers took on the life of an itinerate preacher, traveling from city to city. They understood they may never see their families again. What awaited most was deprivation, loneliness and sorrow. He felt a great heaviness every time an arrest or disappearance was reported.

He still felt remorse over the death of young Joe Stratham. He was eighteen years old and full of hope and zeal. An unlikely candidate with red hair and freckles, he looked frail and had a child's face. He had approached Corbin at the end of a similar meeting.

"I want to be an itinerate," he had said. His voice was deep and did not fit his appearance.

"What is your name?" Corbin asked. Just looking at the boy, he had made his mind up that he was not a good candidate.

"Joseph, Joseph Stratham."

"Well, Joseph, the path you are looking to travel is dangerous and would probably end in your death." Corbin understood the importance of making volunteers aware of the cost. "You will have to leave family and friends behind. The chance of you seeing them again is very slim. We need support staff, those who pray and give to help those on the road. I would gladly get you in contact with a coordinator."

"Reverend Miller, I have already lost everything." The sadness in his voice was palpable, though it did not carry any self pity. "My mother dedicated me to Christ. She died in the food riots last year. She was one of the first to receive cheese and butter. The supply was insufficient for the crowd that had gathered. People were hungry. There was no food in the city and people became desperate. When the supplies were gone, the agent in charge of distribution told the remaining crowd to go home.

"Many there had not eaten in days. They began to throng the supply trucks. The police fired their guns in the air and drove them back. My mother, who was a godly woman, was accosted by an angry crowd. They demanded to know why she received food when they couldn't. Blinded by need, they beat her to death for a brick of cheese and a pound of butter. I have nothing left except to honor her memory and my commission to God."

There was no malice in his words and Corbin was taken aback by his sincerity. Yet, there was something more about this boy. There was a depth and strength in him that Corbin had not seen in many people.

Joe went on to be one of the best itinerates to join the Brothers. A natural leader, he was responsible for the recruitment of hundreds of preachers.

A year after that meeting, Joe mysteriously disappeared. He had organized a prayer vigil in Harrisburg. Thousands attended the event. The gathering lasted most of the day. At the end, he and his volunteers handed out copies of the banned versions of scriptures. The tension had been intense most of the day. The crowd had been surrounded by the police, and unidentified thugs had beaten up many of the attendees, including women and children. Joe was able to keep the believers calm and no one retaliated.

Once the scriptures were being distributed, the Governor ordered members of the NALC to confiscate all the copies. The violence that broke out was all one sided. The NALC waded into the crowd with clubs. Many were hospitalized from the beatings they received. In the melee, Joe disappeared.

Weeks passed without word of his location. Corbin feared the worst. He and Jedediah hounded the authorities without success.

In the middle of May, Joe's body was discovered in a ditch along I-79. According to the police report, his body was severely mutilated and he had been tortured for several days. The newspapers reported the killing was gang related.

When Corbin received the news, he wept. Having been impressed with the young man, he commissioned him to serve in the Brotherhood and it had cost him his life. The funeral was solemn and attended by thousands. Over a year later, no arrests had been made. Corbin knew there never would be. Zealots in the government had perpetrated the crime and there was no one to turn to for aid.

Corbin shuddered at the thought that this gentle young man could have suffered such a cruel fate. Others questioned the mercy of God, but Corbin understood that the servant is not above his master. This was not a question of God's mercy, but man's cruelty and indescribable capacity for evil.

"We send them out as sheep among wolves," a familiar voice said over his left shoulder.

"They are soldiers, Jedediah, fighting a war without malice or hatred." Corbin turned toward his friend. Jedediah looked frail and tired. Corbin wondered how long his mentor would be on earth. His health had been failing him the last few months, but he continued to labor with an energy that made Corbin feel ancient.

"Warriors, Corbin. These men and women are brave and dedicated. They face indescribable hardship. I fear many will not return. The Lord's martyrs have increased in the last six weeks."

"We've lost fifteen good men and women. I can't help but feel responsible for them."

"Nonsense Corbin, these itinerates serve God, not you. They are God's servants, just as you and I are His servants. They do what their heart and faith tell them.

This is their choice, not yours. You rightly grieve and mourn their loss, but don't be so self important as to carry the blame. That belongs to the monsters that harm them."

"I can always count on you to keep me humble," Corbin said with a small chuckle. He breathed a prayer giving thanks for his friend.

"How are the preparations for the vigil in Washington?"

Corbin sighed, not out of frustration, but weariness. He had seen too many good people sacrificed. The Washington vigil was certain to meet with resistance.

Since the militia uprisings, the government moved swiftly against anything they deemed subversive. The country's rulers made no distinction between an armed uprising and a nonviolent gathering for prayer.

"Everything is in place. Some of the Brothers believe this is an unnecessary antagonism. Several have refused to participate. I've had my doubts as well. We are leading these people as sheep to the slaughter."

"Corbin, when is the time to stand against evil? Unscrupulous men have manipulated the system to enslave a once great nation. Do you believe we should wait until all freedom has been taken?

"If not now, when? Those who will gather understand the danger. They know what this government is capable of."

"But many of the Brothers doubt the church should lead such a resistance. They say our battle is not with this world."

"Corbin, do not buy the lie that Christianity is only relevant to one aspect of human existence. A man cannot be truly free unless that freedom affects every aspect of his life. Christ is concerned about the spiritual, physical, intellectual and political freedom of every person. It is the whole man that is the focus of God's liberty.

"This truth is what moved the Founders to create this great nation. The dream of a free nation died when the very laws Christian principles created, were turned against it. Freedom devoured itself."

"I know this is the road I must walk," Corbin responded. "I don't feel up to the task. People look to me for direction and I'm not always sure what I should be doing. I don't want this burden."

"That is precisely why God put his hand on you. Arrogant men seek power. They manipulate and eventually enslave. Your lack of confidence in your ability is your greatest strength. Seek His counsel and never lean on your own wisdom.

"I fear the day will come when your faith will be tested. Lean heavily upon the Spirit. You must face the day with wisdom and courage." Jedediah patted him on the shoulder and walked to a group of men by the door.

Wisdom and courage, the Brothers' greeting was stuck in his mind.

****

Corbin stood on the hastily erected stage. The Brothers built it in the midst of the vast crowd that had gathered. Each component of the stage had been prebuilt for fast assembly. As far as he could see, there were throngs of people all waiting patiently for the prayers to begin.

Spontaneously, a small group of people began to sing Rock of Ages. At first, the singing was barely audible. As more voices joined the chorus, the sound reverberated through the city.

"This must be what heaven is like," Jedediah whispered in his ear. "Behold the power of hope!"

Corbin looked at the faces lifted toward the heavens. Many with eyes closed and hands lifted. Every person was sharing in the moment. Corbin closed his eyes and listened. The beauty of the harmony, the power of the amplified voices removed any doubt he may have harbored. This was the will of God.

Rock of Ages transitioned into Amazing Grace. The atmosphere was solemn. Members of the New America Liberation Corp gathered in groups amidst the crowd. Their crisp military uniforms made them stand out from the poorly clad throng. Some of the NALC were yelling and threatening those around them. Corbin saw an elderly woman knocked to the ground. The worshippers gathered around her to protect her. No one made an aggressive move. Men in the crowd locked elbows to wall in the aggressors. The sheer numbers present made it nearly impossible for the NALC to navigate. Still the singing continued. It reached a crescendo. The crowd began to chant, "Freedom, freedom."

Standing on the platform he felt so small. He understood that the price paid by Joe and others had not been an empty gesture. This mass of rejoicing humanity had found its voice.

Corbin stepped forward holding a megaphone. "Friends," his voice rang, amplified by the device, "it is time to lift our voices to almighty God." Silence fell over the crowd in a wave. "Join me in prayer for our leaders, families and our freedom. You are a testament to the power of hope. This nonviolent assembly represents the best of who we are. Today we pray for an end to tyranny. Today we ask Heaven to awaken the thirst for freedom in every American. This day we dedicate our lives to the God of Heaven."

The crowd reacted with a mixture of applause, weeping and huzzah's. Corbin raised a hand to silence the crowd. This only increased the noise. He stood amazed. These were not belligerent malcontents, but ordinary men and women longing for liberty. His eyes moistened as he raised both hand to try to gain their attention. Slowly the chanting stopped. Lifting his eyes toward the skies, he began.

"Almighty God," Corbin's voice trembled with emotion, "we honor you today..." A searing pain tore through Corbin's right bicep and into his chest. He staggered sideways, disoriented by the pain. The megaphone hit the platform with a clatter. Someone in the crowd screamed.

"He's been shot," Corbin recognized the voice, but could not remember who it belonged to. He sensed his body hit the wooden platform. Darkness was biting at the corner of his eyes. His breath came is gasps. He tried to speak, but the words seemed to be stuck in his throat. Everything was going dark.

****

Jedediah scanned the crowd. This vigil would be the catalyst to force change and bring back freedom.

Something caught his eye on the left of the platform. The shock of what was unfolding seemed to slow time. One of the NALC, a young woman, was raising her weapon. Jedediah saw the muzzle flash and heard the report. Disbelief had frozen him. He watched as Corbin's body folded to the right. He and the megaphone hit the platform almost in unison.

"He's been shot," he heard himself yell. He and the Brothers surrounded the fallen preacher.

Young men in the crowd tackled the shooter. The other members of the NALC drew their weapons and fired into the crowd. The screams were horrifying as participants scattered to avoid being shot.

The presence of the NALC, and the sound of gunfire caused the crowd of nearly five hundred thousand to panic. The elderly and small children took the brunt of the stampede. Once the panic ended nearly three hundred were dead and thousands others injured.

While the panic was building, four Brothers carried Corbin from the platform and hurried him to safety.

With his arms over the shoulders of two men, they conveyed him through the crowd. Using the distraction of the crowd's panic, they were able to escape without raising suspicions.

****

It took twenty minutes to reach the safe house. Though conscious, Corbin was in extreme pain. Jedediah inspected the wound and found that the bullet had passed through the bicep, stuck a rib and exited through his back. His struggle to breath seemed to indicate a broken rib.

"We have to get him to a doctor," Frank, one of the Brothers, said.

"We could take him to the hospital. It is only a few blocks from here," injected another Brother that Jedediah did not know.

"We cannot," Jedediah said plainly. "The authorities will be looking for him and us. His injuries are painful, but not life threatening. We'll bandage him and stay put for a few days. I'll make arrangements for us to get out of D.C."

"If you stay here, you put us all in jeopardy!" The fear in Frank's voice was obvious. Jedediah knew him as

Frank, but was not certain if this was his real name. Many of the Brothers used aliases to protect their families.

"What do you suggest, Frank?" Jedediah asked, "Should we throw him to the wolves?"

"Of course not. I'm only saying you can stay here for the night, then you must move on. The police are everywhere, and the NALC are searching door to door for dissidents. It's not safe to stay in one place very long."

Jedediah understood his fear. The Brothers were hunted without mercy. Many had already been killed or arrested and never seen again. The treatment of the Brothers was far more brutal than other designated dissidents. Under normal circumstances, dissidents were either arrested or heavily fined. Sometimes they suffered both penalties.

Those fortunate enough to escape arrest were levied heavy fines, and since most could not afford to pay, they had to opt for community service which lasted indefinitely.

Jedediah had known several so-called dissidents who were guilty of voicing their opposition to government excess. Each had all their assets confiscated. Their homes were sold at auction or declared public property. This meant their families were left homeless. Their community service was indentured servitude to the state. They were forced to work ten hour days, six days a week without payment. While fulfilling their sentence, they, along with their families, were forced to live in squalor.

Their hours were logged against their debt until the judge deemed it to be enough. In most cases their servitude lasted over a year. Most became compliant after their punishment.

Jedediah was weary. He felt as though he could sleep for a millennia. He watched as the Brothers bandaged Corbin's wounds and taped his ribs. Corbin winced several times but never complained.

Sitting in a tattered, but still comfortable easy chair, he marveled at the man Corbin had become. The first time he had seen the boy, he was an eager student. He was full of questions, and quite timid around others. He was not an exceptional student, but he would not give up. Jedediah spent hours tutoring the boy. The remembrance of that made him smile.

"I can't get this!" Corbin had said in frustration.

"Of course you won't. Not with an attitude like that," Jedediah scolded.

"I'm not smart enough. This is too complicated." Corbin was trying to translate John chapter one.

"Smart has nothing to do with it, Son. Persistence and dedication are the key. I have dozens of so-called smart students. They breeze through these lessons, but learn nothing. It is those who persevere that excel. You have the ability. Now stop whining and do it."

Corbin's unwillingness to quit made him the man that he was. He found strength in his struggles. He became one of Jedediah's brightest scholars.

A father's pride filled his heart. The young man lying on the davenport was one of the most important men of the time, and he did not even know it. Humble to a fault, Corbin always placed others and their abilities above himself. Yet he had inspired the most profound movement toward freedom the country had seen in years. Multitudes were fed, clothed and comforted because of Corbin's vision. Jedediah had to protect him. Corbin had to remain free.

Once his bandages were applied, Corbin had fallen into a deep sleep. Jedediah sat by his side watching the rise and fall of his chest with every breath. *Holy Father*, he prayed silently, *keep this man safe.* Corbin stirred and opened his eyes.

"God was with you today, Son," Jedediah said.

"I know," he replied with difficulty. He sat up slowly, favoring his right side. His left hand was sympathetically holding his damaged rib.

"What happened to the people?" His voice was near panic. "They were shooting into the crowd."

"It was bad," Jedediah said softly.

"How many dead?"

"Last count was over one hundred."

"Oh, Jedediah, what have we done? What are we going to do?" Corbin's face twisted in obvious pain. Jedediah was sure it was a combination of physical and emotional discomfort.

"We carry on," was his simple reply.

"Carry on!" He uncharacteristically raised his voice. "Over one hundred dead and we just carry on? How many more lives will be sacrificed? Have you no heart, no conscience?"

Corbin's words grieved him. Sometimes he asked himself the same question. They were embarked on a journey that bible school and seminary never prepared them for. There was no direction, no clear guidelines. Yet, Jedediah was certain of their path. To stand by and watch the enslavement of millions was wickedness and gross weakness.

"Should we encourage people to suffer and die as slaves, or live their lives as free men?" Jedediah did not try to hide the anger in his voice. "I do not believe that God would have us meekly submit to slavery. You blame yourself. Yet you cannot afford the luxury of self pity. Weak men wallow in self guilt. Yes, many died today, but they died free. How many have died as a result of submission?"

"They are suffering! We have contributed to that. I'm not sure we have the right to ask this of these people."

"Nonsense!" He raised his voice and cut him off. "They suffer indignity, penury and subjugation. All of our lives are a struggle. Evil men have stripped away their wealth and property. Look at the cities and townships. They are full of zombies groveling for existence. The people that stood with us today did so because they long for freedom. Those that died today understood the danger, yet they came anyway. Do not think for a moment they came because of you, or for you."

Frank rushed into the room. "We have to go," he said breathlessly. "The NALC will be here soon. They are searching every house on this block."

****

Corbin struggled to breathe as they made their way down the alley. The sun was beginning to set. They would have the cover of darkness to help them with their escape.

He heard a woman shriek behind him followed by a gun shot. He stopped and leaned against a dumpster. The smell was nauseating.

"Corbin, we must keep moving," there was urgency in Jedediah's voice.

"They are looking for me," he said calmly.

"Yes, and that is why we must..."

"I'm going back," he said interrupting him. "I'm turning myself in."

"Corbin you can't!" Jedediah's face was drained of color. At that moment he looked older, frailer. The weariness in his voice was evident.

"Listen to that! Those people are dying because I'm running. Is my life so important that we would sacrifice a child's mother or father?"

"Corbin, you are too important to the movement. Your leadership is indispensable."

"But I'm not indispensable. You were right, Jedediah. I cannot carry the guilt of other people's choices. I am responsible for my own choices. If I run and a hundred people die protecting me, is that price really worth it? I cannot carry their deaths, not like this.

"I know what God requires of me, Jedediah. I have been running from that. I now know it is time to embrace my fate. I must go back."

Tears cut hot tracks down the old man's face. Jedediah saw the determination on Corbin's face. He knew it was not a fatalistic resignation to fate. Somehow he also knew this was the will of God.

He embraced Corbin and tenderly kissed his cheek. "Go with God, Son," was all he said. He turned to the Brother known as Frank and said, "We must keep moving."

Corbin watched as they headed to the end of the alley.

"Corbin," Frank whispered loudly, "move it!"

"He's not coming," Jedediah said. He turned one last time to look at Corbin. Then just as quickly turned and headed out of sight.

"Father, give me courage," Corbin prayed aloud.

Moving as quickly as his damaged rib would allow, he headed back to the sound of the commotion. Members of the NALC were beating an old man.

"Where is the traitor?" The obvious leader of the group demanded. "Where did he go?" The old man cowered on the sidewalk.

"I don't know. I swear, I don't know."

The mercenary began to kick him in the back and stomped on his head.

"Tell me you old fool, or I'll kill ya."

"He's here," Corbin said as he approached. The terror on the old man's face caused Corbin to stop.

The soldier pulled a photo from his pocket and studied Corbin's face.

"So, he is here," he sneered. He then kicked the old man in the ribs one last time. The man rolled holding his side. "So you're Miller? You don't look like much to me. What do you think boys? He look dangerous to you?"

The young men with him all laughed together. The leader was older than the rest by at least ten years. Corbin noticed he had Sergeant strips on his sleeves. His hair was closely cropped and his nose had obviously been broken at least once. He had a perpetual squint which had created a web of wrinkles around his eyes. His barrel chest and muscular arms told Corbin this was not a man to take lightly.

"Please leave him alone, he's done nothing to you."

The sergeant walked toward Corbin. He stared into Corbin's eyes. He knew immediately, the man was dangerous.

The blow came unexpectedly. Corbin went to his knees. He gasped for breath and was crippled by the pain in his side. He cradled his ribs trying to ease the pain.

"Get up!" The sergeant ordered. His voice was menacing. Corbin struggled to his feet. The effort made him stumble and he used his left hand to brace himself against the mercenary.

The man drove another powerful blow into Corbin's injured rib. "Never touch me!" he snarled through gritted teeth.

"Get him," he ordered his men.

Chapter 19

Manny had reviewed every tape and video from the Whitaker surveillance file. He saw nor heard anything incriminating.

Manny watched in fascination, intrigued by the old man's reaction when he discovered his injured dog. Manny was not sure why he had let the animal live. Ordinarily he would have taken his time dispatching his quarry, but somehow he felt a connection with it. In some ways, he respected the animal. No other man or beast had ever injured him, or fought as ferociously as it had.

After he had planted the bugs and cameras, he had stood over the animal and when it sensed him, it struggled in vain to rise to fight again. With knife in hand, he had knelt beside the dog and pressed its head to the floor. Too weak to fight, all it could do was growl. It's determination and lack of fear made Manny pause. He stood to his feet, sheathed the knife and exited through the back door.

After watching the tape, he envied the connection the dog and the old man shared.

He was finishing his report for Thurman. He hated paperwork. It was beneath him. Someone like the incompetent Barnes should be doing it.

Should be, but Manny had made that impossible. He had confronted the fool about his faulty report on the dog. Manny surprised Barnes by coming to his apartment. He reluctantly invited Manny in. Manny stepped in and closed the door. Barnes started into the living room.

"Barnes," was all Manny said.

Barnes turned to reply. Manny took a step toward the man and plunged his knife deep into his stomach. He twisted the blade, and with both hands, ripped the knife from his navel to his sternum. Barnes gasped as his eyes went wide.

Manny put his hand on the man's upper back and lowered him to the floor. Barnes gasped for breath. Manny smiled at his anguish. He removed the blade and plunged it once into his chest. He then sat on the floor beside him and watched him slowly die. The agony Barnes endured filled him with euphoria. He stayed until he sensed his spirit leave his body.

So now he was stuck doing the paperwork. His meeting with Thurman was at three o'clock. He had a little under an hour to complete it. He would be done long before that.

After showering and having a quick lunch of tuna salad and chips, he gathered his report and left.

****

It was Saturday, and the Department of Verbal Equity and Faith would be officially closed. Manny's official title was Chief Facilitator. The other staff understood his job to be strictly analysis. His role as Thurman's enforcer, was neither official or obvious to the others.

Thurman demanded these Saturday meetings for security reasons. He did not want anyone to know the true nature of his and Manny's relationship.

The office was eerily quiet when he stepped off the elevator. Thurman's office door was slightly open, and he could see the gaunt man at his desk.

Manny walked into the office just as Thurman hung up the phone.

"Ah, sit," he said curtly. "I have good news. Corbin Miller has been arrested. You are aware he led a subversive rally in Washington today. The NALC captured him. He is now being interrogated."

"What of the old man?" he asked.

"Oh, yes, Whitaker. He is still roaming free. The NALC had no interest in him, but I do."

"Seems Miller turned himself in. Left the old man to fend for himself."

Noticing the folder in Manny's hand. He leaned forward and asked, "What do you have for me?"

Manny tossed the file on his desk. Thurman had his office swept for listening devices three times a week. Manny was certain they had been there today.

Thurman eagerly opened the file. Manny's synopsis was on top. Typed all in caps it read - NOTHING. Thurman glanced up and scowled.

"What is this?" he demanded, obviously irritated. "Is this a joke?"

"No," Manny replied.

"It says, nothing, Manny! This isn't a report. This man is dangerous and I need something on him."

"He is an old man. He's done nothing wrong." Manny was surprised by his defense of Whitaker. Soon after he had nearly killed the man's dog, Manny was watching a surveillance tape. The old man sat on the couch to read his Bible. Manny was amazed he could stomach reading it for over an hour. When he was finished, he knelt to pray.

Something the old man said while praying made him rewind the tape several times. In his prayer, he forgave the man who hurt Samson and asked God to do the same. He prayed for the person's happiness, peace and health. Manny was troubled for days over this. It was new to him. His mother had been irascible and vindictive. When she would lock him in the closet, or when she beat him, she would ask her God to send him to hell. Maybe if the old man knew him, he would do the same, but he could not convince himself that Whitaker would react in the same way.

Manny did not intend to be protective of Whitaker, but he was different from the others, and did not deserve to be harmed.

"Well, it doesn't matter anyway. I have other plans for him." Thurman turned sideways in his chair and pulled open the lower drawer in his desk. Manny was familiar with the routine. Thurman kept the names in that drawer. Manny shifted uncomfortably in his seat. He knew what was coming.

"Here," he said gruffly, "this is your new job."

Manny mechanically took the paper. He unfolded it and read what was written.

Jedediah Whitaker

Manny folded the paper and tossed it on his boss's desk. "No," was all he said.

"No?" Thurman asked in anger. "Did you just tell me no?" He rose from his seat and leaned toward Manny. "Do you realize that I could send you back to that hole I saved you from? I own you Manny! You're mine, and you will take care of this!"

"No," he said again, his gaze burning into Thurman's eyes.

Still hovering over the big man, Thurman's face twisted in anger. "You will do what you are told!" He emphasized his words by pointing his finger in Manny's face.

Betraying no emotion, Manny used his powerful legs to propel himself from his seat. With swift, graceful movement, he planted his right fist on Thurman's jaw. The power of the strike sent the man back into his chair, which would have tipped over, had it not struck the wall.

Manny watched the dazed man regain his focus. He smiled. He had wanted to do that for a long time. Thurman was a small arrogant man. Manny despised him more than he had hated his mother. Thurman did not profess a love for the Christian God, but that did not make him irreligious. His religion was the state and power. He groveled at the feet of the powerful. For that weakness, Manny detested him.

Thurman held his chin and rocked forward. He surprised Manny when he came up with a .38 snub nose. Thurman used both hands to pull the hammer back. *This is new,* Manny mused. He smiled derisively as Thurman's hands trembled. His finger touching the trigger.

The percussive sound of the hammer striking the primer was disorienting at first. Manny felt as if he had been struck in the right breast with a small sledge hammer. Still in shock, he looked down at the flowering plume of red that was growing on his shirt. He blinked and looked across the desk. Thurman's eyes were wide with fear and disbelief. The gun had obviously been fired by accident.

It took seconds for Manny to regain his reason. With a rush of adrenaline, he shoved the desk toward Thurman. The edge of the desk struck him in the thighs as he was starting to rise.

Another explosion rang in Manny's ears. A searing pain ripped through his abdomen. Still propelled by an increase of adrenaline, Manny's massive right hand wrapped around Thurman's thin neck. Simultaneously, he ripped the revolver out of his grasp with his left hand and threw it to the floor.

Manny could feel Thurman struggle against his grip. The wheezing sound told him the man was fighting for air. Manny smiled and Thurman's eyes widened in fear. Years of weight training had given Manny unusual strength. He had pinned his prey against the wall. The man's blows were useless. His flailing became weak.

Manny squeezed the fragile cartilage of Thurman's trachea. He slowly squeezed until he felt it pop beneath his fingers. The corresponding crunch told him he had collapsed the man's windpipe.

His prey was gasping for air as Manny fell to the floor. Manny saw the fear in Thurman's eyes. He relished it. Reaching into his pocket, he removed the piece of paper that had been there for many months. With shaking hands, he unfolded it and tossed it into Thurman's lap.

Manny watched the dying man's face as it twisted with recognition. Inexplicable, Thurman grabbed the paper and held it in his hand. He struggled for a few more seconds, then expired.

Manny knew he would die. He was not afraid. He smiled, knowing that the last words his prey had seen had been his own name.

"I'm still the king of the beasts," he whispered to himself.

He then lost consciousness and was soon gone.

Chapter 20

It had taken Jeffrey three hours to reach his destination. Ordinarily, the trip to Conemaugh Dam would have taken a little over an hour. He had taken back roads and backtracked to make sure he was not followed.

Before leaving, he had removed the battery from his smartphone and checked his car for tracking devices. It was dangerous for him to meet Jedediah, but he had been insistent. If he was caught meeting with members of the Brotherhood, his punishment would be severe and his wife would suffer greatly.

The Division had sent him to a training seminar in Charleston. He did not get to see much of the city. Every day had been loaded with meetings. He did learn much about the Division's strategy, and needed to pass that on to Jedediah anyway. He had heard about the shooting in D.C., but the details were sketchy. That was expected. The government only gave the media what they wanted them to have. He assumed the meeting was about the shooting.

"Corbin has been arrested," Jedediah said before Jeff could greet him.

He could hardly believe what Jedediah had said. Jeff Arbino had been Corbin's friend since college. Corbin had always exhibited leadership qualities, and Jeff was not surprised when he had easily moved into the leadership of the Brotherhood.

He and Jedediah had manipulated Corbin's election as president of the Evangelical Christian Union. When the Facilitators had been appointed, Corbin had been an effective buffer between them and the preachers. By design, Jeff had worked behind the scenes to support Corbin's efforts.

He knew this was inevitable, but was surprised it had happened so soon.

"Where have they taken him?"

"I'm not certain. We have received conflicting information. All we know is he was taken into custody by the New America Liberation Corps. Those men are brutal. I fear for his safety."

"Corbin is strong, Jedediah. He will not be easily broken."

Jeff knew that when others were involved, Corbin struggled with his decisions. When his decision affected him, he was uncompromising in his purpose. Jeff's greatest fear was that Corbin would be tortured. The rumors could not be proven, but he was certain that

Brothers who had disappeared had been tortured, murdered and disposed of. The information Corbin had could bring the resistance to its knees. Men like Corbin had great resolve, but could he withstand months of torture? It would be impressive if he could sustain days of torture without breaking. Everyone's life rested in Corbin.

Though he had been investigated, no footprints led him back to the Brotherhood. He and Corbin had orchestrated a rift that had convinced everyone that Jeff had betrayed the gospel. Jeff's cooperation with the Facilitators had earned him the ire of the conservative preachers in the denomination. This had given him opportunity to gain the Division's trust. After many months of feeding them information, he had been recruited to act as a liaison between the Division of Verbal Equity and Faith and the pastors in the denomination. All the information could be validated, though none was incriminating. The veracity of the data gained him the trust of his handlers.

He had recently been appointed Facilitator of western Pennsylvania, West Virginia and the eastern half of Ohio. This gave him access to valuable information that he passed to Jedediah.

He had struggled with the deception, especially having to hide the truth from his wife, Katie. Jedediah and Corbin had assured him that his role was crucial for the success of the Brothers' mission. The price was high. Many of the conservative preachers avoided him and those who did communicate with him, did so formally.

Within the last year, most of these preachers had lost their licenses and were forced to give up their pastorates. Jeff resigned his church. He was unable to preach the drivel that the government approved.

When he told his wife his intentions, she slumped into a chair and cried uncontrollably.

"Honey, it will be all right," his words were gentle, intending to sooth. She shrugged his hand off her shoulder. She looked into his eyes and shoved him away.

"You have betrayed everything you believed in," her tone was accusing and angry. "How could you? How do I explain your new job and our affluence to our friends who barely have enough to eat?

"I have lost all my friends. They're polite, but avoid me. We have taught our children to love God above all things, and you have destroyed all of that."

"Katie," he said softly, "you don't understand..."

"Oh, I'm afraid I do. You have sold your soul for a few pieces of silver. You have become a Judas."

She sat up straight and defiant. He could see the disdain in her eyes. He felt her anger. He could not tell her the truth, that he had been recruited by the Brotherhood to infiltrate the government. His cover had to be unimpeachable. He had access to documents and information that were vital to the movement. He was one of hundreds, if not thousands, of infiltrators. The identity of these people was known to only a few in each region.

"Please Katie," he pled.

"I shall not leave you," she injected. "I made a covenant with God and I will not break it. You will have my presence, my body and my pity, but you will never again have my heart."

She stood and walked toward the kitchen. She stopped and turned. With great courage she said, "I will never cease to serve Christ, I will help the poor, feed the hungry and defy tyranny all the days of my life. If you wish to arrest me, so be it. I will not deny my Lord."

Spinning on her heels, she went to the kitchen to begin preparing lunch.

Jeff had never experienced such pain. He stood silently trying to wish it all away. He knew her well enough to know she would never change her mind, at least not while he had to deceive her. He could not risk telling her his secret. Her safety was at stake.

He walked past her in the kitchen to go to his office in the basement. When he approached, she turned her back.

He entered the study and scanned the books that lined the shelves. There were the works of Wesley, Luther, Calvin and a myriad of other authors. These men of faith had faced untold sorrow for the sake of the Gospel. Was he any better than they?

He closed the door, locked it, and fell to his knees. For the next two hours he wrestled with God. When he rose, he was confident in his path. If freedom would be reborn, his sacrifice was necessary.

"Can you find him?" Jedediah's question broke into his thoughts.

"I will see what I can do. I have higher clearance now and the leaders of the division trust me. I'll contact Thurman and see what he knows."

"You haven't heard? Thurman is dead. Seems he died defending himself against one of his agents."

"I'll contact his boss, Lambert. We have hit it off well. He's the one that got me the Facilitator's position."

"Jeffrey, do not wait. Please call him immediately."

"I have to be careful. If I show too much interest in Corbin, it could raise suspicions. I will call you in three days for official business. I'll let you know then."

Jedediah rose quickly and walked to his vehicle. Jeff heard the engine start and waited thirty minutes before he left. The bench where they met was situated in a stand of trees. He was able to see the complete parking lot. The park was empty except for a few workers, an old man emptying trash and someone lazily mowing the grass.

Satisfied no one was watching, Jeff went to his car and made the long drive home.

****

Jeff pulled in the parsonage driveway. He would be leaving soon. The Division would supply him with a townhouse in a nicely developed area in the South Hills near Pittsburgh. He knew Katie would be packing. He would take time to help her once his business was done.

No one from the church had stopped by to say goodbye and that saddened him. Most of his old congregants believed he had left the faith. Some were angry, most were frightened by him. He put his forehead on the steering wheel and sighed. His was a lonely task, but one God had called him to endure.

There was a time when he could not wait to get home. Now it was a chore. Katie's greeting would be cold. He was hurt, but proud of her moral courage. Though her stance had softened because of her love for him, she would not let him forget what she perceived he had become. Still he loved her deeply and longed to be able to share his secret with her.

He walked through the front door. Katie had been busy. There were boxes stacked everywhere. Katie was wearing jeans and one of his old pocket tees. She looked so beautiful. Coming up behind her as she stood from placing some memento in a box, he gently kissed her on the cheek.

"Hello," she said pleasantly, but did not reciprocate. "There is a message on your desk from William Lambert." She then moved to the next box without looking at him again.

The pain of these encounters was getting less difficult to bear.

"Thank you," he responded. He took off his shoes before crossing from the hard wood floor to the carpeting. This was a rule Katie had made long ago, and one he always respected.

The carpeted steps creaked under his weight as he walked downstairs. His study was spacious. He had paintings on his walls depicting various religious themes. His favorite was a black and white print entitled *John*

Wesley at the Market Cross. The simple print was of the famous preacher standing in front of a crowd with his hands raised, obviously preaching the gospel. Of all the Christian heroes he admired, Wesley was one he related to most. *I wonder what you would say to my deception,* he thought as he stopped to look at the print. It was something he did every time he entered his study.

A pang of guilt stabbed his conscience. *How could you ever forgive me?* He walked over to his desk. A note lay on the desk written in Katie's unmistakable calligraphy. She had the most beautiful handwriting he had ever seen.

Call William Lambert ASAP, was all that was written.

"Thank you Lord," he whispered. All the way home he tried to think of a reason for calling Lambert. He was not the kind of man you called on a whim. Jeff had only met him on two occasions. Thurman had passed on Lambert's praises several times. He could not imagine why Lambert would call him.

This is no coincidence, he told himself, *nothing happens by chance. Providence is at work.*

He dialed Lambert's phone number and after several rings, he picked up.

"Hello," Lambert said in his nasally tone, "Lambert here."

"Mister Lambert, this is Jeff Arbino. I am returning your call."

"Jeffrey, thank you for calling me back. I assume you are aware of Thurman's death yesterday? A nasty affair. One of his associates apparently was determined to harm him. Thurman bravely fought him and died in the process of killing the man."

"I was in a meeting all week, no time for news. I'm surprised it wasn't mentioned at the meeting."

"No need of depressing the morale of our constituents while going through such important instruction. Now then, I am on a limited timeframe here, so I'll get to the point. I would like for you to take Thurman's job."

Jeff was stunned. He had not been sure what to expect, but this never would have entered his mind.

"Well sir, this is an honor. I don't really know what to say."

"Arrangements are being made to move you to Philadelphia. We have a penthouse leased in your name. If it's not to your liking, you can get what you want. We need you here by next Friday. Can you be packed by then?"

"May I ask, Mister Lambert, why me?"

"I've been watching you. You're sharp and loyal. I need that. Plus, you know how these relics think. I need a man that can communicate with them. Can you be ready to be here by Friday?"

"Of course, I'll tell my wife."

"That's not my problem," he said with a chuckle. "I'm in Philadelphia the following Monday. We'll have a briefing then." The phone went dead.

Jeff leaned back in his chair. He knew God's hand was in this. Now he had to break the news to his perpetually angry wife.

Chapter 21

The room was white. There was a window along the wall in front of him. He made the easy assumption that it was a two-way mirror. The table in front of him was stainless steel as was the chair he sat on. He had tested the table and it was fastened to the floor by half inch lag bolts.

His hands were chained to loops that had been welded to the table. His ribs ached. The NALC members that had captured him had taken advantage of his injury. After the initial beating, they handcuffed him and dragged him to a waiting van. While conveying him to this place, they had kicked and punched him at will.

Licking his lips reminded him of the cuts his teeth made when he was repeatedly punched in the face. Looking at himself in the mirror, he was certain his nose had been broken. His right cheek was smeared with blood, and his shirt was stained as well. His right eye was slightly swollen and made it difficult for him to see clearly.

He was extremely thirsty. The metal seat he sat on was cold and uncomfortable. He had been in this room for a while, or at least he thought it had been a long time. He had no idea what time it really was.

"Hello?" he said in a normal voice. "Hello?"

He heard nothing except the whoosh of the air being forced through the vent above him.

"Hello?" he dared to raise his voice slightly. After several attempts to get someone's attention, he began to feel panic.

"Hello?" he screamed loudly. He jumped to his feet and began pulling at his bonds. Simultaneously his wrists and ribs throbbed from the effort. "Hello?" His voice cracked from the effort. Frustrated and frightened, he fought to hold back tears. Soon exhaustion overtook him and sunk back into the chair. He ached from head to foot, and an extreme exhaustion embraced him.

He was about to doze when he heard the lock on the door clack open. He lifted his head in anticipation. The door opened and a slight man entered the room. There was an odd smile on his face. It wasn't menacing, and neither was it friendly.

"Hello Corbin, my name is Alexander. You may call me Alex if you'd like." He extended his hand expecting Corbin to take it, which he did.

"I have been assigned to your case."

"Are you an attorney?" Corbin asked.

"Oh, my goodness, no. I'm your interrogator. My job is to extract information from you. I would prefer you volunteer what I need to know. But, you and I know you won't do that. So, I wanted to review your schedule with you."

He said this so casually that it sent a pang of foreboding through Corbin.

"Don't look so surprised, Corbin. I have my job to do. This is not personal. I have nothing against you personally. You have chosen to make yourself an enemy of a benevolent state. Whatever transpires is your fault, and yours alone."

Fear made it difficult for Corbin to breath. He could not think. *This is not real,* he tried to reassure himself. However, the pain from his recent beating told him it was.

"Are you thirsty?" Alexander asked him.

"Yes," his voice croaked.

"Jack," Alexander called. A large man with tattoos covering his forearms and neck appeared in the door. "Get Mister Miller some water please. You see, Corbin, we are not barbarians.

"Oh, and Jack," the big man turned at the door, "bring him some crackers and cheese as well."

Jack returned several minutes later with a small bathroom sized paper cup filled with water and a large plate of crackers and cheese.

"Eat up, Corbin," Alexander said pleasantly, "it would be rude to leave anything on your plate."

Corbin understood the underlying threat. He ate the large snack, then tried in vain to wash it all down with sips from the tiny cup of water.

"May I have more water, please?" He asked. He was more thirsty now than he had been originally.

"Let's not be piggish, Mister Miller. Jack will escort you to your room." He gave Corbin the same odd smile, then nodded in Jack's direction.

Jack walked to Corbin and unlocked his cuffs.

"Hands behind your back," he ordered. Corbin complied. Jack pinched the cuffs closed tighter than necessary. He wrapped what appeared to be a leather strap around the chain between the cuffs and pulled up. The tension caused pain in Corbin's shoulders and forced him to march on the balls of his feet to his room.

Once at the room, Jack removed the cuffs and said, "Strip."

"Excuse me?" The words barely passed his lips when the powerful man punched him hard in the lower back. Corbin gasped for air. His knees buckled and he hit the floor hard. Jack bent over and grabbed Corbin's ear. He twisted it with such force that Corbin was certain he had torn it off. He howled in pain.

"Please, okay, okay, I'll do it," he panted. Corbin stood and disrobed.

Jack pulled out his keys and unlocked the door.

"Get in."

"Do I get any clothes?" Jack raised his knee quickly, striking him in the groin. Corbin doubled over and was met with a knee to the face. Blood flowed freshly from his nose.

"Get in," his voice was monotone. This time Corbin complied. The room was barely three foot square. The walls were painted a high gloss white. Corbin's eyes hurt from the brightness of the ceiling lights. He looked up. The ceiling was at least fifteen feet above him. Looking at his feet he noticed there was a large grate that covered most of the floor. He could not imagine why that was there. There was no plumbing or light switch in his room.

The four spotlights above him were hot on his skin. He stood for as long as he could. Then he tried to sit with his knees pulled tight to his chest. After sometime, his knees began to ache. The pain became so unbearable that he stood again.

He had tried to kneel once, but the grate hurt his knees. The cycle of standing and sitting went on interminably. At odd intervals, a high pitched whine filled his room. Corbin put his fingers in his ears but it did not help. After a while the sound seemed to cause nausea. At one point he vomited down the wall.

Intermittently, he sang hymns and tried to quote the scripture. Each time he was rewarded with the high pitched whine.

"Please, I have to use the restroom," he yelled. "Please, may I use the restroom?" No one answered. When he reached the point of extreme discomfort he relieved his bowels and bladder on the floor of the room. He now knew what the large grate was for. The heat from the lamps enhanced the stench from his waste and vomit.

Please Lord, he prayed inwardly, fearful that if he spoke aloud, some other torment would be added. *Give me the strength to endure.*

Soon his legs and lower back began to cramp. He was not able to maneuver the small room enough to stretch out the cramps. The pain was excruciating and he began to weep.

Unbidden he began to plead, "Please, please." Soon he was in constant motion, his body writhing and seeking solace. Sleep eluded him.

Corbin endured the agony for what seemed like hours. Overcome, his body and mind were incapable of sustaining anymore pain, and consciousness slipped away.

Chapter 22

It had been seven days since Corbin had surrendered to the NALC. Jedediah had tried in vain to gather information as to his location or safety. The phone call he received from Jeff held some promise. His appointment to Thurman's position gave him access to all but the highest levels of the Division's information.

He had returned home briefly to arrange for the Kesslers to care for Samson. Since the intruder stabbed his friend, Samson had not been the same. He had difficulty rising and spent most of his day lying on his side.

It was a tearful farewell. Jedediah knew he could never go home again. Jeff had informed him that Lambert had ordered Jedediah's arrest.

"I will delay issuing the warrant for seven days. Make whatever preparations you need to. I won't be able to delay it beyond that. Godspeed Jedediah." Jedediah understood the sacrifice that Jeff was making for the cause.

"You are doing God's work, Son. Please look after Corbin. You must free him if you can." Jedediah's heart broke for his student.

"Jedediah, I will do everything I can for Corbin. I cannot interfere with the interrogations, but I will try to lessen his suffering."

"I know what this has cost you, Jeffrey. You will always be in my prayers."

Jedediah put the last small bag in the backseat of his car. He turned again to get one last glance at the house where he and Lydia spent most of their married life. There were so many memories and so much laughter and love there. None of that had any meaning. Those days were gone forever.

The cruel ambition of powerful men had subjugated a nation. Everything was different. When President Freeman first won the election running on the New America Liberation Corps ticket, accusations of voter fraud were rampant. Investigations were launched in twenty states, but nothing could be proven.

Within three years, the President had greatly curtailed personal freedom through executive order. Once the confiscation of personal weapons was underway, armed resistance erupted across the Midwest. The NALC took advantage of the furor to seize control of the federal government. President Freeman declared marshal law and suspended the Constitution. That week he announced the formation of the New America

Liberation Corps law enforcement agency. The agency initially recruited former gang members. The average age of the corps members was twenty-two and each had to pledge loyalty to the President and the NALC. Defending the constitution was eliminated completely. Their authority superseded State and local law enforcement.

News outlets across the country criticized the move. Within three months, the owners, editors and writers involved were arrested for sedition.

The last move by the NALC was to silence the Church. Systematically, conservative pastors and church leaders were forced to resign. Preaching the gospel was now a criminal offense.

Jedediah sighed. He shut the back door on the driver's side of the car. He climbed behind the wheel and headed for a prearranged meeting. The Brother's would transport him to Arkansas. From there, he would escape to the Republic of Texas. He had to find Abbie. She had a right to know what was happening to Corbin. He had an obligation to watch over her for Corbin's sake.

****

Abigail had settled into her new life. They had changed her identity to Nancy Schumaker. She hated the name. The Brothers had rented an apartment in that name near Abilene. They had also gotten her employment at a local restaurant.

"Nancy," she said the name over many times. *Why couldn't they have given me Abigail Schumaker for a name? Schumaker,* the name sounded so rough and angry.

The apartment was luxurious by American standards. Most of her friends in the States lived in hovels compared to this. Yet, the accommodations would have been considered dilapidated forty years ago in the old country. She had not been able to bring any photos or personal memorabilia. The Brothers had stressed the importance of her not having any connection to the past. This, they had told her, was for her's and Corbin's safety.

Earning her own money gave her a sense of security. At first, she hoarded food and pinched every penny. She felt guilty taking a shower every morning. She saved every scrap of food left over from a meal. Over time, she became less frugal, but never wasteful.

It took awhile for her to adjust to her new environment. In the States, she had to watch her every word. Waiting in line to get a meager supply of food was a weekly occurrence. Limited electricity was another inconvenience she dealt with on a daily basis. The blackouts were so frequent, she had to resort to hand washing clothes and hanging the wet garments on a line outside to dry.

Texas was different. Food was in ample supply. The first time she went to the grocery store she broke down and wept.

"You okay, ma'am?" Asked an elderly gentleman in a cowboy hat.

"I'm fine," she sniffled.

Soon a middle aged woman stopped and put an arm around her shoulder. "Do you need anything sweetheart?" Abigail looked at the sincerity and kindness on her face and broke down again.

Under normal circumstances, she would have been embarrassed by her public display. At that moment, she was overcome with joy at the abundance of food and the sincere kindness of these strangers.

When the Republic of Texas was formed, they created a Constitution designed to protect the rights of the individual from government. The legislature was part time and dealt with security and infrastructure. No income tax was instituted. Revenue to fund the government was raised through tariffs, and a national sales tax of two percent. Raising the sales tax required a two-thirds majority vote. Then the individual provinces had to approve the measure by a two-thirds majority of citizens voting in each province.

The Constitution prohibited the legislature from instituting social programs that would take the wealth of one person for the benefit of another. Property rights were protected, which included a prohibition of taxes on property.

Freedom of speech was paramount. There was no provision in the national law that designated anything as hate speech. Words were not illegal, even if they offended a specific group or person. Religion was free to flourish. The right to worship was foundational.

Over the last several months, Abigail learned to flourish in this new environment. She was still in awe of God's providence in Texas.

She grew to love her new job. Waiting tables had never been on her radar of career choices. Yet interacting with people helped her get over her loneliness. She missed Corbin terribly, and the cryptic notes she received and had to send gave her little comfort, though finding a folded letter in her mailbox always made her giddy. She would run her fingers over the words imagining Corbin writing them. She extrapolated the "I love you's" from the generic script.

She had grown concerned over the last few weeks. The letters had appeared every month, but she had not received any recently. Corbin wrote religiously, but his letter was three weeks overdue.

Each night before bed, she knelt and prayed, "Father, watch over my Corbin. Keep him safe and give him the boldness of a lion." She would pray the same prayer tonight.

She sat down at her desk and composed a note to her beloved. Once completed, she folded it neatly and placed it in an envelope. She put it in her mailbox and clipped a clothes pin to the lid. It would be gone in the morning.

****

The trip to Arkansas was grueling. Jedediah's age was catching up to him. It had been ten days since he last spoke to Jeffrey. Raids on two of the Brothers' homes had forced Jedediah to hide at a safe house for several days.

"Why are we stopping?" He asked the driver. He did not know the woman's name, nor would he ask. She was part of the Brotherhood, and he was assured she could be trusted.

"Roadblock ahead," she said over her shoulder. "Do you have your papers?"

"Yes, everything is in order."

"You don't have any other ID?"

"Of course not, this is not my first mission." He said that more brusquely than intended. The pressure was mounting throughout the country. There was a reward of ten thousand dollars offered for information leading to the arrest and conviction of any member of the Brotherhood. In this extremely depressed economy, that could be a temptation even to the most faithful.

Traffic slowed down to a crawl. The NALC was making the occupants exit their vehicle as they reached the checkpoint. The process was slow. The guards had a photo and were scrutinizing the faces of each person. They then pulled the driver aside and questioned them at some length.

"Exit the car," the scruffy faced youth ordered as they pulled to the checkpoint. The female driver exited first. Jedediah stepped out and stood by the rear fender.

"You!" an armed guard said looking at Jedediah. "Over here now." Jedediah moved as quickly as he could. He detested the power of these thugs, but knew that belligerence could get you killed.

"What's your name," the young thug demanded.

"Mark Caruthers," Jedediah answered. That was what his new identification claimed.

"This is him," he stated emphatically.

"No it ain't. The guy in the photo is younger and fatter," his superior replied. The younger guard turned toward his boss. Jedediah glanced at the picture. It was indeed his picture. Jeffrey had already put out the warrant for his arrest. The photo he supplied was at least fifteen years old, when he was younger and more robust.

The years under the rule of Freeman had aged him considerably. Jedediah had lost thirty pounds since that picture and his hair was snow white, rather than auburn.

"I'm tellin' ya, it's him."

The boss grabbed the boys face between his thumb and forefinger and pinched. "Look at 'im! Does this scrawny old man look like him?" He held the photo up to the youth's eye level.

"I suppose not," he said glumly. His superior slapped the back of his head. Obviously depressed, he rubbed his head and leered at Jedediah. "Get back in your car and get outta here."

Jedediah and the driver climbed back into the vehicle.

"We lucked out on that," the nameless woman said.

"No, God has blessed our journey." *Thank you, Lord, and thank you Jeffrey.*

The rest of the journey was uneventful. They crossed into Texas without incident. The driver handed him an address she had neatly printed on the back of a receipt.

"Go to this address and they will help you find Miller's wife."

"Thank you, and Godspeed."

Chapter 23

Sitting in his new office, Jeff felt small and alone. He was one of the most powerful men on the East coast, yet the thought of it sickened him.

Thurman's memorial branded him a hero. Each speaker extolled his courage and determination. The man who had crushed his windpipe was identified as a member of the Brotherhood. The files Thurman left behind told a different tale. Manny, the man who ended Thurman's life, was a sociopath who, according to the hidden files Jeff found, assassinated people Thurman deemed to be a threat. One thing was certain, Thurman was no hero.

Once he settled into his new office, Jeff began pulling all the information Thurman had collected on the Brothers. From what he could see, it was quite extensive. Fortunately, Thurman was niggardly with his intelligence. Like so many participants in tyranny, Thurman kept his knowledge close to the vest and only revealed what information would advance his career.

"Gladys, would you come here please?"

Gladys appeared in the door nearly out of breath. Since he had moved into the office, she was unnecessarily eager to please. Her behavior had become so vexing, he finally called her in to assure her she was secure in her job.

"Yes, Mister Arbino," she said respectfully.

"Gladys, please, you may call me Jeff. There is no reason to be so formal."

"Yes, sir."

Jeff sighed. He was going to have to get used to the kowtowing. Fear ruled the lives of everyone around him.

"I need copies of these files. Oh, and these are for my personal use so there is no need to log a job number." It was not unusual for men in his position to make such a request. The department used job numbers to track the work of employees. People at Jeff's level were not required to log their activities. Jeff was certain this gave the powerful wiggle room in case of a scandal. The needs of the unscrupulous gave him an advantage in gathering information for the Brotherhood.

It had taken some time, but Jeff had finally located the interrogation center that housed Corbin. He was surprised to learn that he was being held four blocks from his new office. Each time he attempted to contact the facility, his calls were routed to a generic voicemail. He would have to make a personal visit.

In the files Thurman left behind, Jeff discovered that Thurman had signed the original arrest warrant for Corbin. This gave Jeff an advantage. Since he was successor to the office, the arrest and interrogation of Corbin fell under his jurisdiction.

Corbin, please forgive me. There is a greater purpose here. Sorrow engulfed him. If he intervened too much for Corbin he would compromise his safety.

****

"Jeff Arbino to see the Director," he demanded.

It had taken Jeff two weeks to get the necessary documents that would ensure that Corbin's case would stay under his jurisdiction. Armed with these papers, he would be able to keep track of Corbin's condition.

He was surprised by the nondescript building that was used for interrogation. It was situated in the middle of the office district in downtown Philadelphia. The sign on the outside identified the building as a data storage facility. At first he thought he had the wrong address.

People exited and entered the building continuously. Inside the lobby well dressed people conversed, laughed and made plans for lunch. The average observer would never believe the savagery of its true business.

"I'm sorry the Director is not seeing anyone today." The woman behind the desk was portly. Her red hair, obviously dyed, was pulled into a bun on the back of her head. Her makeup had been meticulously applied, but did not enhance her appearance.

"He'll see me," Jeff said with authority as he handed his identification to the stunned woman. Once she verified his identity he handed her the letter from Lambert giving him jurisdiction over Corbin's incarceration.

"Let me see if he is in." She immediately picked up the phone and dialed a four digit extension.

"A Mister Arbino to see you, Sir," her voice was subdued.

"Yes, Sir, I understand, but he has authority from William Lambert, and the matter is marked urgent."

Her head bobbed as she listened to the Director. After several minutes of silence on her end, she looked up and said, "He will see you now. Please take the elevator to the tenth floor. His office is Suite 1021."

"Thank you." Jeff headed toward the elevator. He called the elevator and within a few minutes, the doors slid open. He pressed the button for the tenth floor. The box lurched upward.

He felt overwhelmed by the evil around him. *Do these people know what goes on in this building? How could they not?* He breathed a silent prayer for Corbin and each of the prisoners being robbed of safety and dignity for the convenience of the powerful. He despised his job. In the end, he hoped he would not lose his soul.

****

In the sub basement of the Data Storage building Corbin lay on a hard mattress in the infirmary. He was still groggy and disoriented. As he regained his senses, the pain in his body raged.

Becoming more cognizant of his environment, a deep sense of dread engulfed him. He tried to move but his hands and feet were restrained. He did not try to pull loose. After more than a dozen trips to the infirmary he knew it would be wasted energy.

There was an IV in his arm. The heart monitor registered his pulse and blood pressure. His heart began to race. *Why can't this be a dream,* he screamed in his mind. He would not dare verbalize what he was feeling.

He made that mistake three times. He was not permitted to speak unless bidden to by Alexander.

He had cried out for help and Jack walked to his bedside. The memory of him made Corbin look around the room in panic. He had inflicted excruciating pain on Corbin for over an hour.

I mustn't speak, mustn't speak, he repeated the phrase to himself continuously.

Corbin recognized the man in the white coat. He was the doctor. After his first session in his room, he had been brought here and the doctor revived him.

"I am so sorry." That was what he had said as he leaned down to shine a light in Corbin's eyes.

"Please, help me," Corbin had pleaded. The doctor never spoke to him again.

"Please someone help me!" Corbin strained at his restraints. That was when Jack came in.

Jack! The memory made him look around the room in near panic.

The doctor set down whatever was in his hand and began to turn.

I must pretend I'm asleep. Keep your eyes closed. Don't let him see.

"He's awake," the doctor said into the intercom.

Corbin began to cry.

Jack came into the room and removed the restraints. Corbin struggled to sit on the edge of the bed. No one moved to help him. When he placed his feet on the floor, his legs were unsteady and he fell, hitting the ground hard. He lay there absorbing the coolness from the tiled floor.

He grunted as Jack kicked him in the small of the back.

I have to get up. Please Lord, let me get up! Another kick in the back and he forced himself to his knees. This time Jack punched him in the short ribs. Corbin almost collapsed. Instead he urged himself up.

Mechanically, he held his hands behind his back to be cuffed. Jack applied the leather strap and Corbin was marched down the hall on his toes.

"Stop," Jack ordered. Corbin immediately halted. To do otherwise would bring him pain.

Jack opened the door and removed Corbin's cuffs. The room was furnished with a metal table and chair. Alexander was sitting on the side of the table opposite of where Corbin stood.

Alexander looked over the top of his reading glasses and smiled. "Ah, Corbin. Please come in and sit down."

Corbin did as he was told. He never knew what to expect from Alexander. He was always cordial. Even when he ordered Corbin's torture, he made it appear he was doing him a favor.

"I hope you've taken the time to think about what you are putting yourself through. Quite frankly, I'm beginning to think you like it." he chuckled.

Corbin looked at the table. The scratches seemed to resemble something. He just could not quite think of what it was.

"Corbin, do you know why you are here?" Alex's voice was soothing.

Corbin tried to focus on the words. He heard Alexander speak, but he could not focus.

"Do you understand why you are here?" He raised his voice a little.

"No," Corbin slurred. *My voice sounds strange,* he thought.

"You are here because your actions have been seditious. You can make this end by signing this confession," he slid a paper and pen toward him, "and telling us what you know about the Brotherhood."

Corbin began to read the paper. As he read, he shook his head. "No, no, no! I have not betrayed my country! No!" he cried as he rocked in his chair. His mind was beginning to clear. *Drugs,* he thought, *they have drugged me.* He struggled to concentrate. *Father, please help me to resist this. Give me clarity.*

"You are breaking our laws. You consort with the Brotherhood and you preach illegal views. Doesn't that make you a criminal?"

"Your laws are immoral. I cannot obey laws that violate the laws of God." Using his fingertips he pushed the paper back to Alexander. "I cannot confess to a lie."

"So we've come back to this again," the sadness in his voice seemed real. "Why do you punish yourself? Now I will have to schedule another session. I want you to consider that you have the power to stop this."

Tears trickled from Corbin's eyes. He feared what he would face. He feared more that he would not endure. He sat up straight ready to bravely face what would come.

Unbidden, this thought came to him, *And ye shall be hated of all men for my name's sake: but he that endureth to the end shall be saved.*

Emboldened by this he answered Alexander, "No this is your doing. You try to quiet your conscience by distancing yourself from the heinousness of your actions. Understand this Alexander, that in the end, God is judge. Will you be able to endure His scrutiny?"

Alexander chuckled nervously, "I don't believe your superstitions, Corbin." His words were even and clear. "Right now, the State is your master and you will answer to it."

He nodded to Jack. Corbin began to pray.

****

Jack worked methodically strapping Corbin to the chair. The hard wood of the chair was uncomfortable under Corbin's emaciated body. His feet were strapped to a wooden stool. Jack had pulled the restraint so tight that his ankles ached.

"I forgive you," Corbin said to his tormentor, "I forgive you for everything."

Jack paused briefly to slap Corbin hard across the face.

"No talking," he stated as he went back to his task.

Corbin's cheek stung. Whatever Jack was up to would not be good. He closed his eyes and in his mind he sang, *Blessed assurance Jesus is mine, oh what a foretaste of glory divine...*

Corbin's whole body jerked from the pain of the first blow. Instinctively, he squirmed, though he knew it was futile. His eyes were open now. He cringed as Jack pulled his right arm back for another swing.

Jack held a one-half inch piece of PVC in his right hand. The implement was approximately four feet long. Semi rigid, it sent shock waves of pain through Corbin's feet with the second blow.

Gritting his teeth, he tried in vain not to scream. His effort was unsuccessful. After the third blow, he was howling in pain.

Jack hit the bottom of his feet nearly ten times before taking a break. He showed no emotion. Corbin could not sense hatred in the man. Maybe he had seared his conscience and convinced himself it was only a job. He never spoke except to give orders. Corbin wondered how a human being could become such an emotionless monster.

Jack took a drink of water. Then picked the PVC up again.

"I forgive you," Corbin panted. Strangely, Corbin felt no animosity for his tormentor. He pitied him. Corbin's pain was physical, but he was certain Jack suffered the agony of emptiness and self loathing.

Jack did not respond. Instead he continued to strike the bottom of Corbin's feet again. Again Corbin's body tried to retreat. He struggled against his bonds. He wept and screamed.

After ten more strikes, his feet were bleeding. Mercifully, numbness was alleviating the excruciating pain. Jack placed the blood stained tubing on the table. A spray bottle sat on the end of the table which he picked up. In two strides, he was at Corbin's feet and sprayed the liquid in his wounds.

The smell of rubbing alcohol assaulted his nostrils simultaneously with the nerves in his feet coming to life. His feet were on fire. Corbin strained at his bonds until the veins stood out on his neck.

"Why?" he screamed. "Why are you doing this?"

The pain began to subside and Corbin panted as he relaxed his taut muscles. Jack sat quietly in a cushioned chair taking periodic sips from his water bottle. He watched Corbin with curiosity. He appeared to be neither happy or sad. Corbin thought instead that Jack looked bored.

"Please, may I have some water?" Corbin's voice was raspy from his parched throat. He was not able to produce enough saliva to wet his lips.

Jack stood with his water bottle in hand. He stared at Corbin for several minutes. Took another long drink.

Then placed the water on the table and picked up the PVC.

"Please, no, please," Corbin heard himself pleading. He knew it would do no good. There was no mercy in this place. Yet he hoped. "Dear Father," he cried as loud as he could, "Father help me! Please help me!"

****

Corbin had lost count of time. When Alexander came into the room, he knew this session was over. The pain told him his feet were badly damaged. He would soon find out the extent of the damage.

Why Father? How much more do you expect me to endure? Corbin was perplexed by his plight. As if in answer to his question he heard, not a voice, but more like an impression. *I gave my all for you. I suffered at the hands of the Romans and Pontius Pilate. I died an ignominious death on the cross. The servant is not above his Master.* Corbin bowed his head and asked forgiveness. Then with a clarity he had not experienced before, these words infiltrated his mind. *No weapon that is formed against thee shall prosper; and every tongue that shall rise against thee in judgment thou shalt condemn. This is the heritage of the servants of the LORD, and their righteousness is of me, saith the LORD.*

"Thank you, Lord," he said aloud.

"What was that, Corbin?" Alexander asked.

Corbin did not answer. Speaking without permission was one of the rules he must follow. Alexander explained to him that he was a non-person, an enemy of the State. He had no rights except what Alexander gave him. Talking when not questioned or spoken to first would elicit punishment.

Alexander nodded to Jack who immediately punched Corbin several times in the solar plexus. Corbin struggled to breathe.

"I heard you call on your God," Alex stated. "Where is he? Why has he not answered you?" There was no taunting in his voice. Corbin thought he detected sympathy instead. This man was a conundrum. He was obviously devoid of human compassion, yet there appeared to be no hatred.

"He is here," he answered breathlessly.

"Where? I'd like to ask him why he would require you to torture yourself like this. Is he not supposed to be merciful?"

"You order the beatings. Not God. You withhold food and water. Not God. God is not responsible for your actions."

"Yet he allows you to be tortured. Doesn't that make him a monster?"

"The servant is not above his master."

"How noble," the derision in his voice was obvious. "You believe yourself to be a martyr. You think you are suffering because you are righteous? Corbin, you are a lawbreaker. You defy the authority of your government. You're no martyr. You are pathetic. Look at you, you cry like a baby. You choose to live in your own filth. You're pathetic."

"Though He slay me, yet will I serve Him."

"He won't slay you. I hold the power of life and death for you. I control your destiny. You are no longer a man. You are my property to do whatever I wish. Do you understand that?"

"You will not go unpunished, for what you do here." Corbin was bolder than he intended.

"Who will stop me, Corbin? Your God? You say he is here, but can he stop Jack from hitting you?" He nodded to Jack who slapped Corbin with a powerful blow. "You see? You're mine."

Corbin blinked away tears. His cheek burned. The strike had split his lip. His mouth filled with the coppery taste of blood. He swallowed it and his stomach roiled. He had learned not to spit out any blood after being punished. Having done so twice, he found the punishment was severe. Nausea was preferable to the pain Jack was capable of giving.

He was helpless. He knew that he had no power. *Therefore I take pleasure in infirmities, in reproaches, in necessities, in persecutions, in distresses for Christ's sake: for when I am weak, then am I strong.* The scripture came unbidden. Rivulets of tears ran down his cheek. God was indeed with him. The renewal of hope strengthened him. He lifted his head and looked Alexander in the eyes. For a moment he thought Alexander diverted his gaze.

"Wait Alexander," he said with renewed courage, "you shall soon see the power of God."

Jack punched Corbin in the face repeatedly. He nearly lost consciousness until Jack held smelling salts under his nose to jolt him back.

"Let's talk about Abigail." Alexander's voice was even.

Corbin's eyes were blurry. His left eye was nearly swollen shut. His lips felt thick and his tongue was dry.

"Did you think you could hide her forever? A beautiful woman like that eventually draws attention."

"No, she's gone," his words were slurred, "safe, safe from you, from harm." Panic began to fill him. *No, dear Lord, no, please not Abbie.*

"Are you aware of the things that happen to female prisoners? The horrible suffering they can be made to endure. Most never leave here pure."

Corbin strained at his bonds. He began to weep. Tears flowed freely. His sobs racked his body.

"No, she's safe, she's safe. You could never find her."

"Don't be so certain. Even now she is being questioned. She knows more than she should. I have been placed in charge of her sessions."

"No, you don't have her," his words were slurred, "why would you do this?"

Alexander walked to him. He grabbed his now long hair and pulled his head back violently. "Look," he said forcefully, "look!" He held a photograph in his hand. Corbin blinked, trying to clear his vision. The woman resembled Abbie, but it was not her. He was certain it was not Abigail. *Jesus, my Lord, please don't let it be her.*

"If you sign the confession, no harm will come to her. She is of no value to us if you sign."

An inner voice spoke to him again, *Fear none of those things which thou shalt suffer: behold, the devil shall cast some of you into prison, that ye may be tried; and ye shall have tribulation ten days: be thou faithful unto death, and I will give thee a crown of life.*

Corbin raised his head. He looked at Alexander then at the photo in his hand. Summoning his last reserve of strength, he looked his antagonist in the eye and said, "Though He slay me, yet will I serve Him.

"Bind his feet and take him to his room." Alexander brushed back his hair with his left hand and tossed the photograph on the table. He never looked back as he left the room.

Jack bound Corbin's feet with gauze and forced him to stand. The pain was crippling and he crumpled to the floor.

"Up," Jack said in a monotone as he kicked Corbin in the ribs. Corbin struggled to his feet only to fall again. He was forced to crawl with Jack kicking and punching him for not standing.

At the door to his room, he struggled to his feet as Jack opened the door. Jack put a hand in Corbin's back and shoved him. The uneven surface of the grate was painful to touch. No matter how he maneuvered, he could not relieve his pain. In a matter of minutes, it seemed like hours to Corbin, he passed out from exhaustion.

Chapter 24

Alexander McCormick arrived home early. It was not because he felt ill. Something else was bothering him. A detail pulled at the back of his mind like there was something he should acknowledge or understand, but could not quite grasp.

He had been part of the Division's interrogation team for five years. He was good at his job. He had interrogated, some would say tortured, over one hundred fifty insurgents. Those who did not understand the threat these people posed called him and his colleagues monsters. They were small minded. You did what you had to do. The ingrates didn't understand that men like him were heroes. He kept the nation safe from evil individuals whose sole purpose was to destroy the progress the nation had made.

The religionists were far more dangerous than violent insurgents. They used words and persuasion to turn minds away from the greater truth of the state. Their repudiation of violence and double talk about being good citizens only made the more ignorant susceptible to their deceptions. What frightened Alexander was their number was growing. Everyday there were new reports of illegal hoarding and sharing of resources. The laws prohibiting this activity were only created for the greater good. The government was better equipped to know who needed help and who did not. Miller, and those like him, drained resources and stole from the truly needy.

Citizens were no longer as eager to inform on these miscreants. The deception was ingenious. Men like this Corbin, even thinking his name brought unease. *Why is that?* he mused. This man repudiated violence and preached unconditional love, then in the same breath encouraged the impressionable poor to violate the law. He, and others like him, did violence to order and security. If he succeeded in stealing the hearts of the people, the sheer weight of their numbers would crush the system. Alexander could not allow that.

Alex walked to his bedroom, removed his laptop from his backpack, and placed it on his desk. Methodically he opened the closet door and put the backpack inside. This was his daily routine, and it brought him comfort. Recently he was having trouble sleeping. He would wake in the middle of the night sweating and frightened. No matter what he did, he could not shake the sense of foreboding that lingered. In vain, he attempted to be overtaken with sleep.

He rubbed his eyes. He was so tired. He would have to put off sleeping. He had too much paperwork to complete. The thought of breaking his routine was bothersome. The order of his life was being interrupted. His duty to the government and the people was his only priority. This unease had never happened to him before.

Corbin Miller was a puzzle to him. He had used harsh methods on others and they had broken within a few weeks. This man was different. How, he did not know. Alex shook his head, trying to clear his thoughts.

He sat down on the queen size bed. The mattress was firm. Alex surveyed the room with satisfaction. Unlike his colleagues, he did not need expensive things. He felt that opulence made one soft. Not that he was austere. His bedroom furniture was light oak. The walls were painted a soft green with forest green carpeting and drapes. The colors were soothing to him. He lay back welcoming the opportunity to relax. *I'll close my eyes for just a moment*, he thought.

****

The fear he felt was crippling. His whole body ached. He felt a presence near him. He tried to move, but his body rebelled. He felt the warmth of it. He tried to move his eyes, turn his head, but even those simple movements eluded him. His heart began to race. The pounding grew louder and his breathing was more difficult.

He felt it smiling. He sensed it leering, waiting. Whatever it was, it was patient, not willing to complete its desire.

Alex strained at invisible bonds. He could not move. Whatever it was had paralyzed him. He wanted to scream. He was not sure if he even opened his mouth. He strained against the fear. He was helpless, a captive of some unseen evil. That it was malevolent, he knew instinctively. Why did it wait? Why was he still alive?

As if listening to his thoughts, it moved again. He felt the pressure of it climbing on the bed. Though it said not a word, Alex could sense its joy at his helplessness. Its satisfaction was sinister.

Alex was still on his back, his hands lying parallel to his head, his palms up. It moved fluidly toward his head. It sat savoring his fear, growing more powerful by his weakness. Alex trembled. He wanted to weep, but even that comfort slipped away.

Its need to torment him was greater than his will to escape. Alex wanted to move, he needed to move. After what seemed like an eternity, he felt its clammy hands touch his face.

The scream was unearthly. Alex sat upright in his bed. He looked all around trying to see what it was. His racing heart seemed determined to escape the confines of his chest.

"It was just a dream. Just a dream," he said reassuring himself. It seemed so real. This was not the first time he had experienced this faceless specter. He had worked with, and broken multitudes in the past. Ever since Miller! This started a few weeks after I began to work with him. Miller had been a problem. Normally, after a few sessions, he was able to elicit a confession. They usually had no depth. The body needed respite and the mind would comply. Once he got a confession, he would continue applying pressure for several months to make sure his subject did not retract. He had learned that a quick confession, and subsequent denial, only gave his subjects more resolve. Once they confessed, continuing the pressure would so break their will that retraction never entered their thoughts.

"They would confess to raping their grandmother after that," he said aloud to himself. This made him chuckle. He was proud of his dedication to excel at his job. He was the best of the best. That was why he was assigned to Miller. Miller was different. During Miller's sessions, he could not read fear in his eyes. That was disconcerting. Nor did he exude defiance. His resistance was different. It was almost a quiet resignation.

During the last session he had the bottom of Millers feet beaten with a semi-flexible PVC tubing. As expected, his screams were loud and pitiful. However, he did not beg for mercy. Nor did he promise to do anything in order to make the pain stop. Instead he prayed.

"Father," he cried, "please help me to love even those who would harm me."

Watching through the two-way mirror, Alex was intrigued by the prayer. Jack hit Miller's feet again. His feet were already bleeding. Jack knew to allow time between beatings so the subject could sense some relief. Then periodically, rubbing alcohol was sprayed into the wounds that would inevitably appear. This cycle of pain and relief would keep the subject's senses on high alert. Alex watched him intently.

Jack continued his assignment. Miller cried and screamed. The pain had to be unendurable, yet, when he was given a respite he would offer the same prayer.

"Corbin," he said in a soft soothing voice, "this could all end if you would only admit your subversion."

"I-I-I cannot confess to a lie," his breath came hard. There was no anger in his voice.

"I have the power to stop this if you will only cooperate. Wouldn't you like for this to end? Wouldn't you like to be happy again, to see Abbie again?"

This made him cry. He sobbed and moaned at the mention of Abigail's name. In between reflexive sobs he simply said, "Though He slay me yet will I serve Him."

Even when he tried to convince him they had his wife, the man's resolve was impressive. Alex had never had a subject that presented this much challenge.

The memory of that session haunted Alex. For the first time since he began his career, he felt fear. It was irrational and unwarranted, yet he could not shake it. That was when the nightmares began.

Wait Alexander, you shall soon see the power of God. Those words still haunted him. That sentence filled his mind with dread. He tried hard to shake it, to distract himself from thinking about it. Nothing seemed to assuage his foreboding.

The bedroom became stifling. His apartment was eerily quiet. He walked swiftly in to the living room and turned on the stereo. The mild jazz filled the room with warmth. Few could afford a stereo system. "That's what you get for being good at your job," he said, congratulating himself for his good fortune. He spoke louder than he might have ordinarily. His voice echoed back to him in spite of the rich bass and clear trebles coming from the speakers.

He shuffled to the kitchen. He opened the door to the left of the sink, and pulled out an unopened bottle of whiskey. He had been drinking more than usual lately. He then opened the cupboard door and found a shot glass. He turned it repeatedly in his hand staring at it. After a few moments he put it back and grabbed a juice glass that had oranges etched around the rim. Alex opened the whiskey, filled the juice glass, and drank its contents quickly. The warmth from the fiery liquid slowly permeated his body.

Glass in hand he picked up the bottle and walked slowly to the living room. He positioned himself in his favorite overstuffed chair. He lit a cigarette, picked up the remote to turn up the music, and settled down for another night of inebriation.

Chapter 25

Living under an alias was difficult. Remembering to answer to Mark Caruthers was more challenging than he originally believed. Jedediah knew that maintaining anonymity would save his and Abigail's life, once he found her.

Texas was free soil. The differences between the two nations were stark. Jedediah had grown used to living clandestinely and adjusting to real freedom was hard. His first week in Texas was an adventure. He marveled at the stocked shelves in the stores, the smiles and greetings of strangers.

This was a revelation to him. Even before President Freeman, America had devolved into a nation of isolated human beings. Friendships were difficult to build. Everyone was enamored with pleasure and ease. In Texas there was an ease and friendliness that, at times, seemed surreal. After the layers of oppression of the States, Texans had learned to value Freedom.

He looked at the directions again. The hotel clerk was a friendly enough fellow, but Jedediah was not convinced he was very bright. According to the hand written map the Church should be two blocks ahead. He had traversed ten blocks already. The clerk offered to call him a cab, but Jedediah had politely declined. He wanted to walk and absorb the free sun and breathe the air. Somehow it was different here. The sun seemed brighter, the air smelled sweeter.

His calm was shaken when his thoughts went to Corbin. The last communication he received from Jeff indicated he had located Corbin. The rest of the report was not good. He had already endured more than a month of the cruelest torture Jedediah could imagine. He could not read it all, it was too disturbing.

Other news that accompanied the report on Corbin was unsettling, yet not totally unexpected. After Corbin's arrest, several chapters of the Brotherhood had begun an armed resistance. Jedediah was not sure how he felt about that. Until that point, their opposition had been nonviolent. Yet, Christians were being arrested and murdered at alarming rates.

"There it is!" he said aloud with some surprise. The building was fairly new. The brick church sat on a three acre lot. The spire was topped with a large bronze cross. Steps led up to large double doors in the front. The sign in front told him he had reached the correct location. *Our Redeemer* was in large bold letters. Underneath the marquee announced this weeks sermon *Living in Freedom*. Jedediah sighed. A pastor in America would be persecuted for even considering such a message.

Though only a few years old, the hinges squeaked as he opened one of the double doors. To his surprise, there was a receptionist's desk. Churches back home could never afford such a position.

"Good morning, sir," the voice was cheery with a melodic southern accent. Jedediah guessed she was in her thirties. Her hair was short and neatly styled.

"Good morning, miss. Je..." he stopped himself, "Mark Caruthers. I am here to see Pastor Fleming."

"Yessir Mister Caruthers, Pastor is expecting you. Please follow me."

Jedediah followed her down the hall to the left. She stopped at the first door on the right. She tapped lightly, then pushed the door ajar.

"Pastor, Mister Caruthers to see you."

"Thank you, Sandy. Send him in. Oh, and Sandy," he stopped her before she walked to her desk, "would you please brew a fresh pot of coffee?"

She nodded and headed toward the kitchen.

Jedediah waited until she was out of hearing distance then shut the door.

"With wisdom and courage, Jedediah." Pastor Fleming fixed his dark eyes on Jedediah as he took a seat.

Joshua Fleming had been a Pastor in Indiana when the fighting broke out between the government and militia. The Brotherhood was in its infancy and Joshua was traveling back from Wisconsin after a charter meeting with Jedediah.

The little town of Otwell was the focal point of the first armed clash. The battle lasted only a few hours. The militia was poorly armed and undisciplined. Government forces suffered fifty dead and many others wounded. Civilians killed reached six hundred. Among the dead were Joshua's wife, Clair, and his three children. His oldest boy was ten, the middle boy seven, and his precious Amanda only six-months old.

When he and Jedediah arrived, martial law had been declared ranging from Jasper to Vincennes. The military authorities had refused Joshua's request to bury his family. All dead civilians had been interred in a mass grave. The military presence lingered for more than three years.

After allowing himself to grieve, Joshua dedicated his life to serving the Brotherhood. Several months later, Texas declared its intent to vote on secession. The brotherhood sent Joshua to coordinate the Brothers' efforts to influence the legislature's decision. He was now Jedediah's equivalent in the Lone Star nation.

"With wisdom and courage, my old friend. It has been a long time. You're wearing a ring, have you remarried?"

Jedediah watched him roll the ring on his finger. Joshua's gaze went to his left hand.

"No," he said with resignation, "no one could take the place of Clair."

Clearing his throat and sitting straighter in his chair, Joshua changed the subject. "What news do you have?"

"Not good I'm afraid. Corbin has been arrested and is suffering greatly. The Division of Verbal Equity and Faith has unprecedented power. Brothers all over the states are being arrested. Many have lost their lives.

"What is more disturbing is that several of the western branches have begun collecting arms. I fear there could be renewed bloodshed."

"Jedediah, pacifism is not an edict of our faith. I think these men and women have a right to defend themselves."

"Joshua, we're talking armed conflict. Up until now we have resisted peacefully. This could bring the whole thing crashing down."

"It's already gone Jedediah. If the reports we receive are accurate, Christians throughout the states are being hunted, starved and martyred. Do these people not have a right to defend their lives against an immoral government?"

Jedediah knew his friend was right. He detested violence. He feared what might become of those who tasted blood. How could one rise up from that pit? Yet, to allow your spouse and children to face the horrors of tyranny would be a worse fate. The scriptures allowed for defense of life and property.

"Yes, they do have the right. Heaven help us that it has come to this. The brutality of the Freeman regime knows no end. What Corbin and others are facing is worse than facing a firing squad.

"Joshua, you know why I am here. I need to see her."

"Jedediah, you know the rules. This is a free society. Operatives from the states have already extracted several fugitives. All of them were executed soon after they were returned to the states. You will put her in jeopardy."

"She has a right to know. Her husband is facing imminent death. Should she not have the time to pray and prepare?"

"I'll have a message prepared and delivered."

"Seriously Joshua, you cannot be that cold. Such a message would destroy her and I know Abigail. She will head back to the states, no matter the consequences to her. She needs to hear this from me."

Joshua picked up the phone. "Sandy, get Pastor Winston for me. I need to talk to him immediately.

"I do this against my better judgement." he said fixing his eyes on Jedediah, "You must follow protocol. You cannot communicate with anyone from the city in which she lives. Do nothing that will identify you. Once you meet with her you will be brought back here."

"I understand." Jedediah had coordinated enough covert activities to know that secrecy and extreme caution were necessary. It would be good to see Abbie again. Her heart would be broken. She would need him.

****

Tired after a long day on her feet, Abigail looked forward to going home. Waiting tables was taxing and she scolded herself more than once for having been a stingy tipper. She would take a long hot bath to help her relax. It had been weeks since she had expected to hear from Corbin and her anxiety increased with each day.

She had toyed with the idea of heading back to Pittsburgh to see him. She knew that was not possible. Her presence would be a liability to his work. She was also aware that she could be used against him if he were ever captured.

She could not shake the feeling that something was wrong. Her last letter received no response. That was not like Corbin. Her dreams had been disturbed at night, mostly with premonitions of something awful, though it was just a sense or feeling with no specifics.

She had spent hours praying for her husband. She believed that God would watch over him. She also believed there was power in prayer.

Abigail climbed the stairs to her apartment. When she reached the third floor she stopped on the landing. A man was standing at the hall window. His back was to her and the window backlit his form into a shadow. He was wearing a trench coat and a hat. She noticed immediately it was not a cowboy hat, although it had a wide brim.

She took one more step and the floor creaked under her foot. She froze as the man turned toward the noise. It took a moment for her eyes to adjust, then she squealed.

"Abigail," a familiar voice said softly. It was more like a whisper.

Abigail dropped her purse and rushed toward him. Throwing her arms around his neck she wept out of shear happiness. "Oh, Jedediah, how have you been?"

"I suppose we should address each other by our new names." He said this softly in her ear. "For your protection, my dear, and mine."

"Nancy, it is very good to see you again. You remember me don't you, Mark Caruthers?"

She wrinkled the nose at the name. Jedediah never would fit the name Mark Caruthers.

"Please come in," she said over her shoulder as she returned to the landing to retrieve her bag. She fidgeted with the key, trying to get it into the lock. Her hands shook out of shear excitement. Jedediah was a connection to Corbin. He would have news. *Something is wrong,* she thought, her stomach roiling with fear. *Why else would he have come?*

When Jedediah cleared the threshold she closed the door and set the lock. She turned toward her old friend and plainly asked, "What is wrong, Jedediah? Something has happened to Corbin." Her voice cracked as she tried to maintain her composure.

"Abbie, please sit." His tone was fatherly. "I needed to tell you this in person."

Abbie sat on the couch, her hands clenched between her knees. She tried not to panic but that seemed almost impossible. Jedediah sat next to her. He took her right hand and pressed it between his bony fingers.

"Abbie, about three months ago, Corbin was arrested." She gasped. She understood what that meant. Reports were rampant of ministers who had been arrested and never heard from again. Of others, whose battered bodies were found discarded like trash along the road.

"Is, is he dead?"

"No, my dear. He is being held at an interrogation facility in Philadelphia. He is too well respected for them to eliminate him in secret. I don't think they want to make a martyr of him."

Her body relaxed. Jedediah was always honest with her. Yet, she new this was not the whole story. He was holding something back.

"Doctor Jedediah Whitaker," she scolded, "I have given up everything I ever knew for the sake of Corbin and the Brotherhood. Do not think I am so weak that I cannot bear to hear the whole truth. Please do not treat me as a child!"

"Oh, dear Abbie, I would have been disappointed if you had not challenged me. Though, I had hoped I could spare you what I know.

"We had a large rally in Washington," he began.

"I saw a report on that in the Abilene Guardian."

"What you probably didn't hear was there was an incident. The NALC had a strong presence there. One of their members tried to assassinate your husband."

Abbie stopped breathing for a moment.

"The bullet penetrated his arm and bounced off a rib. God spared his life. In the panic that ensued hundreds of innocent people died from gunshot wounds, and more from being trampled to death.

"While we were making our escape, Corbin turned back and surrendered. His actions saved others from brutal beatings and possible death."

A sense of fear and pride filled her thoughts. Her poor Corbin. He was never physically strong. His greatest strength was his character and mind.

"Is he well? Have you seen him since then?" She had a thousand questions.

"He is undergoing intense interrogation."

"You mean torture?" Her voice was clear and strong.

Jedediah nervously rubbed his fingers together while staring at his hands. Without looking up he simply replied, "Yes."

Abbie broke into tears. She tried to imagine the horror Corbin must be facing. She realized that the dreams that woke her in the night and caused her to pray for her husband were from the Lord.

"Oh, Corbin," the words escaped as a moan. Her body convulsed with sobbing. "Oh, my poor Corbin."

She felt Jedediah's arms wrap around her as he drew her near. She sobbed into his shoulder. She did not want to be comforted. She needed to mourn.

Abigail could no longer produce tears. She stood and walked to the bathroom. She washed her face and breathed a prayer. She had to be strong for Corbin. She could not give up hope. The same God that delivered Daniel from the lions could free Corbin from the cruelty of wicked men.

When she walked back into the living room, Jedediah stood to his feet with an anxious look.

"Abbie, I'm so sor..." She held a hand up to silence him.

"What do we need to do? Is there anyone we can contact?" The questions carried conviction. She was determined not to be helpless. She would do what was necessary to free Corbin.

Jedediah tilted his head as though he were trying to figure out who she was.

"There is a Brother who has infiltrated the Division. He is working now to try to protect Corbin. It won't be easy and there are no guarantees. He will contact me in a few days with an update. I will pass on whatever I get to you."

Abigail nodded in agreement. Jedediah was the one man beside Corbin that she would trust with her life.

"First things first," she said as she sat down next to him again. "I want to join the Brotherhood."

Chapter 26

Getting Corbin's case moved to his department was the easy part. Jeff needed to conceive a plan that would allow him to stop the interrogations.

His last communication with Jedediah had troubled him. His trip to see Abigail and her subsequent initiation into the Brotherhood could spell trouble. Abbie could be a stubborn woman. His fear was that she would try to come to Philadelphia to see Corbin. If she were captured, all bets were off for Corbin's future. He stressed that to Jedediah who reassured him that Abbie would pose no issues.

"She is a strong woman, Jeffrey," Jedediah said. "She understands what is at stake."

"Jedediah," Jeff retorted, "if she slips up, it is more than Corbin's life on the line."

I sure hope Jedediah knows what he's doing. She is too emotionally attached, and her love for Corbin could cause her to do something stupid.

"Mister Arbino." Gladys interrupted his thoughts. He sighed. He long ago gave up trying to get her to call him Jeff. He supposed old habits were hard to break.

"What is it, Gladys? I am extremely busy." It was not exactly a lie. He was busy, but not about work.

"Mister Lambert is on line one."

"Thank you, Gladys." Jeff rubbed his face with both hands. Although his mission was to learn as much as he could, he loathed rubbing shoulders with men like Lambert. Taking a deep breath, he lifted the handset from its cradle.

"William, how can I help you?" His voice was cheery, a hypocrisy that made him cringe.

"Have you read the morning's briefings?"

"Why, no Sir, I just arrived at the office. Anything in particular I should look at?" It was not unusual for Lambert to call him about issues that disturbed him. Jeff hoped another Brother was not being targeted. He stalled issuing the arrest warrants so he could at least try to warn the subject so they could make an escape. Unfortunately, it was not always successful.

"Yes," his voice was angry, "there are large protests in every major city concerning the arrest of this Corbin Miller. The NALC doesn't have the resources to deal with it. It's out of control."

Thank you, Lord. This was a situation he might be able to manipulate in Corbin's favor. The interrogation reports he received everyday were disconcerting. He could not imagine that Corbin had not broken. One report in particular had been so gruesome, and the torment so cruel, that he was unable to sleep.

Jeff thumbed through the various briefs until he found the one Lambert had mentioned. According to the report, the protests were massive, and the protestors were demanding Corbin's release.

"William, since Miller is under my authority, give me a little time to think of a remedy."

"The government's resources are stretched to capacity. We cannot sustain a protracted resistance. The NALC did what they do best. Instead of running, the protestors locked arms and sat on the ground. These protests are highly organized. I can only imagine that this Brotherhood is behind it."

You have no idea, Jeff thought with a silent smirk.

"I'll get back with you in a few hours. I think there is a way to calm the protests without losing face." He already knew what he would do. He had to get word to the Brothers.

"Gladys, I need some air. I'm going out to get a late breakfast. Cancel my meetings for this morning. "Oh," he added as an after thought, "contact Alexander McCormick and tell him to move Miller to an intermediate cell."

"Yes, sir," she called after him. He had already pushed the button for the elevator. Providence was working in his favor.

****

"I'm sorry, what?" Alexander was incredulous. Miller was about to break. He was certain of it. Why would they decide to move him to an intermediate cell? This was unbelievable. No one was moved to an intermediate cell until long after they had been broken. It was protocol, his protocol. He was not quite comfortable with this Arbino. Something about him was not right.

"All I know is that Mister Arbino told me to call you and give you these instructions. If you have a problem with that, call him. I don't make the decisions." Her voice sounded irritated.

Though normally in control of his emotions, Alexander slammed the phone down in anger. This Arbino was too soft. Miller was one of the most dangerous men in the nation. His appeal was not isolated to a small group of fanatics.

Corbin was recovering in the infirmary from his last session. Alex had made sure it had been brutal. Jack had done a thorough job of crushing the tips of Miller's fingers with a forty-eight ounce ball peen hammer.

Alex watched through the two-way mirror. Miller's resolve was impressive. His pitiful cries would have been heart rending if he had been worthy of sympathy. His attachment to his superstition seemed unwavering.

Alex had watched the sessions of other dissidents. None had ever resisted this long. Even the religionists soon admitted their guilt and renounced their faith. No one could resist such torment by their own will. What was different with Miller?

The receiver in Jack's ear allowed Alex to orchestrate each session. He fancied himself a conductor. His symphony, the screams and moans of his subjects.

"The forefinger of his right hand first," his voice buzzed in Jack's ear. Corbin's hands had been immobilized. Jack strapped his other fingers to the side. He picked up the hammer and without hesitation raised it above his head. When his arm swung down, the forefinger of his right hand was bloodied and twisted.

Corbin's scream was typical, doleful and filled with despair. His body writhed, and his face contorted from the pain.

"I forgive you, I forgive you." He breathlessly said through clenched teeth.

"Wait," Alex's voice squelched in Jack's ear. Obediently Jack leaned against the wall and watched Corbin. Alex waited ten minutes allowing the shock to dissipate and the pain to reach its apex. "Next finger."

The process went on for hours until each finger had been damaged. Once he was certain Corbin's condition was unbearable, he entered the room.

"How long will you continue to torture yourself?" Alex needed his subjects to understand that what they suffered was their doing. He was only the instrument of the government. Neither guilty nor innocent. *What about the dreams*, his mind rejoined. That thought distracted him. The dreams became more real, more frightening. This man was somehow the cause.

"You are more of a victim than I." Corbin's voice was weak. "I pray God will forgive you."

The arrogance and boldness of this man was perplexing. Alex involuntarily became angry. He took a slow breath to calm himself. None of his other subjects ever affected him like this. He nodded to Jack. He watched as Corbin's head snapped back, his crooked nose leaking blood. *He could not endure much longer*, Alex told himself. *Soon, very soon... Four months, no one had ever lasted that long.*

A shudder ran through him. The presence was there. He pushed down the rising panic. *It is just a dream,* he told himself. *If it is just a dream,* an inner voice said, *why does it follow you?*

Alex shook off the thought. Reluctantly he picked up the phone and called the interrogation center.

"Interrogations, Jack."

"Jack, Alex. We have been ordered to move Miller to an intermediate room."

"I'll make the arrangements right away."

"No, make them tomorrow. Put him back in the room tonight."

"The infirmary says he's not ready. He hasn't healed from the last session. Doc says his heart may not stand the added stress."

"Do as you are told." If he could not break him, the chance of him dying was acceptable.

Chapter 27

Corbin's feet ached even though the outward wounds had healed. His hands were bandaged, and the slightest use of them was painful.

The meager meals he received twice a day were just enough to keep him alive. Each day he received the same fare. For what he assumed was breakfast, he received one-half cup of oatmeal. It was thick and pasty without any milk or sweetener. The first few times he had been given the meal it was difficult to eat. After dozens of days he relished each morsel. His second meal consisted of several small chunks of boiled potato and a small portion of meat. It had dawned on him to count the days by the number of bowls of oatmeal he received. Since he started his tabulations he had eaten forty-seven of the meals. He was not certain how many meals he had had previously.

His whole body felt weak. He knew his weight had dropped. The jumpsuit he wore outside his room was extremely baggy. When he arrive it had fit him perfectly. Everyday he prayed that Christ would take him home. Yet, he was resigned to whatever God's will was for him. He did not know how much more he could absorb.

He longed for a shower or bath. He could not remember the last time he had bathed. His hair had grown below his ears and he had a full beard.

He had no value to these men. Every human courtesy was taken from him. He was not allowed to speak unless questioned. Sometimes scratching an itch could elicit a beating from Jack. He lived in constant fear of reprisal. That uncertainty created a torment of its own.

The doctor entered the room. Corbin closed his eyes. If he appeared too lucid they would take him back to his room. Dread filled him. The doctor never spoke except once when he whispered to Corbin, "I am sorry." Corbin never learned his name.

He had learned from bits of conversations that the doctor in the infirmary had been a prisoner. Technically, he was still a detainee, but his willingness to patch up other subjects saved him from future sessions. Corbin now knew why his left ear was missing. He did not blame the man. His heart went out to him, and when he was healing, he prayed for his redemption.

After his first few sessions, Corbin's inward struggle rivaled the pain he suffered. He found it difficult to forgive Jack and Alexander. Both these men seemed devoid of the most basic human empathy. Neither man appeared to see him as human. Corbin struggled through the physical pain to pray and maintain his humanity and connection to God.

He knew it would have been easy to just quit, to give Alexander what he wanted. Something inside him would not allow it. Giving in would only justify their evil. *Yes, evil,* he thought. *Why else would one human being systematically torment another.* Corbin had known that evil existed, but intellectual understanding could never reveal the horror that the depraved were capable of perpetrating.

Corbin stretched on the thin mattress. Jack had stopped cuffing him to the stretcher long ago. Corbin did not have the strength or desire any longer to try to escape. The freedom of movement was invigorating. His room restricted his movement and his muscles were perpetually sore and cramping. He was surprised at what he was able to tolerate.

His eyes were still closed when he heard the infirmary door open.

"Get him up," Jack's unmistakable voice demanded.

"But he's not ready yet. His wounds are too fresh."

"Now," there was menace in Jack's voice.

Corbin jerked away from the smelling salts.

"On your feet." Jack's voice was neutral, betraying no emotion.

Corbin obeyed. To hesitate meant more pain. The flesh wounds in Corbin's feet had healed. The internal damage made it difficult for him to stand. When his feet hit the ground he staggered forward.

"Disrobe. You're going to your room."

Corbin wanted to weep, but the tears never came. He knew he was going to his room. *My room. Why do you call it that? It is a torture chamber, a coffin.* He dare not say it aloud. These men used euphemism to mask their dirty deeds. Corbin wondered if this was their way of buffering their conscience from their nefarious actions.

Lord of heaven and earth, I long for your salvation. The Lord is my shepherd... he repeated this psalm as a prayer. *I shall not want...*

"Stop." Jack's monotone voice interrupted his meditation.

Corbin no longer felt the shame of his nakedness. This was not his fault, not his choice. He stood motionless waiting for Jack to open the door. The lights had already been turned on. The heat and stench from his room assaulted his senses. Without hesitation he stepped inside.

Corbin heard the door lock behind him. He knew he could not escape the smell or the heat so he resigned himself to the situation. After a few minutes, the damage to his feet became a throbbing pain. He thought of Paul and Silas who were beaten unjustly, their feet placed in stocks. In their discomfort and pain they praised God. Corbin was alone. No, not alone. God's Holy Spirit was with him. Jesus' love filled his heart.

Corbin's voice croaked at first as he began to sing. Immediately the room was filled with a painful noise. He continued his song.

"Holy, holy, holy..." the sound became more intense. "Lord God almighty..." The noise seemed to fade away. He was swept away in worship. His mind focused on his Savior and friend. The pain became a distant throb. He felt strong. In his tiny prison, his mind and soul were free.

Corbin stretched his broken hands toward the ceiling. His voice growing stronger. Tears exploded from his eyes. For the first time in this torment, his tears were not bidden by pain. Joy had filled him. This act of worship freed him. God seemed to speak to him in a quiet inward voice, *Lo, I am with you always, even until the end of the world.* Somehow Corbin knew it would end. He believed that. He had to believe.

He did not hear the door open. The pain was brief. His naked body slapped against the hall floor. Through bleary eyes he saw Jack. His tormentor's right hand was pulled back. Corbin saw the club. It moved toward him and everything went black.

Chapter 28

Against the wishes of the Brothers, Jedediah remained in Abilene so he could be close to Abbie. After taking the Brotherhood's oath, Abigail became an indispensable member. Her zeal was driven by her desire to help Corbin and other believers who were being persecuted by the new American government.

Once privy to all the information the Brothers had gathered on the plight of Christians in the states, she was appalled. She developed a program to bring relief to disenfranchised families. Hundreds of wives and children were forced to live in the streets. Abbie traveled throughout Texas raising money and collecting care packages to relieve their suffering. Nancy Schumaker was becoming well known throughout the state. This caused Jedediah to fear for her safety.

When he cautioned her about her actions, she responded, "are men the only ones capable of hazarding their lives for the cause of Christ?"

"Well no, but..."

"No!" she interrupted him. "There is no, but! Jedediah, God has called me to this as assuredly as he called you to the pulpit and teaching. I am not a child.

These people need me and the Brotherhood has done a poor job of alleviating their needs."

"Ab... Nancy," he glanced around the restaurant where they had met. "Please keep your voice down. You don't know who might be listening." He leaned in lowering his voice. "I am concerned about your safety. Your face is too recognizable. Many have been kidnapped and taken back to the states. This is a free nation and the borders are open. Do you understand?"

"Yes, I am well aware of the risks. Oh, Jedediah, you are like a father to Corbin and me. But, don't you understand? I have to do this for Corbin and the myriad others who have suffered simply because they love Christ and freedom."

He knew she was right. A heaviness settled down on him. He had to leave her in God's hands. Jedediah knew he was not capable of keeping her safe. Her path was between her and God.

"I will help you in anyway I can," his voice was subdued. "I wish we never had to face days like this. Men are so foolish, they would trade their lives for comfort, and wicked men are always willing to oblige them."

Abbie took his hands in her's. He saw the tenderness and compassion born of her own suffering.

She had lost everything. He could not imagine what she must be suffering. She reminded him of his Lydia. He would have moved heaven and earth to spare her life. His grief had been intense. She died from a debilitating disease. He was by her side the whole time, comforting her, consoling her. Abbie did not have that luxury. She knew Corbin was being tortured by cruel men. Heartless animals whose humanity had long ago left them.

"Any news of Corbin," she asked quietly.

The waitress came to their table and refilled their coffee. Jedediah added cream, picked up his cup and took a sip. The satisfaction of that simple act surprised him.

"I received word from Jeff last evening." Once Abbie had taken the oath, Jedediah had told her of Jeff's role in Corbin's situation. That was another breach of protocol, but she deserved to know. "As you know, there were large gatherings in every major city protesting Corbin's arrest. The Brothers organized them to bring attention to the plight of Corbin and others. Jeff took advantage of that and had Corbin moved to an intermediate cell. Prisoners moved from the subbasement to the upper level of the subfloors are no longer subject to torture. Their living conditions are still Spartan, extremely regimented, but no physical violence."

He watched her body relax.

"Mark," it was hard for her to call him Mark, it was too impersonal, "thank you."

"Child, I did nothing, Providence worked for Corbin. The protests that precipitated this were a shot in the dark. None of us were certain it would work and it wouldn't have without Jeff."

"Jedediah," she said his name so only he could hear, "what offense did the church create that has brought such hatred against believers? I know churches and believers have sometimes failed to live what they preach, but is that an offense worthy of torture and death?"

"For years, Abbie, I believed the animosity that powerful men had toward believers was due to the light that was shone on their evil deeds. Though that may be part of it, recently I have been convinced that these wicked men need disorder and anarchy to move them into power.

"Christian principle was the keeper of society. During the Great Depression, people were poor and many destitute. Though, as in any generation, there was crime during that period, most people existed with decency and honor. Society detested theft and avarice. That was due to the basic respect people had for

Christian principle. It kept them. Instead of taking advantage of one another, most helped each other.

"The assault on the Church that began in the early sixties set the stage for a societal breakdown. When Katrina struck in 2005, anarchy ruled. Roving gangs of thugs raided homes and stole property. It was a stark difference from the time of the depression. Once Christian principles had been marginalized, it was easy for men like Freeman to completely annihilate freedom.

"The good news is that the oppression in the states has awakened an interest in the Church. The Brotherhood has been instrumental in reviving biblical teaching."

The waitress came back to their table. "Aren't you Nancy Schumaker?" She asked excitedly.

Abbie smiled, "I am."

"Oh, Miss Schumaker, you spoke at my Church several weeks ago. I never knew how bad it was in the old country..."

Jedediah groaned inwardly. As the waitress prattled on other patrons looked on in curiosity. This was the very thing he wanted to avoid. You did not hide someone by letting them become a celebrity.

Chapter 29

Alex sat staring intently at the drape covered window. Though the sun was bright and the sky a cloudless crystal blue, he could only focus on the various shades of gray and the black crevices where the light dare not go. He was amazed at how colorless his world had become, darkness became his friend. There was no depth to his life. He felt two dimensional as though he were living an abstract existence where color had given way to mottled grays and ever darkening hues that made his skin crawl with fear.

It had been this way for many months, ever since the monster inside him showed itself for the first time. The first hints of it were small, hardly detectable. The pain that accompanied it was almost imperceptible and he dismissed it as insignificant. Yet, over time its presence was undeniable and he knew now that its existence would lead to the end of his.

Alex was still in the pajamas he had put on three days before. The stubble on his chin was course and painted his face with a perpetual shadow. His greasy hair had not seen a comb in nearly a week. All the blinds and curtains had been drawn tight. The light hurt his eyes.

He had still not opened the letter from Regional Director Arbino. He feared its contents. He could not help brooding over the debacle with Miller. Moving him to an intermediate cell meant he would no longer be under Alex's care. That meant he had failed.

He could not shake the image on that last day of Miller in his room, hands raised and singing. Alexander was troubled. In the nearly six years he had performed his service to the people, he had never seen anything like that. Normally, after months of Alex's sessions, detainees were begging to please him. Not Miller.

Since that day, Alex's sense of foreboding had become unbearable. He was unable to sleep. In truth, he was afraid to sleep. Every time he began to doze, he felt the dark presence. His dreams had become worse and were assaulting his waking hours. His nightmares seemed to be more than mere dreams. His silent tormentor had taken control of his waking thoughts as well. Whatever it was, he believed it was malevolent, and had taken residence inside him.

Miller had been a challenge, and the new Director had taken it away. He was certain he could break Miller if given enough time.

"Amateur," he said aloud. "Another bureaucrat with something to prove."

It was seven A.M. and he had already opened a bottle of whiskey. Alex rubbed the stubble on his chin and poured another drink.

"I'm the best of the best," he protested to himself.

"Here's to Miller." He raised his glass in an imaginary toast and downed the contents in one swallow.

Alex wondered what made Miller different. His technique was flawless. He had broken men that others could not. His sessions lasted for days alternating between administering pain and seclusion in the room. The number of sessions varied so his subject would never know what to expect.

After weeks of torment, he would allow the subject to have a respite. This would last for an indeterminate time. This rest time allowed the subject the false hope that the worst was over. The duration of the rest depended on who he was interrogating.

Alex prided himself on understanding the resolve of his subjects. For him, it was an intricately orchestrated art form. No one was as successful as he. Miller was a puzzle he wanted to unravel, but now that opportunity was taken from him.

Putting Miller in his room for the last time was vindictive, and that was not like Alex. As a professional, he never let his emotions dictate his process. The men and women he worked with were the worst of humanity, and their lives had no value. Even after they were broken and compliant their value was minimal. He was disturbed at how this insignificant man had affected him.

He felt the monster again, and uneasiness settled over him. Since his first session with Miller, a pall had clung to him. It was imperceptible at first, gnawing at his subconscious and easily ignored. It had grown over time. The dreams revealed it to be malevolent and alive. He felt pursued. It had invaded his sleep, and now it was relentlessly assaulting his waking hours.

Alex gently placed his glass on the end table. He was straining to listen. Every noise seemed to be magnified. He thought he saw a shadow moving in his bedroom.

"Fool!" he scolded himself. "It's just your imagination," he said as he poured himself another drink.

Alex was weary. The lack of sleep had made him jumpy. The past four nights of limited sleep had forced him to take time from work. He had not taken a sick day or vacation day in five years. His work was too important.

Involuntarily, his eyes, heavy with sleep, began to close. His chest rose and fell in the cadence of slumber.

He was standing in the infirmary. His feet were cold. Looking down, he noticed he had no shoes. Then he realized he was naked and standing near a gurney. His hands, chest and thighs were covered with blood. Fear gripped him. He carefully inspected his arms and chest. With a sigh he said, "Not mine." A white towel lay at his feet.

"Where did that come from?" he said perplexed. Stooping over, he picked it up and began wiping the blood off his body. When he finished, more blood appeared. Using the already bloodied towel he tried to clean himself again. The towel became soaked. His efforts only smeared the now foul smelling liquid.

"No, please, no," his pleading echoed back to him.

Miller's broken body lay before him, his eyes open and lifeless. Alex stepped closer to the cadaver. Miller's skin was pallid with gaping wounds that no longer bled. Miller, or what was left of him, turned his head and looked at Alex, his eyes an empty vortex. "I forgive you," it rasped.

"You cannot forgive me!" he screamed. "I have done nothing wrong." He held up his hands. Blood ran down his forearms and dripped off his elbows. He stepped back and slipped in a growing pool of blood. He wallowed in the gore. The puddle became deeper and the gore thicker.

He looked up and Corbin's broken body now sat on the edge of the gurney.

"Help me, please help me. Corbin, you can't let me go like this, please." He was helpless and at the mercy of the man before him.

"Let go," Corbin's voice rasped. "You must let go." Corbin's gaze moved up. "Ask for His help."

Alex followed the empty eyes. Above him was a figure emblazoned in light. Its eyes were fire, and though the light was bright, it did not hurt to look.

"No, there must be another way." Panic filled him. This being before him frightened him more than the blood; more than his guilt and helplessness. Its penetrating eyes saw into his very soul. It knew him, understood him.

"There is no other way."

"I cannot. I will not."

The blood became deeper and he sank within it. There was no bottom, no escape. He was surrounded by corpses. He recognized each one. All had been his subjects. He tried to scream and his mouth filled with blood. Frantically, he tried to swim to the surface. He longed for escape, for succor. His effort only took him deeper. He was drowning in the blood of those he had made to suffer. There was no escape.

Alex wanted to wake up, but the presence had immobilized him. He felt it moving, stalking, and circling. Alex was surrounded by pathetic soulless screams. The voices were familiar and the faces of his victims appeared before him. Each of them was accusing him with just a look. Alex could sense their suffering; suffering that he had created.

"I was just doing my job," his mind cried, trying to plead his cause. "I was protecting innocent people from your hate," his words echoed back to him.

He tried to scream, but could only manage a low throaty groan. He had no strength. He wished himself awake. He was cognizant of the chair on which he sat. He could hear the ticking of the ornate cuckoo clock that hung on his wall. The smell of whiskey filled his nostrils.

He was stuck in twilight. Not quite asleep and neither was he awake. His hand twitched and the glass it held struck the floor. Alex opened his eyes.

Guilt and fear clung to him. *Guilt?* That was impossible. What he did was for the good of the State, for the people. *I am a hero!* his mind screamed. *I save lives, I preserve the peace.*

His protest could not dissipate the emptiness that flooded him. He stood and began to pace. He could not clear his head; the voices mocked and accused him.

His hands shook as he stooped to pick up the glass and pour another drink. The alcohol no longer gave him relief. He could no longer escape the inner turmoil.

His subjects rose in his mind, one by one. He closed his eyes and cradled his head in his hands.

"What do you want?" His voice trembled. "I have done what was necessary to protect progress."

His words seemed hollow. Everything he had mocked him. He was empty inside. He knew he had no hope. The weight of unfamiliar emotions was crushing him.

The letter lay on the end table next to him. Alex stared at it for a long while. He had heard the rumors and was fearful to read its contents. He downed another glass of whiskey, and after three days he finally mustered the courage to pick it up.

His hand trembled as he held the envelope. He crushed it to his forehead in anguish.

"Just open it, you fool," he scolded himself. "Open it."

He walked to the desk in his bedroom and switched on the desk lamp. The brightness of the lamp caused him to squint. His letter opener was where he expected it. Meticulously, he slid the edge of the replica of a sword down the outer seam of the envelope.

He hesitated before removing its contents. Taking a deep cleansing breath, he unfolded the letter and began to read.

****

Alex stared for a long time at the letter. He began to laugh uncontrollably. He rocked back in his seat and almost lost his balance. He stood up and staggered to the living room to fetch his bottle.

He returned to the desk and continued to snigger. He took several long drinks from the bottle and sat down. He knew his life was no longer his own. All his years of faithful service had been negated by this one man. He had been demoted. He would no longer lead the interrogation team. His life was over, and he knew what he had to do.

At first, the thought of his demise frightened him. It was not so much that he feared to die. No, dying would free him -- no more pain. He instead feared the process of death because he could only experience it once. He was not sure what to expect. Would it wash over him in a tide of peace or would it be a turbulent explosion of pain. Pain, the thought made him shake his head. He was the master of pain. Hundreds had suffered under his direction, pain meant nothing to him.

Alex slowly rose from his seat sighing, wearied by the effort. Since the monster came, small things became painful. The simple act of rising from bed, so natural to most, was a sheer test of will.

Suddenly the monster stretched inside him, reaching, groping, and digging for more ground. It became a battle he realized he could never win. His legs became weak and he tried to steady himself on a nearby chair. He wished for death. He could not continue on. He looked inside himself for strength, but what he saw was no longer recognizable. The shadow he saw was slightly familiar, yet the substance of it was grotesque, twisted and foreign. As quickly as it came, it dissipated. He knew the time was nearing and there was so much to be done.

He shuffled to the stove and put on a kettle of water. He needed something besides the whiskey. Then he unsteadily walked to the bed to keep vigil over his turmoil. At times he would rock back and forth, hugging himself as a child seeking comfort in his own arms. His tears would flow freely, unashamedly. Yet, even that only increased what he felt, and made him realize with more clarity his helplessness.

Dizzy and weak, he staggered from the bedroom and sat down in his overstuffed chair, its tan arms stained from grease, sweat and dirt. He wiped the perspiration from his forehead on the tail of his pajama. His hand was still shaking. Closing his eyes, he tried to calm himself, taking several deep breaths. The pain came crashing in an unyielding torrent. It had the mastery and he could never escape. Time was against him. Soon this thing would consume his very essence.

He reached for his journal where he kept his innermost feelings. He wrote quickly, afraid to lose a thought. The beast would not leave him for long. Each day it gained more ground. His journal would be his testament and he would leave it to those who followed. It had been four months since his life began to disintegrate. It was the most difficult thing he had ever experienced. His life was no longer his own. He was slowly being dominated by the monster.

He brushed away a tear with his sleeve. The thought of losing prestige and control of his life was unbearable. He had found strength in purpose, and yet he knew that the force of this beast would eventually destroy him.

His body shook from weeping. His sobs came in floods of sorrow and isolation. He had to fight this battle alone, and yet he no longer had the will to fight. The battle had been too long and the monster had all the advantage. It fed off his fear and weakness and as time slowly crawled by, fear was all Alex had left.

The high pitched squeal of the tea pot startled him away from his introspection. Painfully, he rose from his seat and shuffled to the stove. Turning off the burner, he mechanically made himself tea. Two lumps of sugar, no, today he would have three. He stared blankly at the steam wafting from the hot water as he dipped the tea bag up and down. The effort made him breathe a weary sigh. The monster moved, breathed and gained ground. It was alive, and eventually, the battle would be lost.

Taking his tea and picking up his journal, he went back and sat in his overstuffed chair. The time was drawing near, it hung in the air like a black cloud. Alex shivered and pulled a quilt across his rounded shoulders. He groaned, he had lost his dignity.

He slowly opened the top drawer of the stand next to him and removed it. It felt cold to the touch. Gripping it in his right hand, he turned it over and over inspecting the fine machine work that had gone into making it. The smell of lubricant was slightly distasteful, and yet it was the smell of salvation.

He took a sip of tea and burned his mouth. He set it down and briefly watched the wisps of steam.

Yes, the time was very near. Alex sat back, shifting his weight, trying to get comfortable. Closing his eyes, he raised his right hand to his head.

He heard a voice speaking, "Let Him help you." It was Miller's voice.

"No." was all he said, then there was an explosion of light, bright and white hot. The pain ceased.

Chapter 30

Corbin opened his eyes and slowly turned his head. The room seemed unfamiliar. With effort, he sat on the end of the narrow cot where he lay.

His head hurt, and trying to survey the room was difficult. This area was different, he had never been in here before. He approximated its size at ten feet long and five feet wide. The light coming through the small window near the ceiling forced him to squint.

He rose and walked toward the window without taking his eyes off the light. He stretched as far as he could but did not come close to reaching the portal. He wondered if he was dreaming. He found refuge in his dreams. Abbie was normally in these dreams, smiling and tenderly touching his cheek. Though he rarely had periods of calm and rest that gave him hope, his dreams of Abbie seemed to strengthen him.

There was a shaft of light that terminated at the far wall. He watched in awe as particles of dust danced and glittered in the sunlight. He ran his fingers through the beam and the particles scurried away. He did this several times and smiled as he watched the spectacle.

"Thank you, Lord," his voice was hoarse. He cringed at the sound of his words. Reflexively, he shrunk back from an expected blow. Jack was not there. No one came rushing into the room to beat him.

"This is a trick." The soft whisper of his words seemed to echo back. He stared intently at the door, expecting the stoic face of his tormentor. Nothing.

It only took three halting steps to reach the door. Corbin pressed his ear tight against the metal and listened intently. He heard nothing but the soft rumbling of the ventilation system. He was perplexed at this new tactic.

It was then that he noticed the second door. It was slightly ajar and decidedly more narrow than the exit. He tentatively approached the door and grasped the knob, then cautiously pulled it open.

Startled, he guiltily looked around. He noticed a small camera in the corner to the right of the smaller door. Corbin left the door open and stared into the room. The stainless toilet sat in the left corner with a small sink above where the tank was. To the right was a small, walk-in shower. Corbin blinked in disbelief.

They're watching, he told himself. He gave a furtive glance to the camera then backed up and sat on the edge of the bed. He had to use the toilet but was afraid to enter the small room. He looked for a grate in the floor and was surprised to see a small nap carpet instead. He rubbed his bare feet on the carpet. Tears came to his eyes as he felt the texture underneath his toes.

They're watching, his mind screamed. Remembering the camera he pulled his feet onto the cot and scurried back to the wall and sat motionless. His breath caught in his throat as he waited for the door to open. *Nothing,* he thought, *Alex is testing me.* The camera was an unwelcome intruder.

His need to relieve himself was becoming painful and urgent. He stayed in the same location and watched as the beam of sunlight made its way up the wall. The urgency to use the restroom began to overcome his fear of reprisal.

Inching his way to the edge of the bed, he stopped short of putting his feet on the carpet. He sat quietly waiting. He stole glances at the door and camera. The uncertainty of what was happening disturbed him. He was uncomfortable with this change of routine. Getting up the courage, he again placed his feet on the floor. The sensation of the carpet filled him with satisfaction. He became fearful that Alex knew he felt pleasure.

Several times during his sessions, Alex had allowed him small pleasures. During these breaks in his punishment, he spent days without pain, only to be punished for taking advantage of small luxuries. This was different. During those lulls in his sessions, he would be placed in a room that allowed him to sit, and even lie down. He still had the floor grate to relieve himself, and had no clothing to wear except for a thin gown.

At times when the breaks were granted, he would be taken to a room with a wooden chair and a recliner. It also had a fully furnished restroom as well as a grate in the floor. When first placed in the room and the door was shut, he immediately sat in the recliner. The softness of the chair caused him to fall asleep. When he woke up he used the restroom then splashed cold water on his face. He then went back into the room and slept in the chair. Two trays of food were delivered, one with his usual meal, the other tray had steak and potatoes.

After the first break, Alex met with him in the interrogation room.

"Did you enjoy your rest, Corbin?" His smile seemed genuine.

"Yes," Corbin replied without making eye contact, "thank you."

"I see. Did anyone give you permission to sit in the recliner or do any of the things you took advantage of?"

Corbin blanched, "I assumed..."

"Assumed? You are nothing, Corbin, don't you understand that? You don't have the ability to choose. You do not deserve better than what you have been given."

Alex picked up the phone. "Jack, please come in here."

"I'm sorry," Corbin pleaded, "I didn't know, I thought it was okay."

"No, Corbin, you didn't think. In fact you have no right to think. You are an animal, my pet, you only do what I allow. Do you understand this?"

"Yes."

Jack entered the room and walked over to Corbin. The blow was swiftly delivered knocking Corbin off the chair. His tormentor took off his belt and began to savagely beat Corbin with the buckled end.

Corbin rolled on the floor trying to avoid the blows. Jack continued to whip him with powerful strokes. Corbin crawled into a corner, trying in vain to protect his battered body. Restrained by the corner all Corbin could do was scream and hope the torment would soon end. His arms obviously fatigued from the effort, Jack began to kick his helpless victim.

After that first experience Corbin never again took advantage of comforts within his grasp.

His discomfort became unbearable and ended his musing. He decided he would accept the consequences, and rushed for the restroom to use the toilet. The anxiety he felt made him queazy. He used his left hand to steady himself, his knees felt weak. He was certain the door would open and Jack would stride in and administer punishment for relieving himself without permission.

Once he was finished, he flushed, and was puzzled that no one had entered the room. After a few moments, Corbin haltingly reached down and turned on the faucet. A weak stream of water ran freely into the small stainless sink. Ignoring the bandages, he put his hand into the stream. The water was cold and clear. He giggled at the sensation and then put both hands into the flow.

Splashing water on his face was luxurious. He did this several times, savoring the wetness and refreshing coolness of this oasis.

The noise at the door brought nearly crippling fear. Backing away from the faucet, he anxiously moved toward the bed. The perpetual pain in his feet made it difficult to move quickly.

Halfway toward his goal, he noticed a tray of food had been delivered through a small hinged gate at the bottom of the door. Corbin stopped and watched the door. Satisfied that no one would enter, he knelt on the floor to inspect the tray.

The smell of turkey and gravy was intoxicating. He dipped his bandaged finger in the gravy and tentatively touched it to his tongue. Saliva flooded his mouth as he savored the familiar taste. Fearful that he was being tested, he scooted back and sat staring at the tray.

Finally overcome with a need to eat, he crawled back to the tray and voraciously consumed the meal. The small portions of turkey, mashed potatoes and corn made him feel full. Unashamed, he lifted the tray and licked the remaining gravy.

The light from the window was slowly dimming. Corbin lay down on his cot. The thin, lumpy mattress felt exquisite as he allowed himself to relax.

Abbie filled his thoughts. Soon he drifted off to a world where hope still lived.

Chapter 31

Everyday had been filled with constant activity. Abbie's work at the restaurant and her role with the Brotherhood gave her little time to rest.

"Is the shipment ready?" Jedediah had been her constant companion since his arrival in Texas. He ate at least one meal at the restaurant and worked by her side in the evenings.

"Almost," she replied as she placed the last of the nonperishable goods into the cardboard box. She wiped the sweat from her forehead with the sleeve of her shirt.

It had been nearly four months since Corbin disappeared. She needed him home, especially now.

"You be careful with that, young lady," Jedediah gently scolded. He grabbed the box and placed it on the truck.

"I'm not fragile, Jedediah. I am capable of carrying a box." She smiled at his kindness. She knew he felt guilty for Corbin's arrest so he doted over her. She assumed it was his form of penance. "But, thank you, nonetheless," her smile was broad and genuine.

"You shouldn't be doing this kind of work in your condition after all the baby is due soon."

Abbie smiled. She placed her hands on her stomach and lovingly caressed the life inside her. This child carried a part of her beloved Corbin. It was God's mercy to her. For years she and Corbin had tried to conceive without success. A trip to the doctor confirmed their fear, that they would never have children.

She and Corbin's last night together had been one of passion and genuine intimacy. God worked a miracle that produced this child. Abbie was certain that the baby growing inside of her was designed by providence to give her hope.

"Jedediah, God did not give me this child to take it from me. Besides, there is work to be done."

"You are a stubborn girl, Ab.. Nancy. Complain if you like, I will not let you do any heavy lifting."

Abigail looked into the eyes of her kind old friend. His face showed his age. His gray hair was combed straight back just as it had been since she first met him. His eyes held an unmistakeable kindness and betrayed a keen intellect. She hugged him and gently kissed him on the cheek.

"Corbin is fortunate to have a friend like you," she said affectionately. "You have done far more than I deserve."

"Abbie," he blinked back tears, "I owe you everything, Corbin wouldn't be where he is, if it hadn't been for me."

"No, Jedediah, he chose his own path. This is not of your making. He is in God's care and we have to leave him there."

"Nevertheless child, I shall not leave your side." He picked up the last box and set in on the truck.

"Where is this shipment going?" she asked.

"Montana. The Brothers there are under siege. Last I heard the military had moved there in force. Hundreds have been rounded up, and many executed."

Several factions of the Brotherhood had relocated to Montana, near Lewistown. Their total number was unknown, however there were rumors they had armed themselves.

Information trickled slowly into Texas. The government in America was jamming radio and television signals making it difficult to glean information. American media could no longer be trusted to give accurate news. All the major networks were under the direct control of the Department of Communication and Speech.

There had been several skirmishes reported that had ended in the loss of life on both sides. The Brothers in Texas were torn over the violence that had erupted.

The last meeting had been heated.

"We cannot afford to lose perspective. Our's is a nonviolent resistance. Our weapons are love, kindness and persuasion." Brother Cantor was one of the charter members of the Brotherhood. He had fled to Texas when several of his associates had been arrested. There was a warrant for his arrest in the States and Texas was his only refuge.

"With all due respect," answered a younger man that Abbie did not know, "we are here in safety. Our Brothers are battling for their survival. Not only should we supply food and medical equipment, but weapons as well. Pacifism only works in a nation that respects its own laws."

Abbie sat and listened as the debate raged. The group was being torn apart. Her mind went to Corbin who was suffering at the hands of evil men. His right to exist, think and believe had been stripped away. Her husband was a nonhuman to these monsters. Their only goal was to break him and take away the part of him that gave him value. She understood that a person's life was more than eating, sleeping, working or relaxing. It was the sum of a person's beliefs and the courage to live them out. Without the right to self determination, a man was a mere shell, an automaton without purpose. Corbin was the strongest man she knew. His ordeal would have ended long ago had he confessed.

Jedediah rose to his feet. "Gentlemen and Ladies, I have listened to this debate long enough. We cannot forget who we are or who we serve. Are we truly willing to sanction the taking of life, no matter whose it is? I, for one, believe that love will win the day. We can ill afford to become what we detest."

The room became quiet after he spoke. No one rose. Abbie was certain it was out of respect to the venerated man. *Is he right,* she asked herself? Then she rose to her feet.

"You all know who my husband is. You know what he has endured. When the Brotherhood first formed, there was hope that working within the law would eventually force change. That was predicated on the assumption that those governing the country still respected their own laws. We were wrong.

"I do not assume I have the answers, but I do know that the American government will pursue believers until all have been silenced. Most of us are here because we have fled the tyranny and persecution.

Others have stayed in the States to carry on the fight. We who have fled have lost the right to judge those left behind.

"People have a God given right to defend themselves, especially against an entity that seeks their destruction simply because of their belief in Jesus Christ. The government in America has lost its right to exist in its present form. The desire to be free has been placed in the soul of man by God.

"We do not have the right to ask men and women to be docile while their loved ones are being slaughtered. That the slaughter is sanctioned by a governing body does not make it any less onerous or any more legal. The law of God supersedes the law of man.

"I for one, in honor of my husband's sacrifice, will do everything I can to ensure that my friends and family in the States are secure and unmolested by unscrupulous men."

When she sat down she felt Jedediah's frail hand on her shoulder. Leaning in, he whispered, "well said."

The debate continued for another hour. A compromise had been reached before the meeting ended to supply both the factions with food, clothing and medical supplies. There would be no distinction, the group would not take sides.

This was the first shipment to be readied after the meeting. One group of the Brothers was developing plans to supply ammunition and tactical equipment to those involved in the resistance. They dubbed themselves the Miller Brigade.

Abbie watched as the last truck pulled away. She said a silent prayer for those who would receive the supplies. Her thoughts went to her baby and Corbin. "Lord, watch over my family.

****

Jeff had stumbled upon the files by accident. His office had a large picture window on the south wall and he was moving his desk to better take advantage of the view. To make the move easier he decided to remove the drawers from the wood desk.

The desk was solid oak with a flawless finish. *One of the benefits for despots,* he said to himself. He was having difficulty removing the top right drawer. During the struggle to free it from the track the drawer slipped from his grasp and landed hard on its side.

He was surprised to see a file fall to the floor, since he only used the drawer to hold pens, pencils and other small office necessities. When he looked closely, he saw that the drawer had a false bottom and realized the force of the fall must have jarred it lose.

Making sure no one saw the files, he quickly replaced them and reinserted the wooden panel. Now that his move was completed, he locked his office door and retrieved the files.

"You don't know how fortunate you are," he said referring to what he read about Jedediah and Corbin. Jeff quickly logged onto his computer using his passcode. He pulled up the official records on Corbin and Jedediah.

The files he stumbled upon contained an order for the death of Jedediah. Jeff searched his official records to see if it had been formally submitted. He had been Regional Director long enough to know that ordering the death of an individual was both legal and encouraged if the subject was deemed to be a threat to security. That designation was solely up to the discretion of the Regional or Deputy Directors.

No official order had been given concerning Jedediah. Thurman must have been killed before he filed the document. His old friend was safe. The only document he uncovered was the request for a warrant against Jedediah.

This is good, he thought as he placed another order changing the threat level associated with Jedediah. He could not remove the warrant, however, changing his threat assessment meant if he was captured he would only be detained for a few days and threatened. These arrests were intended to frighten and were usually enough to dissuade repeat offenses. Once completed he clicked the save button and relaxed a little.

Corbin's situation was more tenuous. According to his files he was to be detained, interrogated and then neutralized once a confession was signed.

"Gotta love bureaucratic double talk," he chuckled nervously. He picked up the phone and called Gladys.

"Gladys," he said not letting her finish her salutation, "have you been able to reach McCormick? I haven't received any updates on Miller, I need to know if he has been moved."

Gladys entered the office and stood opposite Jeff by his desk. He looked up from the file he was reading, perturbed that she was hovering.

"Yes, Gladys?" He asked not trying to hide the irritation in his voice. "Leave the file on the desk." Realizing that she was upset, he placed Jedediah's file back in the drawer and leaned back in his chair. His position mandated a certain amount of ruthlessness. That was the most difficult part of his ruse. Treating people like chattel was disturbing and caused him internal pain. Alone in his study at night, he would wrestle with guilt. Some evenings he would spend hours on his knees begging God for absolution.

Gladys's obvious pain moved him to compassion. He could not ignore this woman. He would not dismiss her and not offer some comfort.

"Gladys, what is it?" His voice was filled with empathy. This was who he really was, who he longed to be again. The role he was playing was robbing him of the tenderness that he cherished. Infiltrating this agency had marred him. He sometimes feared that his soul was at stake. He had to do detestable things, but not this time. He would redeem a part of his humanity and minister to this woman.

"Haven't you heard about Alex?" It was no secret in the office that Gladys and Alex had been close, although Jeff was certain it was more one sided. What he knew of Alex had convinced Jeff that he was soulless and empty.

Jeff had met with Alex several times to debrief him on information received from interrogations. Alex would dispassionately discuss his process and any relevant information he had garnered.

Jeff's first meeting with him was unexpected and shocking. He was aware of the work Alex did, but was not prepared for the coldness of his demeanor.

Though he did not betray his emotions, Jeff had been sickened by the report. The details of torture and subsequent confessions made Jeff's stomach roil. He looked Alex in the eyes and knew that the man was a monster. His business as usual approach only accentuated that opinion.

At one point, Jeff stopped Alex and said, "I do not need to know the details of your nasty business. All I need to hear is the results." Alex was nonplused.

Looking at this frail woman before him Jeff's voice became tender, "Gladys, what is it?"

She struggled to speak. Her voice was soft and tremulous, "They found him this morning in his apartment. He, he, shot himself."

She began immediately to weep. She collapsed into the visitor's seat and buried her face in her hands.

Jeff snatched several tissues and sat on the edge of his desk and handed them to the grieving girl. Though Alex was a beast, this girl was not. She was trying to survive in a world of avarice and lost opportunity. Her position with the Division made her more fortunate than others, but did not make her equal to the Alexes of the world.

He let her sit and cry herself out. Jeff whispered a silent prayer that she would find hope. Though he did not rejoice in the news of Alex's demise, yet he thanked God for judgment given.

The dark deeds of powerful men will always have a reckoning. He had to believe that. If wickedness found no recompense, then there truly was no hope.

His heart went out to Gladys. He spent a few moments with the grieving woman then sent her home.

The news of Alex's death reminded him that Providence was again working for Corbin. Jeff was eager to maneuver for Corbin's freedom. First he must manipulate the ongoing events and persuade the Deputy Director to follow his advice. He had a plan and needed to contact Lambert immediately.

****

Corbin knew by the recurrence of the beam of light, that he had been in this new room for twenty days. No one had come to the room except the person delivering his meals.

It had taken him several days to realize there would be no reprisals for taking advantage of the luxuries available. The first time he had used the shower, he wept uncontrollably. He promised himself he would never take such a simple act for granted again.

When he finally mustered the courage to use the shower, he saw his reflection in the polished stainless steel for the first time in months. The gaunt figure shocked him. His ribs were protruding and his hip bones were prominent. The stark change made him question what he was seeing. Though the stainless mirror slightly distorted his features, it was obviously him. He held up his arms and stared at the stranger before him. Months of meager meals and intense torture had wasted away his once robust form.

He stood in the shower for a long time. The warm water washing over him was comforting, and in a small way, gave him hope. For months he had washed himself with a small rag and a few cups of water in a metal bowl. This abundance of water was a gift from God. When he finished showering, he put on the cotton pants and shirt he found on a shelf behind the bathroom door.

He spent his days in between meals trying to occupy his thought. Extreme boredom was taking its toll. His activities became regimented. He rose from bed, knelt next to the cot and spent time in prayer. He would then eat breakfast. His morning meal normally consisted of one egg, one slice of bacon and a piece of lightly buttered toast. Corbin ate slowly trying to savor every bite.

After eating, he would use the facilities and try to brush his teeth using his finger and a small bit of soap. His first attempt left him retching in the toilet. He had now grown accustomed to the bitter taste and continued the practice each morning.

He used the fork he received with his meals to scratch marks on the painted concrete block walls. These he used as a clock to keep track of his daily activities. The small beam of sunlight would track up the wall allowing him to schedule his day.

After taking care of his hygienic needs, he spent time trying to remember scripture. He had not read the Bible in months. He was not sure of the actual time he had been incarcerated, but he was certain many months had passed.

Sitting on the edge of the cot, Corbin noted the position of his beam of light.

"Time to exercise," he spoke this aloud. It had taken him some time to get used to the sound of his own voice.

"Come on, up you go." He still had difficulty standing. The beatings he had received on the bottom of his feet left him with extreme pain, especially when he tried to stand. It took a few minutes for his feet to get used to the weight of his body.

His exercise consisted of pacing from one wall to the other. Today he would try to do push-ups again. Previous attempts had left him a continuous dull ache in his shoulders. Jack had dislocated both shoulders on several occasions. Remembering his helplessness and the pain he endured, caused him to wince.

After several circuits, the pain in his feet began to dissipate. Corbin's thoughts went to Abigail. The woman in the photograph Alex had shown him looked like her. *She's in Texas,* he anguished, *they could not have her, could they?*

He froze mid-step. Someone had inserted a key into the lock. Hurriedly he sat on his bed. His heart was racing and moisture appeared on his forehead.

He did not recognize the man that entered. He could tell by his uniform that he was a guard. Corbin's panic began to subside. *Not Jack,* he told himself. The man strode into the room and approached him.

"Stand up," his voice was firm, but not threatening. Corbin complied. To do otherwise meant punishment. He stood and turned his back to the man and crossed his wrists behind him. He heard the familiar click and the ratcheting sound of the cuffs closing.

"Not too tight, I hope," his voice was almost congenial. This disoriented Corbin. *They're testing me.* He did not say a word.

"Follow me." The man's voice was deep. He was taller than Jack and at six feet five inches, he towered over Corbin. His shoulders were broad and he walked with a slight limp. His hair was cut short in a military style.

The man walked out the door with Corbin close behind. This was the first time he had been out of this room. The hall was well lit with doors evenly spaced to the end. Corbin counted ten doors on each side. They approached a door at the end of the hall.

"Turn around." Corbin turned slowly, fearful of what he would face. The past twenty days had allowed him time to heal and now it would begin again.

Father, I don't think I'll be able to endure. Not now, not again. He lost control of his bladder and wet the front of his clothes. He feared what was behind the door. The hours of pain were long past. The thought of it beginning again drained him of strength.

"What the..." the man exclaimed as he stepped away from the growing puddle. "In here," he said brusquely. He led Corbin into an empty room that resembled his own. "Take those off and don't move."

Corbin removed the pants and tried to dry himself. The man was back in a few moments and threw new clothes to him.

"Get dressed. You're running out of time."

Corbin dressed quickly, and again, walked with the man to the door. The guard grabbed Corbin's shoulders and spun him around. He removed his restraints and opened the door. Light engulfed both men. Corbin had to squint. He had not seen the full sun in months. He raised his right hand to shield his eyes.

"You've got fifteen minutes," the guard instructed as he shoved Corbin toward the door. The concrete building towered above him. He stood in a courtyard that was created in the center of an octagon shaped building. Each side of the octagon resembled where he was standing.

The door opened to a well manicured lawn. There was a twelve foot high cyclone fence with concertina wire on top. The fence was attached to the building and the twenty by twenty foot cage reminded him of a kennel.

After a few moments, his eyes adjusted to the brightness of the sunlight. The blue sky was a welcome sight. He saw two sparrows land on the fence, unhindered by his prison. *His eye is on the sparrow,* filled his mind as he remembered an old hymn. Corbin took a deep breath and exulted in the soft breeze on his skin. He stood silently listening to the sounds around him.

Though his future was uncertain, right here, right now he was free. The great expanse of sky above him reminded Corbin of the greatness of God's power and love. Over the next few minutes, he worshipped and experienced the freedom no man could take away.

"Time's up," the guard's voice pulled him back from his refuge. "Let's go."

Corbin turned and walked to the door.

****

"These are today's briefings. I have underlined what is relevant to you." The cherub faced clerk brought Jeff the daily briefings every morning by eleven.

"Thanks Josh," Jeff said not looking up. The boy was chatty and he was not in the mood for a protracted conversation. The youth was ambitious and, unfortunately, going places in the Division. The few conversations Jeff had with him had made him uncomfortable. Josh was a believer, and his zeal for all things government made him potentially dangerous.

The school system under Freeman's rule was producing students without a conscience. He had dealt with a few and was convinced they would betray their own families if it would benefit the state.

Since classes had been extended to year round, the propagandists had thirteen years to shape future generations. Private schools and homeschooling had been outlawed long ago.

Joshua was a product of that system and was convinced that an oligarchy was the answer. Once the boy cleared the doorway, Jeff picked up the report.

He scanned the highlighted text and found what he was looking for. *This is exactly the leverage I need.* Jeff quickly picked up the phone. He was about to hang up when a familiar voice answered the phone.

"Did you see this morning's briefing?" he asked the Director after a few pleasantries.

"Yes," his voice was grave, "this is disconcerting. The number of protestors is growing every day. This Miller is dangerous. If we don't deal swiftly with him, this is going to get out of control."

"That is why I'm calling. I have moved Miller out of interrogation and into an intermediate cell."

"Why would you do that? We need to break this man. Once broken, we can broadcast his confession to the nation."

"Sir, I don't believe you are thinking long term." Jeff knew he had to tread softly. These protests were the perfect solution for his plan. "It has been nearly five months and no progress has been made getting any information from him. We had our best man on this." *Thankfully he is gone.* The unbidden thought made him feel guilty. He was not supposed to rejoice in the death of any person. Yet he felt great relief at that evil man's demise.

"If Miller's case is handled properly, we can lock him away forever and satisfy the protestors. The last thing we want to do is make him into a martyr. We could create a legend that would be a constant irritant."

"What's your plan?"

Chapter 32

Marcus Fleming had been with the Brotherhood for nearly ten years. When he joined, the Brothers were involved in charitable giving and education.

Marcus had worked training recruits in political action and the history of the American Revolution. He and other leaders still believed that a proper understanding of the Christian values that shaped the nation would eventually save it.

His role in the Brotherhood took an unexpected turn over the last few years. A security guard by profession, Marcus worked at the maximum security prison near Harrisburg. He had an exemplary record and rose quickly to Sergeant. Most of the men he guarded deserved incarceration, but this new position troubled his conscience.

Thirty days previous, he had received a call from Jeff Arbino requesting to meet with him. Marcus knew who Arbino was and had no love for the man. He had turned his back on the Church, and was now working for the most detestable of all the government agencies.

Marcus was apprehensive about the meeting. He accepted, to avert any suspicion directed toward him. They met at a government run restaurant. Arbino was in an expensive suit, sitting at his private table when Marcus was escorted in.

"Please, sit down." Arbino's smile was broad and disarming. Marcus sat and scooted the chair close to the table. He wondered how men like Arbino could be so casual. He had heard the rumors of the atrocities committed by his office under Thurman. Good men and women had been tortured and murdered simply for their faith. Arbino was new, but Marcus did not expect him to behave differently.

"Order what you like. The food here is top of the line."

"Actually sir, I'm not very hungry. I think I'll just have coffee." He could not bring himself to be benefitted by blood money.

"Suit yourself. You won't mind if I eat?"

Marcus did not answer. He studied the man before him as he ordered his meal. Arbino lived opulently when the average citizen would riot just to get a block of cheese. Men like him were vultures who fed off the lives of the enslaved. Marcus could not wait for this meeting to end. He wanted to go outside where he could breathe clean air.

"Marcus, you come highly recommended. I wanted to offer you a job. This is a great opportunity and could be a career maker."

"I have a job, sir. I'm content there." Arbino was a powerful man and Marcus was apprehensive about his motives. He knew that powerful men did not do you a favor without taking a piece of your soul. "I appreciate the offer."

"Marcus, I'm offering you a chance to enhance your career. As you know, Alex McCormick passed and our Chief of Prisoner Security moved to head the Interrogation Department. I need a new CPS and I'm hoping that will be you."

As a government employee, Marcus already lived better than eighty percent of his neighbors. His sense of guilt was overwhelming even though he funneled twenty-five percent of his income into the Brotherhood's relief fund.

This offer would mean a larger paycheck, and enable him to better support the Brothers' efforts to supplant this illegitimate government. He was tempted, but not ready to bite. As Chief of Prisoner Security, he would not be involved with the interrogation team. They had their own guards. He would oversee the care of prisoners released from the interrogation floor. It would be a chance to alleviate some of their suffering. He had heard rumors of long periods of isolation and inadequate food and medical attention. Many of the post-interrogation detainees were waiting to be executed. God could be opening a door for him to alleviate their suffering by offering them kindness and hope.

"There will be a large bump in pay," Arbino continued, "plus extra benefits like eating here. We have some of the best chefs in the country."

"Mister Arbino, with all due respect, I cannot work for you. I am happy where I am."

"Tell me what I can offer you." his voice was earnest, almost pleading.

"Nothing," was Marcus's reply.

Arbino leaned in close to him, placing his right hand on his forearm, "Wisdom and courage, Marcus. Wisdom and courage."

Marcus blanched. He immediately recognized the Brothers' greeting. *Is this a trap? Does he know who I am, who I am working for?* His apprehension became fear. Anxiously, he put the porcelain coffee cup on the matching saucer trying to hide his trembling hand. Furtively, he glanced over each shoulder. He expected to see armed guards moving to spirit him away. Shifting in his seat, he wanted to be on his way.

Arbino's hand was holding tight to his forearm. "Do not be worried, Marcus. This restaurant is swept for listening devices daily. Some of the most nefarious deals are struck here. Powerful men need the assurance of privacy and this restaurant supplies that need. No one but you and I know what is being said."

Marcus drew his arm back, "What is this Mister Arbino? What do you really want?"

"I want to give you the opportunity to save a man who could lead people to freedom."

"Who is this man?"

"Corbin Miller."

This was not what Marcus anticipated. Corbin was a good man. He had met him once at a prayer rally and Miller impressed him greatly. When Corbin prayed, Marcus believed he had come across a man who lived close to God.

There were protests across the nation calling for Miller's release. The NALC had assaulted and arrested many of the protesters. Despite the violent reaction of the government, the protests continued to grow every day.

"Why would I care about this Miller?" he asked trying to feign indifference. Being sympathetic to Miller was dangerous.

"Because you, like I, have been with the Brothers too long not to care." Arbino's gaze penetrated into his eyes. They told Marcus that he knew too much. *How could this man be a Brother?*

Arbino's career had skyrocketed. Within a few short months he had risen from Facilitator to Regional Director of the Department of Communication and Speech. He did not get there because he was a boy scout.

The Brotherhood was rife with rumors about Arbino. He had turned his back on the church, embraced and enforced censorship of sermons. While a Facilitator, many pastors were harshly disciplined by Arbino for daring to preach their conscience. Marcus took in the large diamond ring on his little finger, the expensive suit, his meticulously combed hair. This man was a player. He served the system so he could live opulently.

"I don't know what you are talking about. I apologize for having to leave so abruptly, but I must."

"Be home tonight," he said sternly, "you will be getting a call. I suggest you be there to answer it."

Marcus halted midway to his feet. He was not sure if this was a threat. He valued his life and the life of his family. He would be there to answer the call.

****

Walking in the woods in the evening helped clear his mind. He knew the way and could find the grotto in the dark. His home was situated outside of Philadelphia near Doylestown. The home had been in his family for several generations. His parents and grandparents had lived there. This was home, his refuge.

Marcus inherited the two-story clapboard farmhouse when his mother died twenty-years previous. He and Sadie had been married six months when the tragedy occurred. At first he thought to sell the place, but Sadie loved the country and begged him to make it their home.

"Please Marcus," she said as she scrunched herself against his muscular chest, "let's stay and make a home here. Look at all the room the children will have to play."

"Sadie, I've lived here all my life. I need a change. There is a whole world out there, bigger and greater than this run down farm."

"Please," she pouted. "We could get some chickens, plant a garden..."

"Okay, okay!" Her enthusiasm was electrifying and he always found it difficult to tell her, no. "We'll stay and you can become Old McDonald's wife."

Thinking about that distant memory made him smile. He did not find much to smile about anymore. Sadie always brightened his day.

For the past twenty-years this had been home. His three children Marcus Jr, Mary and Philip were all in their teens. He had watched with sadness as they became increasingly sympathetic to the government's abuses. Many times he had had heated debates with Marc over the tyranny that engulfed his beloved nation. Marc had even denied the faith and proudly proclaimed he was an atheist. Mary and Phil were younger and maybe this proposition would be the answer to saving his family.

The opening ahead was familiar. Marcus had cleared a ten foot circle in a stand of maples. He had dragged a log into the clearing and would sit there for hours reading the scripture and talking to God.

Twigs snapped under his feet as he entered his sanctuary. He knew that tonight this place would become his Gethsemane.

****

When he had arrived home, as usual, Sadie had prepared a sumptuous meal. Many of the vegetables had been produced on their land. Even the fried chicken had been raised on the farm.

Most of the produce grown on the farm was confiscated by the local food distribution committee. When they had first received the certified letter declaring they were in violation of the law for hoarding, Marcus immediately went to the Food Distribution office in Doylestown to protest. He walked into the office and threw the letter on the receptionist's desk.

The whole incident had been a mistake. The police were called and Marcus would have been arrested if Ted Manners had not intervened. Ted and Marcus had been friends since childhood. Ted was the Assistant Director of the Food Distribution Committee and a member of the Brotherhood. His position allowed him to intervene for his friend and keep him out of jail. Once emotions were in check, Ted convinced the committee to allow him to keep thirty percent of his crops, which was far more than the fifteen percent others were allowed to retain.

The meal was delicious and Sadie was optimistic as usual. He and she discussed their day and prattled about insignificant events. It was when Marcus was ready to sit in the living room and read (they had long ago stopped watching television) that the phone rang.

When he answered the phone, he recognized the voice immediately.

"Marcus, I don't have much time. You must accept Jeff's offer. There is more at stake here than you know."

"This man is a traitor to all we believe."

"No, not everything is as it seems. Believe me when I tell you that Providence has brought you to this place. You must meet with him again tomorrow. He will explain everything."

Marcus loved Jedediah and trusted him with his life.

"Where?"

"Same as today, one o'clock. Go with an open mind. Wisdom and courage."

When he met with Jeff the next day, he was not prepared for the elaborate plan Jeff had concocted. After lunch, Jeff took Marcus in his car to discuss the purpose of their meeting. Marcus listened silently.

"Can I count on you?" Jeff asked looking Marcus in the eyes.

He was not certain what to say. This was not what he had expected. If they succeeded, it would cost them everything. If they failed it would cost them their lives. He remembered something he had heard Corbin say at that first prayer rally, *The price of freedom is the willingness to lose everything.* At the time, they were just words, now they seemed prophetic. *Am I capable of giving up everything, of placing my family in jeopardy?*

Marcus sighed. He was no coward. He had spent many years working against the encroachment of a burgeoning tyranny. Those acts would have carried a penalty of a few weeks in jail or a heavy fine. Prices he was willing to pay. This could mean his existence. Could he make that sacrifice for one man? He was not certain he could and his hesitance pained him.

"Mister Arbino, I need some time. My wife and my children are involved. If I were single..."

"I need an answer soon." Jeff turned away and started the car. The trip back to the division seemed long. Marcus wrestled with the request and his courage.

When he arrived home he sat at the kitchen table with Sadie.

"Would you be willing to lose everything for the cause of Christ and freedom?" The question was spontaneous.

"Why so serious?" she asked teasingly. Sadie knew him better than anyone. Looking intently into his eyes she understood that this was more than a philosophical question. "Marcus, what's wrong?" There was now concern in her voice.

"I believe God is calling me, calling us, to a sacrifice greater than we have ever experienced. Do you trust me, Sadie?" He reached for her hand. He felt the strength of her grasp. On more than one occasion she had been his strength. Sadie had a gift for making moral choices, even when those choices brought her pain. She was the bravest person he had ever known.

"Yes," was her unhesitant answer.

"We may have to leave this place. I know how much you love this farm. Would you give it up for a chance to be free?"

"Marcus," her tone was serious, "I would give up every bit of this for a chance to be free again. This place once was our home, now it is our prison. What good is any of this without the ability to make our own choices?"

****

The eventing sun was filtering through the trees when he stepped into the clearing. Two squirrels scampered up a tree in a merry chase. Marcus envied their existence.

The log and ground were still damp from the morning's rain. This was his altar, the place where he wrestled with God. A shaft of light danced on the log every time the wind stirred the leaves.

Marcus already felt the unseen presence. This was holy ground, unsullied by the world and avarice of men. God met him here. Marcus sat down at the edge of this sanctuary and removed his shoes and socks and set them aside. He stood and the dampness of the leaves cooled his feet.

The shaft of light danced again, calling him into the presence of unending love. He knelt, oblivious that his pants were soaking up moisture. Nothing else existed, just he and his God.

Chapter 33

With the recruitment of Marcus Fleming, an important step in Jeff's plan had fallen into line. He was waiting for Deputy Director Lambert's call. Once Lambert signed off on the second phase of his scheme, Corbin's incarceration would end.

Impatiently he picked up the phone and dialed the Deputy Director's number.

"Lambert," the Deputy Director rasped.

"Deputy Director, how good to hear your voice. I wanted to see if we could expedite the Miller case."

"What do you have in mind? I'm growing impatient with these protestors. They have disrupted everything.

"Between them and the fool Christians in Montana, the NALC is stretched thin. You told me you knew how to end this, so speak."

"We give Miller a public trial..." The laughter on the other end cut his sentence short.

"That is your great idea? A trial? Any child could have come up with that."

Jeff kept his anger in check. Lambert was a fool, drunk on his own self importance. Anger would only nullify his chances of getting the trial. If his plan was to succeed, he had to get Corbin out of detention.

"Please hear me out. This would not be an ordinary trial. Keeping him sequestered away is making his legend grow. A televised trial would show how weak he really is and he would lose sympathy from this rabble that needs a hero. The trial will demystify him."

"All right, Arbino, you have my attention."

"This is the scenario as I see it. We broadcast that the trial will take place. Have the media feature his crimes against the people. Those would include hoarding, illegal distribution of food and clothing to a few, in other words we showcase his hypocrisy. This will give us opportunity to focus on the poor citizenship of the Christians. We could deal with both issues at once.

"People are easily manipulated if they are bombarded with constant negative images. We can use the television and print media to our advantage. We can also instruct the Facilitators to mandate that the churches highlight the same message."

The silence from Lambert made him anxious. Selling this to him was paramount. Jeff breathed a silent prayer for Providence to intervene again.

"You are convinced this will work?" Lambert said breaking the silence.

"I'm positive it will work. We can put this whole issue to rest. Once the protests have ended, the ringleaders can be rounded up and face justice." Jeffrey breathed a prayer, *Lord please keep these people safe.*

"We would control the outcome of the trial. The media will feature what we want the public to see. Miller will obviously be found guilty of sedition and treason.

"I will instruct the Prosecutor to emphasize the government will not seek the death penalty, but instead, will place him under house arrest until he dies of natural causes."

"When he is found guilty, why not execute him and get it over with?" Lambert protested.

Jeff always knew this man was a fool. Raw power was all he knew. He was a bully that could use the full force of government to intimidate. He and men like him were more dangerous than any common criminal. They controlled the reins of power and who could restrain them?

"Because, sir," Jeff struggled to control his emotions, "he would be a sympathetic figure. By showing mercy, he will lose his appeal." *And you will lose him.*

"Alright, pursue your plan, but any indication it isn't working and I'll pull the plug."

"Agreed." Jeff replaced the handset and leaned back in his chair. A feeling of satisfaction infiltrated his mood. He would be able to save his friend.

His phone beeped. He lifted it and saw that he had a text from Marcus. He thumbed open the file.

3 new recruits.

Jeff smiled. Everything was falling into place. He wondered if his other plan had been delivered.

****

Jedediah looked forward to a day off. He and Abbie had been laboring ten hours a day for the last three weeks packing relief boxes and loading trucks.

In their last conversation Jeff had requested he stay home today. There was an important package arriving and he did not want it to be unattended.

So he took the day off and was grateful for the opportunity. He was feeling his age more. After a day of hard labor, his fingers, back and knees ached. He knew he would have to retire soon, but there was so much to be done.

The teapot whistled insistently. Its shrill sound made him wince. He turned down the burner on the stove and retrieved his cup and saucer. The chamomile tea would help him relax. Carefully he placed the bag into the cup and poured steaming water over the tea.

Jeff had been very nebulous about the contents of the package. Jedediah was certain his evasiveness was for security.

He took the tea out on the small balcony. The air outside was hot but mercifully not humid. The tattered lawn chair was comfortable beneath him. The tea cup clattered on the saucer as he held it in his shaky hand. The tremors had begun several months ago. A trip to the doctor revealed he was in the early stages of Parkinson's disease. Though devastated when he first heard the news, he had learned over the years to rest in the will of God. *This world was not his real home, he was only a sojourner.*

****

The insistent knocking at his apartment door woke him from sleep. Thankfully he had finished his tea before he dozed. Stiffly, he rose from his seat and half limped to answer the door.

"Mark Caruthers?" The man before him was much taller than Jedediah. He wore blue jeans and a light blue denim shirt. The white cowboy hat he wore had a yellowish sweat stain around the brim.

"Yes," Jedediah did not recognize the man.

"Wisdom and courage, sir." His smile was broad, almost mischievous. "Delivery for you. You'll have to come downstairs to get it."

"What on earth for? Why can't you bring it up?"

The man did not lose his smile. Instead of answering him, he handed him a letter. Jedediah's trembling fingers had a difficult time tearing it open. He blew the envelop open and removed a neatly folded letter.

He missed you,
Jeff

The befuddled look on Jedediah's face made the deliveryman chuckle. Jedediah turned the paper over to see if he had missed anything. He then looked at the cowboy quizzically.

The man shrugged and simply repeated, "Downstairs."

Jedediah navigated the stairwell on painful legs. The man led him behind the building were a large panel van was parked. The engine was still running and Jedediah heard the air conditioner compressor kick on and off.

The man maneuvered him to the rear of the vehicle, grasped the handle and pulled the door open.

The difference in light forced Jedediah to refocus. He leaned forward and came nose to nose with a large black face. Memory filled in the rest. Samson sat before his master with slobber hanging from his jowls. Oblivious to the sticky strings, Jedediah threw his arms around his friends neck and wept. Stepping back, Jedediah's eyes swept the large animal. The ugly scars were still apparent from the attack.

"Thank you," he said through tears to the driver.

The man helped him lead Samson from the van. He walked to the cab and looked back. The satisfaction on his face was obvious to Jedediah. The man climbed into the drivers seat and pulled away, leaving Jedediah and Samson alone.

"Come boy," Jedediah's voice was filled with emotion. Samson padded behind his master. His massive muscles rippling with each step. Jedediah stopped and stooped in front of Samson, grabbed his head in his hands and kissed the dog on his muzzle.

Samson was more than a dog, he was Jedediah's friend and companion. On more than one occasion, he had been the old man's protector. It was good to have him home.

****

"One more," he said encouraging himself. He had become quite adept at carrying on a one sided conversation. Squeezing out one more pushup was a personal triumph. After more than four weeks Corbin's body was beginning to heal.

He had learned to push through the pain and force his body to act. The pain in his shoulders was becoming less of an issue. Fifteen push-ups was his personal best since he had been moved to this room.

His feet posed a different challenge. The beatings he had received from Jack and Alex had altered them. Not only were they tender, but he was sure bones had been broken and nerves damaged. Despite the pain, he had accepted his condition and was determined to overcome it.

He rose from the floor and walked to the bathroom to wash his face. He was already taking these small luxuries for granted. Pausing before the sink he bowed his head and whispered, "Thank you, Father." Then he turned on the faucet and the water trickled out. Though the flow was not strong, it was enough for him to get his face wet.

He dried his face and sighed. The seclusion was difficult to deal with. He had always loved being around people. He enjoyed listening to their stories and sharing their aspirations. He missed debating about theology and politics. More than any of that, he missed the conversations he had with Abbie. He would agonize, trying to remember conversations. He tried to recollect the scene from the environment around them, to what she was wearing and how her hair was styled.

He would sometimes lose himself in their intimate moments. He could almost sense the softness of her skin and the smell of her perfume. He imagined himself holding her and stroking her skin. At times the memories would increase his pain. He ached to hold her again, to see her smile and hear her voice.

"Abbie, remember I love you." He said softly, believing that saying it louder would somehow cheapen the emotion. "I will see you again. I know I will."

There was a light rap on the door. This surprised him. No one knocked on his door, they just entered. He heard the key slip into the lock then just as quickly the door opened.

Corbin had never seen this man before. He was tall and broad shouldered. He wore the uniform of a guard but the stars on his shoulders told Corbin this was no ordinary guard.

Helplessness engulfed him. He backed from the door to the far wall. He lowered his head and stared at the man's shiny boots. Eye contact with the guards was forbidden, even here, wherever here was.

"Corbin," the man said kindly. Corbin shifted uneasily. "I'm the new head of prisoner security. My name is Marcus Fleming. You will be in my care from now on. The first thing I want to say is the camera in this room is off and will not be turned on again."

Corbin nodded, but did not look up. He kept his eyes on the shoes. He had learned that kindness was followed by pain. He began to tremble and stifled back tears.

"Corbin, you are permitted to look at me." He crossed the room to him and lifted his chin. Corbin averted his eyes. "Corbin," he said forcefully, "you are still a man. Look me in the eyes."

Corbin looked up. Marcus's eyes were steel blue and piercing. They were the eyes of one with authority. This man's gaze was too much and Corbin's eyes frantically searched for the shiny shoes.

"What have they done to you?" Marcus whispered. "I will be back. In the mean time, your yard privileges have been increased to once a week and I've arranged for you to receive more rations."

Corbin did not move until the man exited his room and locked the door. He glanced up and the room was empty. He rushed to his cot and huddled in the corner. He pulled his knees to his chest and buried his head in them and softly began to sing hymns.

Soon he was lost in sleep.

Chapter 34

Abbie could not pull herself away from the television. Corbin's face had been on it most of the morning.

The new American government normally blocked transmission of news to Texas, but this was an exception. Jedediah had warned her that this might happen. Corbin's trial would begin in a few weeks and the media was setting the stage.

She had turned up the volume and went to the kitchen to make coffee. The music told her that the morning news program was back. She rushed adding cream and sugar, spilling some. Frustrated she grabbed a dish cloth and cleaned it up. She hated leaving messes.

When she reentered the living room the host was introducing his morning guest.

"And now Doctor Price is going to explain the charges against Corbin Miller. Doctor."

"Thank you, Gary," his baritone voice was laced with authority. "Miller is accused of sedition under the new law. This means that if found guilty he would face the death penalty."

Dr. Price leaned back in his seat and steepled his fingers together. His hair was white and he had a neatly trimmed goatee. Abbie noticed that he sat with perfect posture. Everything about him gave the impression that he was an expert.

"You say he was arrested for sedition. Explain to our audience what this means."

"Miller was engaged in actions that subverted the smooth operation of government. For example," he turned toward the monitor as a video began depicting the rally in Washington, D.C., "here he is encouraging thousands of citizens to participate in an illegal gathering. This incident would be enough to convict him, however, other activities are just as onerous."

The video continued and Abigail was appalled at how Corbin's activities were misrepresented.

"Miller also defied the Division of Faith and Verbal Equity. As you know, this division was created to protect the average citizen from the abuse of anachronistic church speech.

"His other crimes included hoarding of resources such as food and clothing. Some would say that he distributed these things to others, but keep in mind, he only gave these things to people who agreed with his opinions and most of these people were not suffering want.

"The anti-hoarding laws were enacted to ensure the fair distribution of needed goods. I may add that the government agencies involved in redistribution have administered their responsibility flawlessly."

For the next twenty minutes Abbie listened as her husband was impugned for acts of love and charity. Nothing good was attributed to any of his actions. None of this surprised her, yet each new accusation cut like a knife.

The knock at the door told her that Jedediah had arrived. Abigail rose from the couch and opened the door.

"Have they started yet?" he asked before entering.

"Yes, and it is appalling what they are doing to Corbin."

"Take heart, these things have to happen. If Jeff's plan is to be successful, Corbin must be tried by the media."

"But the things they are saying..."

"Are not true!" Jedediah took her face in his hands. "Believe me when I say that, in the end, this will benefit Corbin."

"I miss him," she said softly.

"I know."

Jedediah followed her back into the living room. Both sat on the couch and listened to the ongoing coverage.

****

Marcus had replaced several of the guards with trusted members of the Brotherhood. These three were put on rotation to guard and protect Corbin.

He was horrified at the conditions in the intermediate confinement cells. With Jeff's help, he had already improved the meals and increased the yard time for each prisoner. All the men and women in his care were political prisoners. Each had, in some way, exercised freedoms that had, at one time, been taken for granted. Most were broken shells.

Searching the files on each prisoner revealed the horrific torture each of them endured. Alexander McCormick had been a monster. Marcus felt no remorse that this man was dead. McCormick never released anyone to the intermediate cells until they were completely broken and signed a detailed confession. He would then continue torturing them for months afterward, then recommend intermediate status. The only exception was Corbin. Arbino had intervened.

Marcus had been wrong about Jeff. He had protected his mission well.

The details in the files were so surreal that Marcus questioned their validity. *No one could be this monstrous,* he thought as he read the particularly brutal multiple rape and torture of a Catholic nun. The list of what she endured was written so casually that it made Marcus's skin crawl.

Her name was Anna Marie. She was slated for execution within the next six months. Her crime was rescuing a live baby that had been aborted and thrown into a dumpster. She was also an outspoken critic of the government's two child law. Each family was allotted two children. If the mother became pregnant again, her responsibility, under the Population Stability Law, was to report to a state run Population Clinic and terminate the pregnancy.

Her file revealed that Alex had spent an inordinate amount of time with her. When Marcus went to her room, she rambled incoherently. When he touched her, she screamed and wept.

Her execution would be carried out like all the others. She would get no trial. Her confession was considered sufficient for carrying out the death penalty. Guards would come from the interrogation unit with a warrant and Marcus would have to let them take her. She would be taken to one of the small torture rooms and be shot in the head. He had learned that the small rooms were used for the convenience of the executioners. The grated floor allowed for easy cleanup with a hose.

He closed the files on his computer and wearily rubbed the stubble on his chin. A picture of his family sat on his desk. He ran his fingers across the picture, closed his eyes and let the image burn into his brain. This was not where he wanted to be. Soon this would be over, it had to be.

In his last private meeting with Jeff he asked him how he lived with his new position. His response was troubling.

"Every morning I look at myself in the mirror and pray that somehow God can forgive me. I can only try to alleviate the suffering of these unfortunate people, I cannot save them.

"There are days that I wash my hands dozens of times and I never feel that I can get the blood off them."

Marcus closed his eyes. He had been at this job for several weeks and he already felt tainted. Jeff's words echoed countless times in his mind.

"Father," he whispered, head bowed, "wretched man that I am, who shall deliver me from the body of this death?"

Chapter 35

The trial began early on August 15. Thousands of people gathered outside the Federal Courthouse in Harrisburg. Some had gathered in support of Corbin, many of them arrested or beaten. A large group was calling for his execution for crimes against the state.

Jeff shook his head at the spectacle. Most of it had been orchestrated by his department. The New America Leadership Corps populated most of the groups. None in uniform.

As his chauffeured vehicle turned the corner a protester dented the hood of the car with a baseball bat.

"Enough of these traitors!" He screamed, "Put him to death, put him to death." Others surrounded the car shouting similar demands.

His driver pushed the vehicle through the crowd and kept a steady speed. Jeff heard thumps as protesters were nudged out of the way by the vehicle.

"You okay back there?" The driver asked over his shoulder.

"I'm fine Frank, not so sure about some of the protesters though. Is that really necessary?"

"My job is to keep you safe. If it means bruising a few of these fools, so be it. Besides, they'd kill their own mother if it gave them an excuse to riot." Frank chuckled. "Almost there, sir," he added.

Jeff still had a hard time adjusting to the preference he constantly received. He had always shunned pretentious people. He chafed at how they treated others and took advantage of their position. Now he was one of them and he did not like it any better. He would be glad when this was all over.

Jeff flinched as a bat slammed with great force against the back window. He was grateful for the armored car he was provided.

The media was everywhere. Anchors from all the national news channels were represented. Cabling and satellite dishes cluttered the streets.

Fashionably dressed men and women stood in front of the courthouse, microphones in hand. All of them performing for the camera. One female reporter was gesticulating wildly at a cameraman. Obviously angry, her face was red, but when the camera was switched on she was all smiles and gentle motion.

"Quite a circus, huh, sir?" Frank had been his driver for months. Tall and muscular, he was more than just a chauffeur. Jeff knew that if there was a threat to his person, this man would risk everything to protect him.

He had been thankful on several occasions that Frank was around.

After moving at a snails, pace they reached the parking garage that was reserved for government officials. The parking structure which had been recently completed, had an underground tunnel that led to the basement of the courthouse.

Security was tight in the garage with several checkpoints before entering the actual parking area. Jeff pulled out his identification knowing he would have to show it at each checkpoint. It seemed like overkill to him, but several officials had been assassinated in recent months. Unrest had gripped the nation, especially among those old enough to remember what the nation was like twenty years in the past.

His position as the Regional Director of the Division of Verbal Equity and Faith gave him privileges that ordinary citizens and many officials did not enjoy.

Once the vehicle was parked, Frank and three other armed guards escorted him through the tunnel and into the courthouse. The building was only a few years old and had an institutional feel.

The courtrooms were surprisingly small and onlookers were discouraged. One detail that stood out to Jeff was the lack of any reference to the Ten

Commandments and the absence of Lady Justice. Jeff knew there was no impartiality in these halls. The verdict was determined the day the person was arrested. Any hope of a fair trial died when the Freeman administration suspended the Constitution.

The outcome of Corbin's trial was predetermined as well. Today was a formality, a show for the public. It gave the government cover for its oppression. Jeff never understood why totalitarians needed such subterfuge. Who was going to stop them? He supposed that even the wicked needed a wall to hide behind.

Jeff was escorted into the court and seated in the section reserved for government officials. The seats were extremely comfortable and headsets were provided in case they had difficulty hearing.

Jeff exchanged pleasantries with other officials, cordially smiling and asking about family. He then settled down and looked at his watch. The show would begin shortly.

****

Corbin sat silently as Marcus instructed him to put on the clothes he held on a hanger.

"We will be leaving in twenty minutes," Marcus said as he placed the suit and underclothes on the cot. "I'll be back to get you. I'll be taking you to Harrisburg, your trial is today."

Marcus had mentioned this to him several times in the past week.

Corbin nodded and rose from the cot. He stood motionless until Marcus had exited the room. When he heard the deadbolt slide into place he began to disrobe.

Corbin had not worn anything except the light cotton clothes he had on for nearly five months. The street clothes felt strange to him. He buttoned up the starched white shirt and then pulled on the trousers. The waist was a little loose, but not enough to make keeping them up an issue.

He deftly tied the tie into a Windsor knot and sat on the cot to put on the black socks and shoes. The clothes were strangely constricting. He had worn a suit nearly everyday of his adult life, but now he wished for the pajama like prison clothes.

Once he had laced up the shoes, he stood to walk in them. The shoes enhanced the pain in his feet. He had not worn shoes since he had been incarcerated. All of this felt new.

The slight rap at the door told him that Marcus was back.

"We're ready to go. Please follow me."

It took several steps before Corbin could walk with any proficiency. He followed Marcus down the hall. They stopped in front of a metal door and waited while Marcus unlocked it.

The hallway beyond the door was different. Inside the prison area, the walls were painted a drab gray. Corbin stepped onto the soft carpet that lined the hallway. There were various plants positioned to create a pleasing aesthetic.

They took the elevator that deposited them in a subbasement garage. A white panel van sat idling. The driver was leaning against the front quarter panel smoking a cigarette. When he saw them exit, he dropped the smoke and crushed it under his foot.

Without a word, the driver raced to the rear of the van and opened the back doors.

"Your hands," Marcus ordered.

Corbin extended both arms and waited for the familiar ratcheting of the cuffs. Leg shackles were locked into place and then Marcus and the driver helped him into the van.

"So this is Miller? He don't look like much." The driver's comment brought a stern glance from Marcus.

"You're not being paid to talk," Marcus was obviously angered by the comment. "Now, shut us in and let's get moving."

The driver shut and locked the rear doors without glancing at Marcus or Corbin.

"Corbin," Marcus' voice was soft, almost imperceptible, "do you understand what's happening? You are going to court to be tried for conspiracy to commit treason. Do you understand that?"

"Yes," Corbin's voice nearly croaked. Hours of silence had made it difficult for him to articulate.

"I will be there with you the whole time. Jeff Arbino will be there as well."

This made Corbin look him in the eye. *He's trying to trick me.* He looked down almost as quickly. He sat hunched over, his elbows resting on his knees.

"It's almost over, Corbin. Wisdom and courage."

Corbin did not move. A tear slid down his nose and dripped onto his hands.

****

It took nearly three hours to reach Harrisburg because of increased traffic. Several hundred thousand people were expected to converge on the state capital. Even with a police escort, traffic moved at a snail's pace.

The van was pulled in front of the courthouse. This was by design, Corbin had to be seen entering the building. This would create the attention that Jeff wanted.

Riot police had cordoned off the street running parallel to the entrance. A K-9 patrol walked the perimeter. When the officers with the dogs walked by, the protesters cut them a wide berth.

The driver hurried to the rear of the vehicle and opened the doors.

"Boo, boo, boo," was chanted by the crowd. Marcus stepped out first. His security team exited their vehicle and took strategic positions around the rear of the transport.

The chanting changed to, "Corbin the coward."

Once he was satisfied the area was secure, Marcus nodded to one of the detail to retrieve Corbin. Still shackled Miller exited the van. Corbin squinted at the brightness of the sun. The day would have been beautiful if not for the spectacle around him.

Pandemonium broke out in the crowd. Supporters of Corbin were beaten while the police stood by. One woman was dragged to the ground by her hair and kicked repeatedly.

A chant of, "Death, death, death," began to swell. Thousands of voices joined the cry. The words reverberated among the tall cement structures. Bottles began to break around the van as protester hurled the potentially fatal projectiles.

"Let's go, let's go," Marcus shouted over the crowd. The six other guards surrounded Corbin to form a protective shield. As one, they ushered their prisoner into the safety of the courthouse. The muffled cries of the protesters could still be heard.

Corbin found it difficult to move in the shackles and had to be half carried, half dragged by the guards.

Inside the building, Corbin was deposited into a small room furnished with a table and two chairs. Corbin was seated in the chair facing the door, his restraints still in place. He sat silently with his hands in his lap.

The door opened and a portly man with beads of sweat on his forehead entered.

"Miller? I'm Ben Coburn, your attorney." Corbin shook his damp hand, then tried to dry his palm on his pants. "You're in big trouble. I guess I don't have to tell you.

"The evidence against you is pretty tight, so I'm going to plead guilty and throw you on the mercy of the court. Maybe they won't kill you."

Corbin looked up at his attorney. "No, not guilty," his voice came out in a whisper.

"I'm sorry, what was that? You have to speak up, I can't read lips."

"Not guilty," his voice was stronger.

"That will never do. You have two choices here. Die - not guilty or possibly live - guilty. Simple. You have done a lot of bad things. Not guilty isn't even a choice."

"Not guilty," Corbin was more insistent. He had preserved his integrity through months of torture. He was not going to throw that all away on the chance they might forgive him. If he was to die, then he would do it with dignity. He would not justify their lie by creating one of his own. "You will plead not guilty."

Sweat was trickling down the fat man's face and dripping off his chin. He pulled out a handkerchief and wiped the perimeter of his face, then stuffed it into his pocket. His round face was turning red. He ran his fingers through his combover and seemed perplexed.

He began flipping through Corbin's file. Corbin was certain it was the first time he had ever looked at it.

"Confession, where's the confession," the anxious man said to no one in particular. "Doesn't matter," he finally said after a fruitless search for Corbin's signed confession, "you singed a confession and you cannot retract it."

"I did not sign a confession."

"That's preposterous. No one gets to trial without a confession." He looked intently at Corbin, then pulled out his cell and dialed frantically.

When the party he was calling answered, he rose and began to pace the room.

"Where is Miller's confession? I need that for trial.

"What?" he exclaimed after a brief pause, "what do you mean there is no confession? How am I supposed to do this without a confession?" Coburn thumbed off the cell phone and turned to Miller.

"We will be pleading guilty."

"I am..."

"Not another word!" he shouted. "I am pleading guilty. How else will I defend you?"

Coburn stuffed his files back into his briefcase and slammed the door as he exited.

****

The court was crowded when the bailiff escorted Corbin through the door. Immediately the room was electrified.

The major national news network had been invited to broadcast the trial live. When Corbin broke the threshold the reporters thrust their microphones in his face.

"Miller, tell our viewers how you will plead."

A pretty, excessively made up reporter shouted, "Corbin, what would you say to Abigail if she were here?"

Corbin remained silent. The lights and confusion were disorienting. He had not been in such a large crowd for months. Seclusion had become his companion. He wanted this to be over.

The media was allowed their time as promised by Jeff. After nearly forty-five minutes of chaos, the bailiff called the court to order.

Everyone rose as the three judge panel entered the court. Each ceremoniously took their seat and arranged their paperwork. Once they were settled, the spectators and defendant were seated as well.

"Bailiff, read the charges against the defendant." The judge in the center was obviously in charge. All three judges studied Corbin as the charges were read.

The bailiff read the litany of charges in a monotone voice, "The said defendant Corbin Miller is charged with the following crimes, unlawful assembly...twelve counts of violation of verbal hate crime laws... distribution of illegal printed material...seven counts of conspiracy to commit treason..."

Corbin sat quietly watching a fly walk across the table in front of him. He half listened as the charges were read. He knew what he was charged with and understood that he would not survive once the sentence was handed down.

He had come to peace with his pending death months ago. His only wish was that he could see Abigail one more time before he permanently closed his eyes.

"How does the defendant plea?" The judges voice broke into his wandering thought.

Coburn stood to his feet, "Guilty, your honor."

"No!" A gasp rippled through the crowd as Corbin shakily stood to his feet. "No, your honor, I plead not guilty." This time his voice was strong and clear. This was where God wanted him and he would not allow anyone to believe he had confessed.

Corbin thought of Joseph Stratham who had given his life for the cause of Christ and freedom. He could not dishonor his memory by accepting what evil men willed. He would make them prove his guilt. They would have to work for it, he was not handing them the verdict himself.

"I see," said the head justice, "Counselor?"

"May I have a minute to speak with my client?"

"By all means," his words dripped with sarcasm.

"What are you doing?" he frantically whispered. "Do you want to die? If you insist on this you will find no mercy from this court."

"I choose to die a man and not a slave."

Coburn looked perplexed. He blinked several times and beads of perspiration broke out on his forehead.

He turned toward the bench, "My client pleads not guilty, your honor." His face was pale when he sat down. He glanced at Corbin with curiosity.

****

The trial only lasted for four days. Witnesses were brought in who testified that Corbin was involved in many activities he had never done. Witness after witness pointed an accusing finger at him.

His attorney half heartedly cross examined the prosecution's witnesses. In most cases he had no questions. Corbin sat quietly listening to the evidence presented. He betrayed no emotion. He was confident that in the end, the great judge of all mankind would vindicate him.

On his sentencing date, Corbin was ready to accept his fate. He had faithfully served his God and had no regrets.

As he entered the courtroom for the final time, a youngish female reporter stuck her microphone in front of him. "Do you have anything to say before sentencing?"

"Abigail, I love you," were his only words. Encouraged by this, other reporters converged on him in a frenzy to get just one sound bite. He never complied.

When the formalities of his final day in court were completed, the head justice asked him to rise.

"Corbin Miller, this court finds you guilty of all charges brought against you. In this penalty phase the law clearly states that your crimes against the state and the people deserve death. However, the Prosecutor has petitioned the court to show clemency.

"Upon careful consideration of that request, your sentence shall be as follows. You will be placed on perpetual house arrest in a remote location of the Division of Verbal Equity and Faith's choosing. You will never be allowed to leave the premises for the rest of your natural life. It is also the judgement of this court that during your incarceration you will not be allowed contact with anyone other than officials of the state."

A murmur passed through the crowd. Reporters rushed into the halls frantically dialing their cell phones. Corbin was quickly ushered from the court to a holding cell on the same floor.

Corbin was perplexed. He was ready to die. Somehow the news that he would live was disconcerting. He would live out his days in seclusion. That would be worse than death. The idea that he would continue to exist not knowing what happened to Abigail, and never seeing her again was a torture far greater than anything Alex concocted. Alone in his cell, Corbin wept.

Chapter 36

Abigail never missed a day of the trial. Corbin looked so sickly. She had never seen his cheeks so sallow nor his body so frail. The footage of him shuffling out of the courtroom made her weep.

She cheered when he rose to his feet and proclaimed his innocence. Whatever they had done to him, they had not stolen his honor. She could only imagine the courage it took for him to stand.

The first evening of the trial, after Jedediah had gone home, Abigail cried herself to sleep. She agonized for him. Each day created greater stress as she listened to the witnesses accuse him.

"Oh, Jedediah," she agonized, "how can these people say such things? Corbin never hurt anyone in his life. He has always been a kind and gentle man."

"Abbie, you must trust that God will prosper Jeff's plan."

Jeff's plan seemed a difficult stretch to her, although she knew it was probably the most viable option. Watching the trial had given her second thoughts. The whole scheme hinged on Corbin escaping the death penalty. Everything was stacked against him.

The media had spent the last two weeks destroying his character. They painted him as an anarchist who could not let go of the past. One reporter referred to him as a megalomaniacal zealot seeking to undermine national stability, pointing to the three hundred dead in Washington as an example.

Public polls were touted that showed a decrease in support for Corbin as the trial progressed. Abbie feared the worst. She spent the four days of the trial fasting and praying for her husband. He needed her and she was safely hidden away in Texas. The thought made her feel guilty. She had wanted to go to him, but Jedediah had wisely persuaded her to stay.

Day after day she watched and when it seemed she could take no more, both the Prosecution and Defense were ready for the verdict.

Corbin's attorney was slovenly and obviously lazy. Abbie could not understand why he had passed on questioning most of the witnesses.

"What is he doing?" She fumed at the television. She looked at Jedediah with pleading eyes.

"Abbie, did you really expect that a state appointed attorney would actually try to prove his innocence? This is not the country you grew up in. Even then things were beginning to change for the worse."

"No, I didn't," she answered, frustrated by her own helplessness. There was no justice left in the country she once called her own. Power, control and dominance were all the ruling class wanted. She, like many others, was realizing too late how tenuous freedom is.

"We failed, didn't we Jedediah? We failed to hold freedom sacred, failed to limit the power of ambitious men. Look what we have come to. Corbin has no hope for justice, he is alone, he has no friends."

"No, not alone child. Do you think that He who sees all things has forsaken him? We are never alone, even at our weakest hour.

"Did you forget how Corbin stood and defied those powerful men by proclaiming his innocence? That took courage. Even now he knows he is not alone. That knowledge gives him a strength that cruel men will never understand."

"What good is it? He is still in their hands. Still in danger of torture. Surely you saw, he looks old, broken and feeble. He was barely able to walk. The things they must have done to him." She could hold back no longer. The tears came unbidden. She collapsed on the old man's neck and wept like a little child.

"This should not be," she said between sobs. "Men should not have to suffer so."

"Men suffer tyranny because they forget that they are the defenders of liberty. Abbie, we all forgot that. Every time we look to someone else for succor we give away part of our character.

"Do you think the bravery of Corbin standing alone in his defense was lost on the multitudes watching? Some will be angered by it, still others inspired. Corbin created a legend the moment he stood to his feet. Years of suffering and oppression will help resurrect the desire for freedom in many. Nothing but good will come of this."

"For Corbin? I want him to be free."

"He is already free, can't you see that? The moment he stood to his feet he was a free man. Free men stand when others won't because they will be owned by no one."

The television announcer was speaking loudly to overcome the crowd behind him. Abbie heard him say the verdict would be handed down shortly.

She and Jedediah watched as the head justice read the court's decision. Corbin would live. The second phase of Jeff's plan was complete.

Chapter 37

The ride seemed to last forever. The van slowed and turned left. Corbin could tell by the sound of the engine that they were traveling at a lower rate of speed.

The ride in the back was bumpy. Corbin had to reach out several times to steady himself when the vehicle jostled. Soon the brakes squealed as the van rolled to a stop.

The two guards riding in the back with him sat silently the whole trip. That was what he preferred. Solitude was his punishment. The only person he longed to talk to was Abigail. He prayed she was safe. He was sure that Alex's claim to have captured her was a ruse to get him to sign the confession.

The back of the van opened and Corbin saw a dirt road behind it and trees in every direction. He stepped from the van and his senses were quickened by the beauty around him. Glancing to the left and right all he could see were trees and thick undergrowth.

"Follow me," the guard said without looking at him. Corbin trailed him around the back of the van. The dirt road led up to a fifteen foot tall chain link fence that was topped with concertina wire. As far as he could tell, the fence enclosed a large yard around the small ranch house that sat in the middle. As they approached, the guard swung open the gate to allow them entrance.

This would be his new home. He noticed that each window was barred and the front door locked from the outside.

"Stop here." Corbin complied.

"May I know your name?" Corbin asked trying to make a connection with his captor.

The guard hesitated briefly and looked Corbin over. He started to speak then turned and walked toward the house.

Corbin was puzzled that he felt hurt by this slight. Men like him had broken his body. Why his silence was so painful he did not understand.

"Inside."

Corbin entered his new prison. When he crossed the threshold, the door closed behind him and the familiar sound of tumblers clicking told him he was locked in.

He was standing in an entryway to what, he assumed, had been someone's home. He wondered who had lived there and why they were gone. The house was quiet and he stood, eyes closed and listened. He could hear the guards laughing outside.

He stepped deeper into the house and was astonished that the living room was fully furnished with a couch, love seat and appropriate tables. There were no lamps on the tables, only a modest chandelier in the center of the room. Though it was still daytime the surrounding trees blocked out much of the sun.

He switched the light on and off several times and decided he liked it slightly dark. Light streamed in through the windows despite the bars covering them. That he had windows, made him smile.

He set off to explore the rest of the residence. The one bedroom had a twin size bed and chest of drawers. He opened the top drawer and was surprised to find an adequate supply of underclothes and stockings.

There was a closet adjacent to the dresser that held several pairs of pants and six polo shirts, all of which were the same color. The bathroom he found was adequately furnished. He stopped in front of the mirror. He did not recognize the face staring back at him. When had he gotten so old? His face was gaunt and his lips thin and pale. His hair was grayer than he remembered.

The kitchen was large with enough cabinet space that Abbie would have loved it. *I miss you, my love.*

"Curious," he said as he further surveyed the kitchen. There was no stove to be seen. He began opening the cabinet doors only to find them all empty. There were no eating utensil, nothing that would suggest anyone lived or ate there.

The wooden table in the middle of the kitchen could seat two. That made him chuckle. Who was he going to eat with? Maybe they thought he had an imaginary friend. He was laughing now. He laughed until his sides hurt then the laughter turned to tears.

Corbin sunk to the floor howling with grief. He was certain the guards could hear him but he was beyond pride. This was his lot, to be alone, to never hear a kind word nor share an emotion. His grief was almost overwhelming and he was sinking into despair.

I will never leave you nor forsake you. His inner voice screamed above his mourning. *Are you not worth more than the sparrows I feed everyday? Cast your burden upon me and I will give you rest.*

The first time he had heard his inner voice, he believed it to have been manufactured by his need for hope. After months of its importunity, he understood it to be the voice of God.

"This punishment is worse than death," he protested, his voice feeble and tremulous. "How much more shall I endure?"

The bows of the mighty men are broken, and they that stumbled are girded with strength. Corbin's tears flowed freely as those words echoed in his mind. God had not forsaken him. He still had a purpose for Corbin that no other person or organization could diminish.

But they that wait upon the LORD shall renew their strength; they shall mount up with wings as eagles; they shall run, and not be weary; and they shall walk, and not faint. That was the answer. The solution would never come from his own hand. Nor would he find solace in the mercies of the wicked. This house was not a prison. God had turned it into a sanctuary. If God was present with him, then he had true liberty.

Corbin rose to his feet. He was not a slave or helpless. His freedom stemmed from God. He would stay free as long as he was willing to not bow to oppression. That courage came from his belief in the living God. His was the way of the Nazarene.

He walked into each room and bowed his head and asked for God's blessing. This was his home, his sanctuary. He would worship God unimpeded. Though his tormentors would not allow him a Bible, he would begin to record what he could remember of scripture.

If this was where God wanted him to be, then he would live. Self pity was death and servitude to the will of others. He would rejoice as long as he had breath.

Corbin slowly walked to the living room and fell on his knees before the couch. He lifted his head and looked out the large picture window behind the davenport, his eyes fixed upon the sky and began to sing.

****

Jeff looked at his watch again. Marcus was late. He paced in his study concerned that he had not arrived yet.

The door bell rang and Jeff bounded up the basement steps two at a time. He pulled back the curtain and caught a glimpse of Marcus on the porch. He quickly opened the door.

"You're late," he said accusingly. "You were supposed to be here thirty minutes ago."

"Traffic, what can I say."

"Katie," he called upstairs, "I will be in my study with Marcus. Could you see to it that we are not disturbed." He hated making that kind of request, especially since Katie was so angry with him all the time.

Marcus followed him to his study. Jeff closed the door and they both sat down.

"Has he been moved yet?" Jeff was eager to put the last phase of his plan in motion.

"Yes, he was delivered to the house around three this afternoon. I had two of my best men escort him."

"What about security?"

"I have six men rotating twelve hour shifts. I figured the less men involved, the easier it will be."

"Smart. I will contact Jedediah tonight and give him instructions. It is imperative that we pull this off with little complications. We only have one shot."

"Did you talk to your wife and is she on board."

"I told her what she needed to know. She and the kids are already on their way south. What about Katie?"

Jeff had put off talking to Katie until the last minute. Given her new disdain for him, he was not certain how she would react to heading to Arkansas, especially if he did not give her a compelling reason.

"I'll talk to her tonight after I talk to Jedediah."

"Are the rest of the plans in place? Nothing can go wrong. If we are caught what they did to Corbin will seem like a picnic compared to what will be in store for us."

"I have arranged for my guys to be on duty next Thursday night. We can be in and out within ten minutes. I arranged for the guard's shifts to range from nine in the evening until nine in the morning. I figure we would go in just after dark. That will give us at least a ten hour head start. No one will know he's gone until after breakfast is delivered at ten.

"I gave implicit instruction that no one was to make any contact or overture of friendship to Corbin. The Deputy Director liked the idea of total isolation. He thought it would enhance Corbin's punishment. Frankly, Jeff, I can't wait to wash my hands of these sadistic monsters."

"We shall be free of them soon enough." Jeff was pleased. *Hold on Corbin, just a few more days,* he thought.

Chapter 38

Marcus waited at the family farm. He took one last look around, none of it really mattered anymore. Twenty-five years ago his greatest fear was that his retirement account would not grow fast enough. Now he feared for the future of his wife and children.

He had grown up here. His parents had been dairy farmers and even as a kid, he worked sunup to sundown. He could still remember the smell of his mother baking bread and how the old metal table rocked with the force of her kneading the raw dough. Meals were bountiful. They ate what they had grown.

He and his siblings spent countless hours milking, putting up hay, and helping their mother with the canning. He participated in other chores like feeding the chickens and bottle feeding baby goats. Life was never dull, and at the end of the day, he slept soundly.

Those days were gone forever and sadly he knew he could not wish them back. He stood under the oak tree where he first kissed Sadie. The memory was as sweet today as it had been then. Being a sappy romantic, he had pulled out his pocket knife and etched their names in the trunk. He ran his fingers over the familiar grooves.

Right on time, Jeff wheeled his SUV into the driveway. Marcus set aside his musing to prepare for the business at hand. He stepped from under the oak and waved Jeff to a stop.

"Let's get loaded up." His tone was resigned.

While Jeff opened the back of the car, Marcus grabbed the gear he needed. He had packed night vision goggles. These were standard issue for members of the Division's security force. He had never needed them until now. He also packed a taser gun, trifold zip tie handcuffs and balaclavas for him and Jeff.

Marcus slammed the rear door shut and climbed into the passenger seat.

"Hold up, forgot something," he said as he flung open the door and jumped out. When he came back he stopped at the car door and chambered a round into his 40 caliber handgun.

"Hey, wait a minute! We're not in the business of killing anyone," Jeff protested. He had never been a fan of firearms. He especially believed that Christians had no use for one.

"Neither are we in the business of committing suicide," Marcus retorted as he shoved the weapon into the holster on his hip. "I don't plan on getting caught, but neither do I intend on being taken alive if we are."

They left the farm at six o'clock, heading to Carlisle, Pennsylvania where Corbin was being held. The trip would take approximately three hours. They needed to arrive shortly after the shift change. Jeff's plan depended on them putting as much ground behind them and Pennsylvania as possible within the twelve hour window.

He knew the protocols, and the first warning issued would be local. The guards were instructed to tell authorities they had been overpowered around four in the morning. It would take the lumbering bureaucracy hours to expand the search.

With Corbin's high profile trial, he was counting on Lambert's pride keeping this quiet to avoid being embarrassed by losing an obviously broken man. Their success depended on everything going as planned. He had lived long enough to know that rarely happened.

****

Corbin opened the living room window and breathed deeply. The smell of the woods was always satisfying. He liked to listen to the wind move through the trees, and hear the buzzing of bees at the ill kept rosebush by the window.

Tonight the sky was glowering and threatening to rain. White light flashed in the distance followed by the low rumble of thunder. Corbin imagined that the voice of God would thunder like that, booming, frightening, and awesome. The wind began to pick up and the crackling of lightening moved closer.

Corbin sat closer to the window. He wanted to see it all. This was God's power and a revelation of the smallness of man. Man's greatest strength was his capacity to love. His greatest weakness was his cruelty and disregard for life.

In the end Corbin knew that God would have the final word. Man blustered and bullied, but the power gained was tenuous at best. *One day,* he mused, *we will all stand before the great white throne of God. Everyone will be equal. Man's power will be seen for what it is, a vain attempt to be a god.*

Lightening struck a tree nearby, thunder exploded like a cannon shot and the house went black.

****

The time they spent on I-78 seemed like an eternity. The storm they met with did little to help. The rain came down so hard that Jeff had to pull off the road and wait it out. Both men were feeling the strain of their mission.

Jeff hoped that Katie had missed the storm. When he first approached her about meeting him in Texas she refused. She poured out a flood of frustration on him.

"Jeffrey Arbino, after what you did to Corbin Miller, I would not meet you anywhere." That was the first time he had ever experienced anger from her. He was dumbstruck. He reached out to touch her and she recoiled. "I might as well tell you now. I'm leaving you, I can't live with the monster you have become. I've heard the rumors of what happens in the Division. How could you? How could you be so cruel?" She began to sob and was inconsolable.

It was then that Jeff decided it was all or nothing. He could bear no longer having Katie believe he was a monster. He had never really considered the consequences his choices would have for her.

"Katie, please let me explain..."

"Explain what? How you tortured your best friend, how you imprisoned him for life? You turned your back on everything you believed in."

His strength left him. How could he not have seen what was happening. His family was being dismantled, and yet he felt compelled to do what he had done.

379

Gently he put his arms around the woman he loved and silently sobbed. He did not weep because she said she would leave. He deserved that. He wept because of her pain, and her anguish made him sorrowful.

When he finally persuaded her to listen, he explained his role in the Brotherhood. How he had moved Corbin to better conditions and recruited Marcus to watch after him. Jeff walked her through the trial and it's purpose. He knew he was revealing more than he should, but he could not chance losing her.

Katie listened silently as he unfolded his story. She showed no emotion other than kneading her fingers.

"Jeff, why didn't you tell me? You let me believe you had turned your back on Christ and us. I agonized over the decisions you made. Couldn't you have trusted me?"

"Kate," his voice was subdued and he avoided looking in her eyes, "I only wanted to protect you. But now we have a chance to leave this place. Some of the Brothers are ready to take you to Arkansas, from there Jedediah has arranged to smuggle you into Texas."

"You talk as if you aren't coming." The alarm in her voice was obvious. She grabbed his face between her hands and looked into his eyes. "What aren't you telling me?"

"I have to remain behind for a few more days. There is something I have to do. I cannot tell you what it is. The less you know, the better. All I can say is that I will be with you in less than a week."

Overwhelmed Katie sat down and buried her face in her hands. Jeff looked on helplessly as he watched her shoulders shake from sobbing. He had put her through more than she deserved. She had always been by his side and he loved her deeply.

Jeff placed a sympathetic hand on her shoulder and this time she did not push it away. Instead she reached up and placed her hand on top of his.

Finally she looked up and said, "When do I leave?"

"Within the hour."

"I won't have time to say goodbye..."

"Katie, you must leave now. Goodbyes will raise suspicions. What I have to do today will make you a target. If they get their hands on you, unimaginable horrors would await you. Trust me!"

Jeff looked at his watch. Katie had been on the road for over twelve hours. By the time he and Marcus completed their mission she would be safely hidden in Texas. *Lord, let it be so.*

Exit 49 was one mile ahead. Jeff felt his adrenaline surge. He had never been involved in anything like he was attempting tonight. His life before the Freeman administration had been extremely normal. He focused all his energy on ministry and his family. The most adventurous thing he ever did was go kayaking with the youth group.

He had always been a student of the Christian Scripture. Nothing thrilled him more than discovering new meanings in the Word of God and communicating those thoughts to his congregation.

In the past five years, he found himself embroiled in intrigues he was ill suited to tackle. He had tried to remain neutral during the insufferable persecution leveled at Jews and Christians. The Jewish community had been the easiest to attack. Anti-Semitism festered among those looking for someone to blame.

When his dear friend Rabbi Cohen had been arrested, tortured and murdered, something changed in Jeff forever. He, like many of his colleagues, had deliberately blinded himself to the abuses around him. When word came that Rabbi Cohen was dead, Jeff began his journey to disrupt the viciousness of evil men.

Marcus took the exit and turned toward Carlisle.

"Won't be long now," Marcus said glancing at Jeff, "You ready for this?"

"Yes," Jeff said, unconvinced he was up to the task.

****

A wisp of sunlight cut through the horizon as they pulled into the compound. Marcus stopped halfway down the drive. He had switched off the headlights before turning into the driveway, avoided touching the breaks and revealing their presence. He let the SUV roll to a halt along the side of the drive.

The compound was dark except for the emergency lighting that was directed toward the building that housed Corbin. The perimeter fence was normally illuminated with bright halogen lights, but tonight everything was black except for the light that leached from the compounds interior. Though unsure why the lights were off, Marcus was grateful for the added cover.

"Something's wrong," his voice trailed off as he stared intently through the windshield. "There are four cars, there should only be three."

Jeff's eyes moved to the parking area. "What do we do?'

"We stick to the plan." Marcus pulled the balaclava over his face to hide his features. Jeff did the same. He then thumbed off the interior lights of the vehicle. He did not want the lights to come on once he opened the door. He needed stealth to determine what was going on.

"Wait here," he whispered looking at Jeff. His peripheral vision caught movement to his left. He reflexively held up a hand to warn Jeff to keep silent.

Two men exited the guardhouse. The man on the left was Scott Johnson, a member of the Brotherhood. He was Marcus's first point of contact. He did not recognize the person to his right. The man was gesticulating wildly and the laughter that reached them indicated a joke of some sort had been told.

He watched as Scott tried to move him toward his car, but it was obvious the man had no intention of leaving.

Marcus reached into the backseat and grabbed the small duffel bag that contained the night vision goggles, zip ties and taser.

"Once this guy is neutralized move quickly," he said to Jeff as he slowly pulled the door handle and moved silently out of the SUV. Keeping his eye on the two men, he slowly pushed the door shut until he heard the latch catch. Neither man reacted. Their loud speech and laughter covered the sound.

Marcus slid silently into the underbrush. Adrenaline had increased his heart rate and gave him labored breathing. He paused trying to allow himself to relax. The last thing he needed was to make a mistake. He took several deep breaths and began to move.

He lowered the night vision goggles and switched them on. The landscape came alive with green light. The lack of perimeter lighting made it unnecessary for him to avoid looking in certain areas. The brightness of the lights would have been intensified by the goggles and limited his vision.

He moved forward careful to avoid stepping on branches or stumbling over objects. The adrenaline and physical effort made controlled breathing difficult. He estimated he was twenty feet away when he stopped and crouched behind a tree.

"My old lady ain't gonna be happy," the man said in an exaggerated tone. Then he began to howl with laughter. Scott laughed as well and glanced up the drive. Marcus knew he saw the SUV when his gaze stopped briefly in that direction. Scott maneuvered toward the gate and leaned against it. This forced the man to further turn his back toward the SUV.

"Good boy," Marcus said to himself. When he had recruited Scott, he had been impressed with his quick mind and attention to detail. All three of the men on guard duty were picked for their loyalty to the Brotherhood and each was aware of the plan.

"She sounds like a real peach." Scott answered.

"She's round as a peach!" This evoked more laughter from the man.

Marcus moved quickly in a crouch. The taser was in his right hand. When he pulled the trigger two needles with wires attached to the gun penetrated the man's shirt and sent forty-thousand volts of electricity through his body. The intensity of the charge interrupted his motor skills and sent him convulsing to the ground.

Scott immediately rolled the man on his stomach while Marcus applied the zip ties. He pulled them tight. He knew it would hurt but he did not want this guy to escape.

"What happened to the lights," Marcus asked as he tethered the man to the fence post. Adrenaline made his hand shake.

"Providence," Scott said simply. "Lightening struck the power lines and the transformer. I've never seen anything like it before."

"If those lights had been on, we would have had issues," Marcus replied, silently thanking God.

"You ready?" Marcus asked. Each of the guards understood that part of the plan meant they would be hit with the taser and cuffed. This would protect them when they were interrogated by the Internal Investigation Division. Each could claim they were ambushed by a group of intruders.

As with all the interrogators in the Division, the members of the IID could use excruciating persuasion if they believed someone was lying. The unknown man he had just cuffed would add to their cover.

"As ready as a guy can be," he chuckled as he raised his hands to present a better target.

"Wisdom and courage," Marcus said as he pointed the taser pistol at his chest.

"Wisdom an..." Scott's words were cut short as his body convulsed. Marcus began to apply the cuffs when the unknown man began to groan.

"Sorry about this." Marcus removed the slap jack from his belt and struck the man hard on the back of the head. The lead filled leather weapon created a soft thunk, and his body going slack, told him it was effective.

Once Scott was secure, Marcus heard the SUV door close. Jeff would be bringing the bolt cutters and the remaining cuffs.

They moved around the perimeter fence quickly. Within thirty minutes all the guards had been tased and secured to the fence. Marcus hoped the bad weather did not return. The last guard they secured was at the rear of the house. Marcus took the bolt cutters and made an opening in the chain link fence. After breaching the fence, they shut down the generator. Once the generators thrumming subsided, a macabre silence fell over the isolated location.

****

Corbin sat silently in the darkened room. The only light filtered in from outside once the generator started. The fresh smell of ozone filled his nostrils as the lightening danced around the compound. Thunderstorms had always just been, but tonight he recognized the potential of God's wrath.

As quickly as the storm began it was gone. A moderate breeze caused the tattered shear curtain to come alive. Corbin was fascinated as it moved ghostlike around him. He was not quite sure how long he had been here. Time no longer mattered, he would die here. How long God willed for him to live was none of his concern. His faith had strengthened, not lessened during his ordeal. If he only new God theoretically before, he was certain of his relationship now.

He heard the guards talking. One of them was laughing gregariously. Unaccustomed to the sound of a human voice Corbin leaned closer so he could better listen. Though he could not understand what was said, the connection gave him some comfort.

The brightness of the perimeter lighting made it difficult to see who was talking. The laughing man stopped abruptly. Corbin could only hear the whine of the generator. He leaned back in his chair and relaxed.

The sudden blackness startled him. He felt his way to the window and strained to see. He could neither hear nor see any of the guards. This seemed strange. The grave like silence made him uncomfortable and he reached out to God. Cautiously he made his way back to his chair.

Suddenly, the door to his prison burst inward. He heard pieces of wood clatter on the floor. Two silhouettes moved toward him.

"Corbin?" The voice was familiar, Corbin could not quite place where he had heard it before. Each man grabbed his upper arms and dragged him toward the door.

Corbin did not try to resist. He had expected to be executed and was resigned to his fate.

****

The thinness of the arm beneath his grip was surprising. When he and Marcus grabbed Corbin it was like lifting a child. Jeff knew from Alex's detailed reports that he had been subjected to inhumane treatment, but the feel of his arm was unsettling.

"Corbin," Jeff whispered as they led him away, "we're taking you home." He was surprised by the lack of response.

When they reached the SUV they gently guided Corbin into the backseat. Corbin had to be told to put on his seatbelt. His docile compliance to their commands seemed unnatural. Corbin had never been stubborn, but neither had he ever been easily swayed.

Even as a college freshman, Corbin had been intensely spiritual. Careful to a fault, he avoided things most would have found harmless. Jeff admired that in his friend.

Once they were back on the road Jeff and Marcus removed the masks. They stopped along I-81 to get rid of their equipment. Marcus threw everything in the culvert except his handgun.

They had been on the road for fourteen hours when they reached Nashville. Jeff's official ID had gotten them quickly through the three checkpoints along the way. If an alert had been issued about Corbin's escape, he would have been notified at any one of the checkpoints. The lack of news was reassuring.

****

Gabriel liked his new job. He had been assigned to the maximum security prison in Jackson, Michigan for seven years. He hated it there.

That prison was filled with some of the worst scum he had ever come across. The last straw for him was when one of the inmates threw urine in his face. He called his union steward and demanded a transfer. Because of his experience he was offered this position.

His shift did not officially begin for another forty-five minutes, but he enjoyed being outside, and liked catching up with Scott. The forest surrounding the compound was relaxing and the prisoner was docile.

This was his third week away from that hole in Jackson. *Good riddance,* he thought.

As he turned into the driveway he knew something was wrong. He saw two men struggling on the ground. He pressed his foot down hard on the accelerator. The distance to the prone men disappeared quickly. As he exited the car, he unholstered his service revolver.

"They're gone," Scott's voice was hoarse from screaming. "They've got Miller."

"Not good," Gabriel said as he moved toward the guard shack.

"Hey, Gabe, come on, cut us loose." Scott's wrists were bloodied from struggling.

Gabriel stopped and went back to free the two men. Then he ran to the shack and called in the escape.

****

When they reached their contacts in Arkansas they were informed that a nationwide alert had gone out about Corbin's escape.

Surprised, Jeff said, "I underestimated Lambert. We have to move fast. It won't be long until they realize that Marcus and I are gone as well. Once they put the pieces together, we'll all be hunted."

"What about Miller?" One of the Brothers asked. Ted was how he introduced himself, but Jeff doubted it was his real name.

Jeff looked in Corbin's direction. His old friend sat quietly in the back of the car. He showed no curiosity in anything around him. He barely spoke during the trip except to say he was thirsty or needed a bathroom. Even then, he spoke at his feet, he never lifted his head.

"He'll be fine."

"He seems off."

"He'll be fine," his voice was filled with anger. "You have no idea what he has endured."

Ted blinked twice and took a half step back. "No offense, just an observation. If you are going to get into Texas, then we better move now."

Jeff was glad he changed the subject. "What do you suggest?"

Ted laid a map across the hood of the SUV. "The security isn't as tight away from the bigger cities." He pointed to an area south of Texarkana, "We'll cross here at Hoot Plant Road. The security there is minimal and will be your best chance."

Jeff left Marcus to work out the logistics with Ted. He walked over and sat beside Corbin. "Corbin, we're going to take you to Abbie."

Corbin's knees were pulled tight together and he fidgeted with a twig he had picked up. He did not answer. Instead tears began to create wet spots on his pants. "Abbie," he whispered and continued to fidget.

Jeff pushed down the anger and desire for revenge that erupted in him. He could not imagine the darkness that must have lived inside of Alex. His clinical analysis of the torture he put Corbin through became more real. His friend had always smiled and laughed. His ability to communicate was uncanny and now he was broken and unresponsive.

"It will be better soon. I promise it will."

"Let's go," Marcus called. "If we want any chance of surviving this, we have to move now."

The three men climbed into the SUV. They rode in silence. Jeff was apprehensive and would rather have been anywhere but here. The Brothers followed until they were certain Marcus knew where to go, then they made a u-turn and headed back the way they had come.

"There it is ahead," Marcus's voice was tight. "Looks like there are only two NALC guards and they are just kids." Marcus removed his weapon from its holster and hid it under his right thigh. He put the SUV into drive and rolled slowly up to the gate.

"ID," demanded the sandy haired kid.

Jeff immediately produced his credentials. The kid scrutinized the photo then stared for a few moments at Jeff.

"Who are these guys?" His remark was addressed to Jeff.

"Marcus is my personal guard and that is my assistant." Jeff hoped he had not noticed the tremor in his voice.

The kid leaned near the back window and stared at Corbin. He pulled a paper from his shirt pocket, unfolded it and glanced from it to Corbin several times.

"Get out of the car," his voice became menacing.

"I'm sorry Son, do you know who I am?" Jeff made his voice authoritative.

The kid stepped back and drew his handgun. "I said get out of the car." The other guard was alerted and he jumped to his feet. His weapon at the ready.

Jeff watched as Marcus placed his hand on the door handle. He quickly glanced to his right then pushed open the door. As he exited the vehicle he brought up his right hand and fired into the boy's face. Brain, blood and bone fragments sprayed behind him as his body slumped to the ground.

Automatic gunfire exploded to the right of the SUV. Glass shattered around Jeff as he tried to duck down in the front seat. Searing heat penetrated his right shoulder.

Marcus side stepped to his left. His two hand grip on the handgun gave him the control he needed. His first round went wide of his target, the second and third caught him in the chest. The guard staggered backward and momentarily lowered the muzzle of his weapon. Marcus moved forward like a tiger, stalking its prey. With each step, he fired into the torso before him.

The guard went to his knees and then fell lifeless to the ground. Spinning quickly Marcus ran back to the SUV. Jeff heard the tires squeal and the thunk of bullets striking the vehicle. The gunfire behind them told him there were other NALC behind them. He felt disoriented, dizzy, then everything went black.

Chapter 39

Abigail paced nervously in her apartment.

"Abbie you're going to wear a hole in the floor," Jedediah remarked. "Sit down and relax, we'll hear something soon."

"What if they don't make it? You heard the reports. They know he's gone."

"Jeff and Marcus are resourceful, they'll make it."

Abbie ran from the room when the baby began to cry. Little Corbin was her only connection to her husband. Already four months old, he had filled the emptiness of the last thirteen months. When she reached the crib, little Corbin's face was contorted as he hit a decibel level that made her cringe. How such a small thing could make such a large noise was beyond her.

Smiling as she scooped him into her arms, she swayed back and forth saying in a soothing voice, "Daddy will be home soon." His screaming soon subsided and he began to gurgle.

The ringing phone startled young Corbin and he resumed his crying.

Jedediah stuck his head in the door, "Come on Child, we have to pick up Katie and Sadie."

Jedediah had borrowed a large van from the Brothers to transport the wives and children to the rendezvous point. Within an hour they were waiting at a prearranged place. Abigail did not know where they were going, only Jedediah knew their destination.

"The Brothers in Arkansas reported that they would be at the border crossing in twenty minutes. It won't be long now." Once the other ladies were in the van, it did not take long to reach the rendezvous point.

Jedediah parked so they could see the Texas checkpoint. The gate was manned by eight soldiers armed with automatic weapons.

Abigail was struck with the stark difference between the two border gates. There was no barbed wire strung out across the border on the Texas side. No one was intimidated either coming or going through the gate. The military presence in Texas was to protect Texans and refugees from harm.

Little Corbin began to fuss and Abigail sang softly to him as she swayed in time. "Hush sweetie," she cooed softly, "Daddy will be here soon."

It sounded like fireworks. She heard the first crack followed by dozens in rapid succession. When the Texas soldiers readied their weapons, she knew that she had heard gunshots. She felt Jedediah's arm wrap around her shoulder. Sadie and Katie huddled close and all watched silently, anxiously to see what was happening.

The firing stopped for a brief moment. Then she knew that more than one weapon was firing. Dust kicked up in the half mile distance of no man's land between gates. In the billowing dust she saw a black SUV traveling at a high rate of speed, weaving from side to side. Abbie could see that the windshield was shattered. Once the SUV was within twenty feet of the Texas line, the soldiers returned fire.

The vehicle sped through the lifted gate and skidded to a halt a safe distance from the gate. The firing from the American side had long ceased. The Texas soldiers lowered their weapons on the motionless SUV and were yelling orders for the occupants to exit.

Abbie broke into a run, holding little Corbin tight to her chest.

"Abbie!" She heard a distant voice yell. Her concentration was focused on the vehicle. It only took a few moments for her to reach the checkpoint.

"Halt," a young voice demanded. "Ma'am, I said halt."

"My husband, my husband is in there," her voice was pitched with terror. "Corbin, Corbin," she heard herself screaming. The SUV was riddled with bullet holes. Only the left rear window was intact. The driver was lying on the ground his left side covered with blood. One of the soldiers was applying a field dressing.

Katie and Sadie arrived soon after Abbie. Sadie ran to the driver and fell to her knees. She was sobbing. Jeff staggered from the car, his right arm hanging limp at his side, fresh blood dripping from his fingers. He was hunched over, obviously in pain, his left hand covering his wound.

"Corbin, where's Corbin!" She was frantic, trying to find her husband. He was supposed to be there! They had assured her. She tried to run to the vehicle but the young soldier prevented her.

"Abbie," a monotone voice came from the SUV.

Though the voice was empty of emotion, she recognized it. "Corbin!" She screamed again. "Yes, Honey, it's me Abbie."

"Abbie," he said again in the same tone.

Two soldiers helped a man out of the back seat. He was gaunt and extremely feeble. His sallow eyes were focused on the ground and he went quietly were the soldiers led him. Abbie blinked back tears. She did not recognize this person.

He appeared to be unharmed. There was blood on his shirt but she could tell it had not come from him. She assumed it must be Jeff's blood. When no one else exited the vehicle, she realized that this old, frail man was Corbin.

"No," she groaned, "no." She stared at him for a long while. Jedediah moved to her side.

"Abbie, go to him."

"Oh, Jedediah, what did those monsters do? I don't even recognize him. Look at him, there is no life in him."

"Go to him, Child. He needs you. He'll get better, I promise you. Go to him." Jedediah took little Corbin. She felt the old man's hand in the small of her back as he pushed her forward.

The first few steps were difficult. Her sense of guilt was crushing. How could she go to him now when she had abandoned him to that fate? As she approached, she noticed the scars on his arms and his bent fingers.

With each step she felt weaker. Emotion exploded in her as she fell on his neck. Her body convulsed with weeping. She felt his hand tentatively at first. It was as if he did not believe any of this was real. Soon his embrace grew stronger.

"Abbie?" he whispered. It was a question of surprise and disbelief.

"Yes, Corbin, my love. It's Abbie. Oh, Corbin," she said between sobs, "I have missed you so much."

"Abbie," he said his voice stronger.

She pulled back and looked into his eyes. His averted immediately. She grabbed his chin with her left hand and turned his face toward her. She looked intently at his face, studying every feature. Her Corbin was still there, only buried beneath a vacuous stare.

Jedediah had joined her at Corbin's side. He handed the baby to her and she held him so Corbin could see. "This is our son, Corbin. Your little boy, God's gift to us."

Corbin's eyes moved slowly from Abbie to the child then back to her again. His stare was not the penetrating gaze of understanding, rather his visage betrayed confusion.

"Oh, Jedediah, he doesn't know me," there was panic in her voice.

"Give him time, Child."

She and Jedediah turned when they heard the ambulance's siren. The soldiers quickly moved the civilians aside. Abbie moved reluctantly. She glanced back and Corbin was staring at the ground.

The paramedics went first to the driver and began to stabilize him. Another emergency vehicle arrived within seconds, and Jeff and Corbin were ushered into the back and taken to the hospital.

Epilogue

"They will be here soon!" Abbie called from the kitchen. "Are you ready out there?"

"Yes, stop worrying." Corbin chuckled to himself. She wanted everything to be perfect and he would do his best to make it so.

"Hey there, Buddy," he said as he picked up the toddler. Little Corbin had grown quickly and was a complete handful at age two.

The smell of the charcoal fire was comforting. He lifted the lid on the grill and flipped the burgers. He anticipated today's gathering.

It had been two years since Jeff and Marcus had risked their lives to save his. It was a purely selfless act, one that distinguished humanity from every other creature on earth. Corbin knew it was that part of people that truly reflected the nature of God.

This would be their second anniversary gathering. The yearly celebration had been Abbie's idea. She had told them all she never wanted to forget those who had given her life back. Corbin never wanted to forget either. Life was not cheap, it was a precious gift and needed to be celebrated.

The first several months after his rescue had been difficult. Hours of physical therapy had begun to rejuvenate his strength. After two years, he still walked with a limp. The doctors told him that the damage to his feet had been extensive and would never fully heal.

The trauma of his incarceration was still a part of his life. Even though he lived in a free state, his autonomic response was to avert his eyes whenever he saw a soldier or police officer.

Little Corbin had been the best medicine. The first time Abbie put him in Corbin's arms, he wept uncontrollably. His response was so profound, Abbie had to take the baby out of fear he might drop him. The unconditional love he received from his wife and child was healing.

When Corbin had received the news that Alex had taken his own life, he was surprised by his own sadness. Alex had been the product of a society that saw humanity as nothing more than a commodity. His detached violence was the logical conclusion to the policy that could waste life to benefit the powerful. The prevalence of abortion on demand, euthanasia and the systematic neglect of the infirm taught the young that neither they nor anyone else, had value.

"They're here," Abbie called excitedly.

Corbin removed his *Kiss the Chef* apron and rushed to the front door and opened it. They had all arrived at once. Corbin and Abbie hugged each guest as they entered. Abbie, Katie and Sadie went to the kitchen to talk and laugh as they prepared salad for their feast.

Corbin led the men onto the patio where each sat in a lawn chair.

Marcus spoke first. "The Brotherhood in Montana has grown stronger over the last two years despite intense fighting."

"I'd heard," Jedediah said softly. Corbin's old friend needed a cane and though his body was becoming weaker, his mind was still sharp. "The face of this struggle is changing. Christians are openly arrested with little public outcry. The resistance needs a leader."

"Corbin," it was Jeff speaking, "have you given any thought to the Brotherhood's proposal?"

The Brotherhood of Texas was still torn over the tactics of the American Brotherhood. The skirmishes between them and government troops were increasing. Montana, Idaho and northern Wyoming had seen the greatest increase in fighting. The Brotherhood had started interrupting supply lines and attacking government installations. The Americans had committed a large contingency of troops to the Middle East where unrest was endemic. The limited resources of the Freeman government made it nearly impossible to deal with the simultaneous uprisings across the nation.

The fighting and mounting death toll had given Congress all it needed to outlaw worshipping in a non-government licensed church. Fragmented reports indicated that the church had gone underground and many of those had aligned themselves with the Brothers.

Though sympathetic to their plight, the Texans were loathe to condone preemptive attacks, many considering it antithetical to Christian doctrine.

Since his release, Corbin had been elected Presiding Elder of the Texas Brothers. This was equivalent to being president of the group. In the past ten months, he had refused to publicly take sides in the debate.

His personal sympathies were with those who desired to protect themselves and their families. Having experienced the wrath and malice of the Freeman government, he was not ready to condemn those who wished to live in freedom.

"You have become a folk hero in Montana," Jeff continued. "The Division tried to keep your escape quiet, but it has become a legend. I've heard the Montana Brotherhood's battle cry is "Remember Miller."

This made Corbin feel uneasy. "I did nothing."

"On the contrary, Son," Jedediah interjected, "you faced the giant and won. It's not your escape that inspires, it is your faithfulness. Not many men could have withstood that much abuse and still remained true to their beliefs. No, don't sell yourself short. God was preparing you for what is ahead."

"Have you talked to Abbie, yet?" Marcus asked in a near whisper.

"No." Corbin sighed and rose stiffly from his seat. He went to the grill to attend to the cooking burgers. Smoke billowed as he opened the lid.

"You have to soon," Jedediah stated.

"I know." Corbin looked toward the kitchen window. Abbie's laughter danced across the yard. He sighed. The hope that he would see her again had helped to sustain him. Even at the end of his incarceration when that hope began to dim, his memories of her gave him strength. He was not sure how to tell her, but he knew it had to be soon.

The celebration was full of laughter. After they had eaten and the sun began to set, they built a small fire and the reflection of the flames flitted across the group. The atmosphere became solemn and this group of survivors bowed their heads to worship. The prayers were spontaneous as was the singing of hymns.

Corbin was acutely aware that his countrymen no longer had this simple privilege. That fact had made a difficult decision easier. He and his three friends were leaving for Montana in three weeks. Tonight he would rejoice with Abbie and little Corbin. Tonight would be unspoiled by talk of violence and war.

He would tell her in the morning...